Last Prom Standing

by

R.H. Bird

Promposal Series

Last Prom Standing

Cover Art by *Teddi Black*

The Wild Rose Press, Inc.
PO Box 708
Adams Basin, NY 14410-0708
Visit us at www.thewildrosepress.com

Publishing History
First Edition, 2025
Trade Paperback ISBN 978-1-5092-6062-1
Digital ISBN 978-1-5092-6063-8

Promposal Series
Published in the United States of America

Dedication

To my wife Lynn. The prettiest and greatest girl ever to come out of Oswego State and my muse, especially for one of the characters. Can you guess which one?

Praise for R.H. Bird

Praise for, 'Promposal

"*Promposal* is not only a delightful read for female readers but also appeals to young men who can relate to Luca's quest for redemption and recognition. It's a quick, enjoyable read that balances humor, drama, and romance, making it perfect for anyone looking to relive the highs and lows of teenage love."

~ *JITHU,* Instagram Influencer *@jithendrajithu01*

"Readers will be gripped until the very end by this endearing and thrilling story that examines themes of adolescent love, redemption, and the desperate urgency of high school romance. Even if the characters aren't gullible, the narrative nevertheless has an air of innocence. Long after you flip the last page, this unusual youthful romance will continue to resonate with you. As much as it will appeal to female readers, this novel will also appeal to young guys who want to be noticed. The *Promposal* sequel has me eager to learn more about Luca and Piper's journey."

~ *Trishita Das, Book Reveiwer*

Chapter 1

Going for a Ride

On the hottest, muggiest afternoon all summer, Piper and I were sticky and sweating like crazy. Her skin glistened like a melting ice-pop. She wore white denim shorts, a cute pink tank top with floral print, and white tennis shoes. Her gorgeous eyes twinkled down at me, and she shook out her sandy blonde ponytail—making me gulp.

"Don't do this to me, Piper."

"Why, when should we do it, Luca?"

I sat on her uncomfortable wicker sofa—and she stood in front of me. Our knees pressed together. My adrenaline spiked every time she moved and they re-connected. Was she doing that on purpose?

My friend Pablo swore that girls always knew what they were doing to us. If he was right, she was up to something.

Tilting my head to the side, I focused on her green eyes, trying to get a read on the situation. Instead, my breathing picked up, my concentration went fuzzy and somehow my gaze drifted to her bottom lip, probably because she was biting it.

"I don't know, anytime but now. Please." My appeal for mercy came out softer than I wanted, and I cleared my throat, trying to hang tough and strengthen my resolve.

"Why?"

I reached around her, and my fingers brushed along her tan and toned calves. Butterflies did a breakdance in my stomach. If she was doing this on purpose, I was a dead man.

She flashed a knowing grin and took a long drink of lemonade, the ice clinking around. I felt the heat coming off her body. She removed a piece of fuzz from my hair. Her tiny touch made my breath hitch.

"Because I'll look like the biggest idiot in the world." I stuck with the pity route, but didn't feel hopeful. My t-shirt and shorts had been soaked for hours. They barely started drying in the air conditioning.

"I thought that already happened," she said, mocking me. She tried holding back her beautiful smile, but I was psyched when it broke through.

"What are you talking about?" I tickled the back of her legs and she giggled.

"I seem to remember you getting down on your knees and telling me that *you* were the biggest idiot in the world for breaking up with me. And you did it in front of the whole school."

"Oh, look who's funny today," I said.

She snorted a laugh, spraying out lemonade.

"Nice. Just what I wanted. Piper's grody mucous all over me." Wearing a sarcastic grin, I wiped off my shirt. "But that's not exactly how I remember things."

We got back together five months ago, on May first, the craziest day of my life. I found out in first period detention she didn't have a date for that night's prom. I was a junior at the time and spent the rest of school going from class to class, pleading with her to let me take her to *her senior prom.* But she kept turning me down.

With time ticking away, and desperation setting in, I literally went down on one knee and begged her—quite possibly the first promposal in recorded history, right here in Big Dune, New York.

It happened in the middle of the hall and to this day, no matter where I go—to school, to a party, even to the drug store, people bust my balls for it. Some girls tell me how romantic it was. Mostly the guys destroy me.

We still had a couple weeks before school started. I'd be entering John Marshall as a senior, and I was on the wrestling team, with a good shot at going to States. "You said I got down on both knees. I only knelt on one of them."

One of the cool things about our relationship was that we could joke about almost anything, even our most embarrassing memories.

"Oh, sorry. You're right. I guess I had it all wrong. So, are you saying you're not man enough to handle this?" She set her glass on the coffee table. An icy pitcher with condensing water droplets rested on a wooden tray. Indoor trees adorned each corner of her sunroom and potted plants hung from the ceiling. Piper nudged the table to the side with her leg. She slid closer. Her knees ended up inside mine and she ran a hand through my black, scruffy hair.

Man, she smelled good.

"That's not going to work again," I said. "How many times do you think you can play the *you're not man enough* card?"

She inched forward, making my stomach jump. The sensation multiplied when her fingers fluttered past my ear and down the back of my neck. I inhaled her body

3

spray. Earlier she told me it was called *Bare Vanilla*. I swallowed. Honestly, she didn't have to manipulate me to get what she wanted. The simple touch of her fingers was enough, and the feel of her leg was a thousand times more than she'd ever need. But why tell her that? I adored these playful tricks.

"Okay tough guy, then let's see how much of a man you are," she said.

"Uh-oh."

She yelled, "Mom, can you come down here for a minute?"

"Ugh. Why now?" My pulse quickened and my mouth went dry as a pinecone.

"Don't you trust me, Luca?" She knew my panicked expression—bulging eyes and the white expanding past the brown.

I had the worst poker-face in the world. She could always tell if I had a full house or was bluffing. "Yes, I trust you. But still." I blew out a long, frustrated breath.

"And you love me, right?" She peered down at me, doe-eyed, still twirling my hair.

When her fingernails grazed my olive skin, goosebumps broke out all over.

"You know I do."

"Then tell me."

"I thought I just did."

"Uh-uh. It's not the same. You have to say it."

I stood up and caressed her arms, gliding up and down. She had goosebumps, too. Glad I wasn't the only one. My fingers tip-toed around her back until they interlocked. I cocked my head and took in everything about her, an infatuated smile curling my lips.

"Piper Kraft, I love you."

She stared at me with those sparkling green eyes. Her arms went around my shoulders, and her whole body tensed when she squeezed a clump of my hair. "I love you, too, Luca Esposito." She leaned in to kiss me; her tongue tasted like cool lemonade.

My anxiety drifted away and for a brief second, I forgot what was about to happen.

"Be right there," her mom called from upstairs.

That snapped the pressure back. I tried to step away, but Piper pulled me in close.

"Where do you think you're going?" She started making out.

"Umm. Your mother is on her way," I said with her lips on mine.

"She's all the way upstairs. We have time." She gave me a quick peck then we resumed kissing.

Wow, was this girl awesome. Since she seemed game, and wasn't worried about getting caught, why not try a move? I always loved a girl's back, especially hers. She chose that moment to rise on her tiptoes and luckily, the bottom of her tank top elevated a tad. I took the opening, reached underneath and lightly tickled her skin, tracing from her lower back upward and down again.

Piper's cute inhale was very audible.

Her mother's feet echoed on the wooden staircase.

My hands drifted toward Piper's hips.

The hardwood floor squeaked as Mrs. Kraft turned one hundred-eighty degrees, heading our way.

Venturing lower on the back of her shorts, my fingertips were almost there. Couldn't stop now if a comet hit the planet.

A cabinet door slammed.

Piper pulled away and slapped my hands off. She

also shoved me in the chest, and I dropped onto her lame wicker couch. A jagged end pierced my hamstring and I covered my head while blue sunflower pillows tumbled on top of me.

"Hey, none of that now, my mom's too close." She had a teasing lilt to her voice. "And don't think I don't know why you always stand to say you love me. Somehow, we wind up making out and you end up copping a feel." Piper bent over and her lips grazed mine as she spoke—one of her favorite moves. "You'll just have to wait until later, mister."

Chills shot down my spine. "I can't wait. But I didn't mind what we were doing before I stood up. I kinda enjoyed that view, too."

"Hmm," she moaned and bit her bottom lip, beaming at me. Was this how it felt the first time we went out? I didn't remember it being this great. Would I have been stupid enough to break up with her if it had? No, this was so much better. We didn't say we loved each other back then. Now, we say it all the time—and mean it.

That's the crazy thing about love. You don't know you're lost until you're found. I stared deep into her eyes, digging every bit of it, and was torn out in one of the worst ways possible.

Mrs. Kraft clomped into the room. "What did you need, honey?"

Piper straightened up wicked fast, adjusting her shorts and tank top. Her mother stopped in her tracks and fired a disapproving glare. My skin may have sizzled from her death rays.

"Umm, it's about tomorrow. Would it be okay if I rode to school with Luca?" Her voice came out quick and shaky and she brushed a hand through her hair.

She was heading to the University of Albany in the morning. She'd be starting college as a freshman, while I'd still be in high school. Time to find out if we could survive a long-distance relationship. Tons of couples have vowed to stay together and failed miserably. I knew we'd be the one-in-a-million, but a whole year without her—without touching her, without seeing her, without holding her hand, and without breathing in her unique scent—all of it was going to royally suck.

We avoided saying "Albany" all summer. Our logic made perfect sense. If no one uttered the name, this day would never come, and we wouldn't have to be apart. If one of us messed up, the other person chose a penalty and you had to do it, no matter what. At first, Piper laid down the law and ordered me to kiss her every time I botched it. It didn't take her long to realize I may have been *accidentally* saying Albany a little too often. Eventually, she switched it to a dollar per violation.

There's a game out there called *Smell and Guess*. The first time Piper slipped up I made her play it. I blindfolded her and placed different items under her nose until she guessed one correctly. I used a jelly donut, and then my brother's hamster. She twitched her nose and got them both wrong. Next, I tried vanilla ice cream, but she said almond extract. I tapped it into her face, and she flipped out. I turned and bolted for my life. That's when we learned Piper ran faster than me.

Earlier, I came over to help pack their car. But as the day went along all we talked about was how much we'd miss each other, and how we wanted to spend every last minute together. I also couldn't stop touching her.

"Frank! Can you come in here?" Mrs. Kraft

groaned. "Now!" She glared at me like a troll making off with her only child.

Great. Her father didn't like me the first time we dated. When I broke up with her, she had cried for weeks, which didn't endear me to the old man. During her prom pictures, he warned me not to show my face around the Kraft homestead. But when we started going out again, it couldn't be avoided. I'd beg her to hang out at my house instead of here, but you could see how far begging got me.

Her humongous home sat on top of a hill deep in the woods. Below us, were tall trees, brown leaves carpeting the ground, giant bedrock boulders and the Hudson River. Did I mention her folks were rich? Her grandfather started Kraft Cement and her father inherited the company.

"Oh, you're still here, Luca." Mr. Kraft frowned as he entered the sunroom, probably ticked-off I hadn't left yet. He dried his hands with a towel and flipped it onto his shoulder.

"Actually, Luca has something to ask you," Mrs. Kraft chirped.

The last time I felt this kind of panic, I had to give a speech in front of the whole school, totally naked. It might have been a dream.

"*Well*?" He sneered. He was lean, in good shape, and over six feet.

I didn't want to ask if I could take Piper. I thought she should do it. Preferably long after I had gone home, where I'd be safe behind my mom. I would have done anything to avoid this awkward situation.

Finally, Piper came to my rescue. "Actually, Daddy, *I* have a question." She scowled at her mother. "Would it be all right if I drove to Albany in Luca's car?"

We lived about three hours south of the college.

"What about all our plans, pumpkin?" He was speaking to her but aimed his grim reaper stare at me. "Seven a.m. for breakfast at the diner. We're going to get sundaes instead of pancakes then hit the road by eight. Don't forget this is a huge milestone for us. Our little girl is going off to college."

His message stung and hit the mark. *This is family time, jag off. You're not invited.* For a second, I felt my throat being squeezed really tight. Was he using a weird mind meld against me?

He pointed at me with his thumb. "If I had known you wanted to go with *Lucy*, I would have hired movers."

My turn to sneer. She told me he calls me that behind my back. He "slipped" once and said it to my face. Ever since, he drags it out whenever he's annoyed. I've learned to deal. She wants me to like her parents, so I gave it the college try. A small price to pay to be in love with her.

"We can still do the diner. *Luca* will meet us there. But can I drive up in his car afterward? If you need me, I'll have my pager. Please, Daddy."

While looking into his daughter's eyes, his resistance melted. Is it possible Piper had the power to outmaneuver all men, not just me? Maybe I should write that down.

"Fine, pumpkin. If that's what you want." But it's not what he meant. His hands fell to his sides, defeated. None of this was fine and it was all my fault.

She threw her arms around him. "Thank you, Daddy."

His daughter had chosen her boyfriend over her

9

father. He glowered at me. I swear, I could tell what he was thinking. *I know exactly where to bury this turd. And with a little extra cement, make it super painful.*

When her parents left the room, so did Piper's sunny demeanor. Her eyes flickered, turned pink, then all the way red. She was barely holding it together. Me, too. This time tomorrow I'd be driving home all alone. She'd be starting a whole new world without me. As confident as we acted, we were both scared to death we might not make it. The idea of breaking up felt like a black hole opening in my chest.

Piper came over and sat on my lap, hugging me. She started to cry. I buried my face in her shoulder, hiding my misty eyes. I wish I knew how to comfort her, but it was wrecking me, too. The pain of her leaving was too much. We fought it bravely all day, eventually losing.

Yesterday by The Beatles played in the kitchen. Paul's voice ripped our hearts out. *"Why she had to go, I don't know, she wouldn't say."* She stroked my hair, and I squeezed her tight. Her sobbing and my sniffles burst through. I'd be stronger for her in the morning when the promise of our future was in her eyes. Right now, my throat constricted for real, and it killed me. The suffering seemed right. Kissing her made the moon rise. We stayed like that a couple hours, way after darkness came.

Chapter 2

The Trip Up

When I arrived at the restaurant, the Krafts already had a table. Two coffees steamed across from her parents. An untouched OJ sat in front of Piper. The pulp floated on top, while the heavy yellow gunk sunk to the bottom—never was a big orange juice fan. Pulp was gross. A couple in their eighties stood at the hostess station, desperately waving to get the girl's attention. She ignored them, yapping on the phone.

The assistant manager grabbed two menus. "Bill, Terri, good to see you. What are you two doing way back there? Follow me to your table." He sounded Greek.

Grinning, they trudged in their walkers.

Piper spied me watching them. Her eyes lit up and she bounded out of the booth. The diner was busy in the morning, and she dodged two waitresses, ducking under a tray of omelets and pancakes.

The dull roar of customers ordering food, an angry bell pinging, and silverware tinging off the floor filled the restaurant. Delicious bacon smoke made my eyes water.

She jumped into my arms and gave me such a tight hug; it knocked me back half a step.

"Whoa, I am so happy to see you." I loved the feel of her body, but her father shot me the evil eye, so I broke our embrace.

She wasn't ready to stop hugging and glared like I rejected her.

"Your dad looks like he wants to kill us. Actually, he'd spare your life and just pour hot coffee down my shorts."

The rims of her eyes had reddened, she'd been crying already.

I brushed a strand of hair from her face. "How are you doing so far?"

She nodded and tried to force a courageous smile. We interlocked fingers. She gave me a huge kiss but no tongue. I put my head down, ignoring Mr. Kraft.

"I love you, Piper. You can handle this. In fact, you can handle anything. You're going to kick ass at that school."

Both of her hands gripped mine. She took tight, deliberate steps, like she was afraid to fall on an ice rink. Probably a good idea on the greasy floor.

They had the temperature freezing in here and goosepimples appeared on my forearms. The weight of her leaving pushed down on my shoulders. We'd both be alone soon. My stomach spun like a fan, but I wanted to be solid and stable for her.

I wore my green John Marshall Wrestling t-shirt with jean shorts and sneakers. Piper had on jeans and an Albany t-shirt from orientation.

"I like your hair down like that. You're going to be the prettiest freshman up there."

We arrived at the table. She rubbed her arms and plopped in.

Her father scowled. "Look, honey, it's Luca."

I scooted into the booth next to her.

The waitress appeared right away, topping off their coffees. "We've been waiting for ya, hon. What'll ya have?"

"Thanks, but I'm not hungry." I couldn't eat if I tried. Way too nervous.

"Don't be like that," her father mocked. "You're not the type of kid who's embarrassed to order food when you're not paying. Are you?"

I shrugged. "I'll take steak and eggs, a large orange soda, and a five-scoop sundae with extra peanut butter cups, please."

She snapped her gum. "Will that be all, sugar?"

"How about two of those the big black and white cookies to go? You know, for the ride up."

****

"I can't believe how slow your dad drives. It's going to take us three and a half hours. I guarantee I could have gotten us there in less than three." I borrowed my mother's silver Plymouth Fury and followed behind her parents lame minivan. "He's rendered my radar detector totally useless."

"Huh?" she muttered.

I motioned at their minivan. "Could you shoot me in the head, please?"

It was the first week of September and a few of the trees started to change colors. This part of the highway had clumps of dense woods, rolling hills, and leaning "55 MPH" signs. An occasional barn sped by.

"Check it out." I pointed at a farm. "We used to yell, 'Corn!' whenever we drove past stalks as kids. Part of me still wants to. I promise, *it's funner* than it sounds. Why don't you try it?"

"Cor…"

13

I barely heard her above the radio. I turned and squinted. "You, okay?"

She shrugged. Anytime I began a conversation, I was met with one-word answers, a sniff, and a sob. I let out a deep breath but didn't push further—she needed her space.

I distracted myself with the scenery. Give it another month and the surrounding Catskills would transform into the prettiest place on earth. Vibrant reds, yellows, and oranges will explode into life.

But after the first frost they decay into browns and dull grays. It's amazing how something so stunning can turn so ugly.

For the past few months, I avoided thinking about Piper going away to college. I wanted to enjoy my time with her, especially our summer nights. I think she did the same.

Right now, her limp posture, unsmiling face, and huge sighs triggered a longing so intense, my body ached, and I tasted stomach acid. Well, peanut butter sundae-ish acid.

I made one last attempt. "It's going to be beautiful up here soon."

"Yeah."

I bit into her cookie—finished mine awhile ago.

We pulled up to the college at 11:30. Piper's eyes sparkled but they were filled with tears. I wish I knew how to make her feel better and I wish I knew how to make myself feel better.

Mrs. Kraft had a large map unfolded in front of her, blocking half their windshield. Her hands jetted in all directions. Mr. Kraft barked at her. I doubted they were sweet nothings. Sometimes Piper'd point when they

14

made a turn, other times she'd attempt to raise her arm, but it fell back to earth when she lost strength.

My head was on a swivel trying to absorb it all. I'd never been on a college campus before, and I felt energized, like I should be reading *MacBeth* or at least sneaking in a bong. But Piper only gazed forward, as if she were afraid to see what life apart looked like.

When I pictured college, I imagined red brick buildings, ivy covered walls and large oak trees. This wasn't it. Instead, Albany had the best, or possibly the worst modern architecture ever. It all depended on how you looked at it. Large glass, gray, and white buildings dotted the landscape. They were surrounded by cold concrete walkways and small, fragile trees. The center of campus held a large quad, with a circular fountain inside a long rectangular pool.

I tried cheering her up. "I hear the frats make pledges put soap bubbles in the fountains and dump in green dye on Saint Patty's Day."

"Mmm hmm." She stared at her feet and rubbed her hands together like she was heading off to prison. We had stopped at a rest area along the way. When she came out of the bathroom, I asked what was wrong. "Just a little nauseous," she claimed, but I could tell she had thrown up.

Albany erected four towers on the outskirts of campus, each twenty-four floors high. Unless they had a place off campus, most kids lived in one.

"What's the name of your dorm again?"

"Dutch."

Her parents pulled up to a long line of cars waiting in front of a tower, and we joined the Dutch queue. Moms, dads, and students carried armfuls of suitcases, boxes of sheets and blankets, toiletries of every kind, as well as desk lamps and office equipment. A poorly hidden box of condoms dropped out of one kid's notebook. His mother scooped it up and smashed it over his head.

A heavyset Black woman with a clipboard approached the minivan and a frantic conversation ensued with Mr. Kraft. I felt sorry for her. She pointed at my car and I waved. She nodded back but appeared annoyed and hustled to the station wagon behind us. A moment later Piper's father walked over.

He rapped on my window even though I was already cranking it down. "That was your residency director. Things are moving on time, and she wants to keep it that way. In a few minutes we'll pull into one of the unloading spots. We have thirty minutes to move you in. If we're not done by then, we have to move our cars to the lot way over there and Luca will have to lug the rest by himself."

Ignoring his dig, I asked, "What's a residency director?"

"Essentially, she's the boss of the dorm. Any other intelligent questions for me?"

I glanced at Piper. Usually, she came to my rescue, but she had drifted into a coma.

"Guess not," I said.

"Good, genius. Try to park in the spot right next to me, then pop your trunk and get to work right away. This is where you earn that expensive breakfast, *Espuzito*." He said my last name wrong on purpose.

It's spelled Esposito but pronounced Es-Poh-sito, with an accent on the second syllable. Teachers have butchered it since kindergarten. Piper has told him how

16

to say it a million times, but he likes treating me like a jerk.

"Aye, aye, sir." I slowly chomped on the cookie and saluted him with it.

He gave me a dirty look. If there's one thing I won't miss during my hiatus from Piper, it's him.

"You okay, pumpkin?" he asked her.

She used her monotone voice. "Fine, Daddy."

"Have you two been fighting?"

She tried to grin. "No, I'm just a little sad."

"What have you got to be sad about? You're starting an exciting chapter in your life, and you'll be meeting all types of people and making all kinds of *new friends*. Who knows, after a while, you might like being with these kids better than your *old friends?*"

I crinkled my face at him and pointed at the line of cars. "I think your fly's down."

"How's that?" His hands shot there, and his knees angled in.

It wasn't down.

"I mean, the car in front of you just pulled away."

"Oh crap." He ran back to his minivan. Unfortunately, he moved with an athletic grace that suggested he was in good shape and wasn't anyone I'd ever want to mess with. Especially after he threatened to have his workers bury me in cement if I ever hurt his little girl again.

I took Piper's hand. "This is it. As soon as you step out of the car, you're no longer a high school senior. You'll officially be a freshman. Are you ready to start college?" I faked the enthusiasm in my voice because my spirits were sinking. I loved spending time with her, seeing her smile, and listening to her laugh.

How was I going to manage without her? Plus, Piper was the best kisser ever. How could I live without that?

She leaned over and started making out. I peeked through the window, worried about her father, but he already took off. When I felt the coolness of her tear-streaked cheek, I put my other hand on the side of her face and wiped the tears away with my thumb. I left it there a few seconds, then played with her hair.

Piper let out a small moan, pulled back, and sniffled. Boy did she look gorgeous. I wish I had a camera to capture the moment. It was so tender and intimate. I felt a stirring from my gut all the way to my choked-up throat. The car behind us laid onto his horn—probably another ticked-off father.

Our lips came toward each other, and we melted into a passionate kiss. I didn't ever want to stop. The weight of our pending separation smashed into me and now I was the one with glistening eyes. When the horn resumed its blaring, we pulled apart, but both started laughing. The next thing I knew, Piper was wiping a tear out of my eye.

"Now I'm ready for college," she said, as her hand cupped my face. She tilted her head at me and smiled.

"I love you, Piper." My chest felt so hollow.

"I love you, too."

Chapter 3

R.A.

Piper lived on the thirteenth floor—room 1313. After my hundredth trip in that cramped, rattling, and possibly haunted elevator, she introduced me to a pretty Korean girl. "Luca, come here. This is my new roommate, Robyn Cho."

I put down a red milk crate containing her mini boom box, about twenty CDs, and a case holder. "Hey Robyn, nice to meet you." I knew a few Korean girls back home, but they were all petite. Robyn was tall, maybe five foot seven, with long black hair tied up in a high ponytail. Her loose t-shirt and baggy jeans hid a curvy body.

"So, this is the boyfriend." As we shook hands Robyn gave her lips the tiniest lick. "Yum… And are you in our dorm, too? I hope you're on this floor." She raised her eyebrows provocatively, and her voice was sweet as syrup. I swear her thumb grazed the side of mine.

My muscles clenched. I'd never seen anyone like her before and felt more than a little intimidated. I wanted to run away and hide in the car.

A taller, tanned guy wearing an Aerosmith t-shirt, gym shorts, and a backward baseball hat entered the room. He put a black garbage bag full of clothes into one of the closets. "Cut it out, Robby. One of these days some guy isn't gonna realize you're joking around. And his girlfriend is gonna kick your ass. Right, Piper?"

"What, huh?" I mumbled. After moving so many boxes I felt dizzy, but it could be from the vibe Robyn gave off. She didn't mind flirting in front of Piper, or two sets of parents, which seemed weird. An older Korean couple bowed slightly to me instead of saying hi. I waved back.

Robyn let go of our handshake. "Oh look, he's turning red. Aren't you cute."

My blushing got worse when everybody started laughing.

"Don't pay any attention to her, Luca. I'm Danny, Robyn's boyfriend, although maybe not much longer if she keeps this stuff up." He towered about six inches over me.

I shook his hand, pointed at Robyn, and let out a rushing puff of air. "Glad to meet you, man. I had no idea what to do with your girlfriend over there."

"What did you think you were going to do?" Piper hugged me from behind, her arms going around my waist. She perched her head on the back of my shoulder and nibbled my ear. I didn't know if she was being playful or marking her territory.

"Go running for you to come save me," I said.

Piper's mom and dad eyed me suspiciously. Robyn's parents ignored us and kept emptying boxes.

"Hmm, good answer." Piper's demeanor had loosened up after meeting Robyn. Her father had me going back and forth to the minivan and dropping things off in the lounge. He'd carry them in from there, so I hadn't seen Piper in a while. She wasn't acting like a scared freshman anymore.

"Sorry about that, Luca, sometimes I can't help myself," Robyn said, still flirty. "But you never told me. Do you live on this floor, too?"

"Me? No, I'm not in college yet."

"Really. Look at you, Piper, with the jailbait," Robyn teased.

Piper's dad glared at me. I was standing in front of a laundry basket filled with her bras and panties.

"Oh." I jumped away like a spider bit me.

Peering at me like I was wacky, Danny slipped behind Robyn and gripped her shoulders—then addressed Piper. "You'll have to get used to my girlfriend's warped attempt at comedy. I feel sorry for you as her roommate, having to live with her twenty-four hours a day isn't gonna be easy."

She elbowed his stomach. "Oof," he grunted softly and stepped back.

"I'm looking forward to it." Piper beamed and hugged Robyn from the side. She returned it with a big smile. "So, do you live on this floor, Danny?"

Seeing Piper relax chilled me out too.

"Nope, I live in Colonial, one of the other towers."

"I have an idea," Robyn said with a lively twinkle. "We all need our student I.D.'s. Well, except for baby Luca. How about we head over to the quad and pick them up, along with our schedules and whatever else they have?"

Robyn's mother replied from the other side of the room. "I think that's a great suggestion."

"You okay with that, Mom?" Piper asked.

Mrs. Kraft stood next to one of the narrow beds pulling out a set of linens. "Absolutely. It'll give us a chance to get your room unpacked. Take your time, honey."

Boxes, bags, and clothes covered almost every inch of the floor. The room was a total mess. It'd be even more cluttered if Piper and Robyn hadn't spoken a couple times over the summer and compared notes on what to bring. Otherwise, they'd have duplicate mini-fridges, microwaves, and plungers. The walls were a boring yellow, but they'd be covered in posters, tapestries, and strings of white lights in no time.

"Okay, thanks." Piper high stepped over to her mother and kissed her on the cheek. When she hugged her father, he giggled like he won a funnel cake.

****

As we strolled past the fountains, a pleasant breeze sprinkled mist our way. It was boiling-hot again today.

"Where are you guys from?" I asked. Piper and I held hands, but I got the impression she was copying Danny and Robyn.

"A small town north of Syracuse. It's called Oswego, did you ever hear of it?" Danny asked.

"Yeah, they have a college there, a pretty good wrestling program, too."

"Oh, are you a wrestler?"

"Luca's actually really good. He's even going to a camp next week and is thinking about wrestling in college," Piper boasted.

"Is that right? You're that good?"

Piper's bragging warmed my chest. "We'll see. Did you guys ever think of going to Oswego?" I swung her arm in a lighthearted way. If it was just me and her, I'd have scooped her up by now and made believe I was dunking her in the fountain.

She smiled and I could tell she was still nervous, but

22

in a better mood.

Danny said, "Not really. We both wanted to go away. Oswego's cool, it's known as a party school, but I hear Albany holds its own."

"Did your parents care that you two were going away together?" Piper asked. "I'm not sure what mine would say if Luca were coming here, too."

That stung. We touched on the idea of me attending Albany next year, and she acted excited about it. But Mrs. Wild, the school's Assistant Principal, told me I had Ivy League potential and she'd help me get into a big-time school. Right now, Northwestern ranked as my top choice. But I didn't know anyone going there. I'd still like the option of coming to Albany with Piper. Was it my imagination or did she just veto that?

"My parents are okay about it," Robyn said. "Besides, Danny's been a fixture at our house since tenth grade. I think they love him more than me. They would have thought it was weird if we didn't go away together."

Piper inquired, "How did your parents take it, Danny?"

"About the same. They didn't even come down with me today. I rode here with Robyn's family. And my parents *definitely* love her more than me. If we ever broke up, they'd give her my room and kick me out of the house."

"Aww, don't worry," Robyn said. "I'll let you stay in the garage."

"Aren't you sweet?" Danny kissed her as they walked.

"But you'll have to pay me rent. And do other things for me, too," she teased.

He grinned and made a face at her.

I creased my forehead and looked at Piper. "Did your parents ever ask if I was coming here?"

"Hmm, maybe."

"What'd you tell them?"

She angled her body away from me, like pairs figure skating, and I was supposed to twirl her. "I said you were looking at other schools, most likely out of state."

That didn't make me feel any better. She kind of dodged the question. No one said anything for an awkward moment.

Finally, Robyn broke the silence. "So, Jailbait, what middle school do you go to?"

"Very funny."

We arrived at the student center. I held open the door and shot Robyn a sideways glance. "I'm a senior," I mouthed.

She stuck her tongue out at me.

It was a madhouse inside and super loud. Parents and freshmen milled from table to table and room to room, picking up different packets.

"Oh, please don't make Jailbait his nickname." Piper grabbed my arm and kissed me on the cheek. Despite her protest, I knew she got a kick out of my new label. Part of her liked being the older woman. She tucked in her chin, and her pouty eyes told me she felt sorry for not discussing the college thing.

"It's okay," I whispered, then gave her a long kiss.

"Too late. Jailbait, it is," Robyn declared. She pulled us apart and pointed. "I have an idea. How about we divide and conquer? It looks like the three of us go in that room for our Student I.D.s. And there's a line at that table to get information about our dorm and meal plan. Do you mind standing in line, *Luca*, and we'll catch up with you in a couple minutes?"

"Yeah, sure."

"Great, we'll meet you in a little bit." She took hold of Piper's arm and whisked her away.

Watching them leave, I hoped Piper would look back and give me a smile. She never did. After a couple seconds, I headed over to the Dutch dorm line.

While I waited, I checked out the room. I'd never seen so many hot girls in one place. It was like high school on steroids. Since it was still summer, the room was aglow in shorts and crop tops. Sometimes I couldn't believe my eyes. Before I realized it, I found myself at the front of the line.

"Dude, those chicks you're scoping are pretty sweet." A guy wearing an Albany t-shirt and a nametag that said *Jamie—R.A.*, nodded and smiled. He was tall, with messy brown hair and in good shape. He caught me admiring these amazing little co-eds, both redheads.

"Tell me about it. Is it always like this?"

"Pretty much. You're going to love it. So many opportunities," he said. "And, welcome to Dutch dorm. What's your name? I'll snag your Welcome Package." He started scanning a clipboard.

Piper and company weren't back yet. I needed to stall. There were about ten impatient people behind me, and I didn't want to lose my place in line.

"What does an R.A. do?" I asked.

"It stands for Resident Advisor. We're usually seniors or grad students. In exchange for free housing and a meal card, we coordinate activities in the dorms and enforce the rules."

"So, what does that mean? If you catch people drinking or smoking pot you have to tell the dean?"

"No, we write students up, we don't tell the dean. But as long as things don't get out of hand, I'll probably join in. If you're cool with me, I'll be cool with you. But if you stink up the hallway smoking a joint, you're going to put me in a sticky situation, especially if the director is around. So, don't do that. But being an R.A.'s not a bad gig, plus I get my own room."

"What's the big deal about your own room?" Personally, I looked forward to having a roommate in college. A lot of people said their roommate became one of their best friends.

Jamie looked around, making sure no one could overhear him. "You wouldn't believe how many freshmen chicks dig a guy with his own room. And the whole authority thing attracts them like flies. Every R.A. I know does really well for themselves." Then he pointed over my shoulder. "Perfect example, check out this little blondie coming our way. If she's in our dorm, I'll bet you anything I hook up with her before Christmas."

"Dude, that's my girlfriend," I said.

"Nice pull. She's pretty tasty. But don't worry, I'll keep my eye on her for you," he said, totally sarcastic.

My lips curled back in disgust. A flush of heat in my neck developed into anger. Why was he being such a jerk? What happened to the bro code?

Stepping closer to the table, I minimized the distance between us. "Don't even think about it. I only live a few hours away and I'll be visiting all the time. I better not find you anywhere near Piper."

He let out a malicious laugh. "You mean you don't even go here? This'll be too easy. And Piper? That's her name? Can't be many of those. Let's take a quick peek." He ran his twisted finger up and down the clipboard.

"And look at this, there's a Piper Kraft on the thirteenth floor, just down the hall from me. That wouldn't be the same girl, would it?"

I'd never met a bigger jackass. I thought Bryce from last year was bad, but this sleazebag was way worse. "Jamie, I swear—"

He raised his hand. "Stop right there, kid. Don't try to intimidate me. I used to play football here. And sorry to tell you, but girls in college stray, cheat on their boyfriends, and have a good time. Why do you think they go away in the first place? There's nothing you can do about it. But there's something I can." He raised his eyebrows and wiped a speck of dirt off his shirt as if he were flicking me away.

"Keep it up, dude. You'll find out what happened to the last two football douches who pissed me off." My fight with Puma and Brayden came to mind and how we kicked the football team's ass at the prom.

He scowled. "Do you really think you're going to be the one putz who keeps up a long-distance relationship?"

We stared at each other for several seconds, then Piper threw her arms around my neck and kissed my cheek.

"Thanks for waiting in line for us, honey. Perfect timing too," she said.

Crinkling my nose, I thought deeply. Had she ever called me honey before?

Danny and Robyn came up behind her. Danny liked the picture on Robyn's I.D.

She corrected him. "You have no idea what you're talking about. Why didn't you tell me my smile was crooked?"

"You must be Piper Kraft. My name's Jamie. I'll be

your R.A. You're on the thirteenth floor, right?" He thrust out his hand and she shook it. Holding on a few seconds too long, he was all smiles, especially at me.

I would have loved to jump over this table and pummel him in front of her. I wasn't a jealous guy. I trusted Piper and she trusted me. I also believed in what we had together. It was too good to be ruined by a tool like Jamie. But Piper had been so emotional and vulnerable today. The last thing I needed was some idiot like him undermining me.

She grinned at her new R.A. "Yes, room 1313, great to meet you. I hope Luca hasn't been telling you too much about me."

"Luca, huh?" He drew himself up to his full height and crossed his arms, nodding at me.

I said, "Actually, Jamie's been telling me about *you*."

She scrunched her face. "What could he possibly say about me?"

"That he'll get in your pants by Thanksgiving."

Chapter 4

Camp

Thirteen days later I was finishing up at the Shultsville, Pennsylvania, Wrestling Camp. My best friend Pablo had been coming here since seventh grade. He claimed it turned him into a state champion—two years running. Everyone expected him to cruise to a third title as a senior.

Whenever he tried talking me into joining him, my answer was always the same. "There's no way my parents are paying for that."

At the beginning of summer, I received an interesting call from our high school coach. "Luca, what are you doing the last week of break?"

"I have no idea, Coach."

"Good, don't make any plans, you're wrestling at Shultsville that week."

"I am?"

Coach Slazne, or "Slaz" as we called him, wrestled in college with the head of the camp. He convinced him to offer me one of their three scholarships. As long as my parents would pay for my room and board, the scholarship would cover the fee.

My dad was less than excited. "There's no way I'm paying for that."

So, I covered it. Whatever money I made waiting

tables at Gino's Café went toward my room and board—about four hundred dollars.

Hopefully, the camp's magic would rub off. As I sat on the mat, lacing up my sneakers, I told Pablo about Piper's R.A.

"So, how did she react when you said that to Jamie?" he asked, coming to the end of his stretching routine.

"Well—"

"Hold on, don't tell me. You kind of pissed her off, right?"

I gazed at him, like he cracked open a safe. "Yeah, really pissed actually. How did you know?"

"Gee. This is a hard one. Umm, girls don't usually like it when you talk about other guys getting into their pants. It especially ticks them off when their boyfriends do it."

"Where were you when I needed you?" I kidded.

He grinned. "You brought her up there almost two weeks ago. Why are you only sharing this story now?"

I shrugged. "I don't know. She was only mad for a little while. By the time I got home, she had already left two messages telling me to call her because she missed me."

"You two are so cute."

I blew him a kiss. "And why does every wrestling mat smell like ass?" We still had a few minutes to goof off before practice.

Even though we were supposed to shower after every session and bring clean clothes each day, it didn't mean we followed the rules. Wrestlers took pride in how hard they worked out and how much they sweat. There was a badge of honor to smelling gross. A guy on my team ate garlic cloves before each match. He wanted to give his opponent the creeps.

"Baby, you're the one who smells like ass." Pablo sniffed me twice then tried running his hands through my hair. He used a seductive voice and started climbing on top of me. I clutched his elbow with mine and rolled him away—one of my favorite moves.

"You're a jackass, you know that?" I finished lacing up. I was the only kid at camp in sneakers. My dad refused to spring for wrestling shoes—too cheap, I guess.

Wrestle-offs were being held today. The top guy in each weight class won a medal and a t-shirt saying, 1990 Shultsville Wrestling Camp Champion. To me, the t-shirt was way more valuable. The medal would sit on my dresser, but I'd be able to wear the shirt to school and practice. It'd get me a lot more respect.

Last year I wrestled in the 134-pound weight class. Even though I probably added ten pounds of muscle, I also trimmed down and lost fat. Hopefully I'd still be at 134 this winter. Otherwise, I'd have to move up to 140 and those dudes were mini-Arnolds.

Pablo finished stretching and slid next to me as I began work on my hamstrings. "You ready to wipe the floor with this kid? He's the only guy that beat you last season."

"Somehow, I think I remember that. Thanks for bringing it up."

"Just shut up and get your revenge."

I won the county championship last year, but when I got to States, I wasn't ranked very high. I made it to the semifinals, but a big ugly guy named Hector Wolfe destroyed me. He was a real jerkoff and happened to be at camp this week. He lived upstate, in Booger Hole County. I hoped I'd never see his white hair and evil, frosty eyes again. But here he was, in Shultsville, and he stood in the way of my cool t-shirt.

The biggest guy in camp plopped onto the mat. "What's up, ladies?"

"Hey, Tex," I said. We met earlier this week. He lived in New Jersey and came the past two years. Pablo already knew him.

"Luca, can I share a secret with you?" he asked.

"Sure," I drew out the word, but he talked loud enough for Pablo to hear.

Placing his head on my shoulder, he looked at me with dreamy eyes. "Do you moisturize? Because you have the softest hands in camp."

"Get the hell away from me." I shoved him in the arm, and he slid off.

Pablo chuckled and asked him, "Any luck dropping the weight?"

"Coach wants me down to two-seventy. He thinks it'll make me a lot faster. I began camp at two-eighty-five."

"What are you at now?"

He smiled a big toothy grin. "Two-eighty-seven."

"How's that even possible?" I asked.

They weighed us last Sunday, then handed out a diet plan to achieve our "ideal" weight. Plus, they worked us so hard, everyone shed pounds. Well, almost everyone.

He raised his eyebrows. "Have you tried that pizza joint next door? Did you know they deliver until midnight?"

Pablo smirked. "You're such an idiot. Final weigh-ins are tomorrow morning. Coach is going to flip when he finds out. What are you going to do?"

Tex checked the area, ensuring no one could

eavesdrop. "A guy over there gave me a bunch of laxative pills. One time he took two pills and dropped seven pounds."

"You're going to crap off the weight?" I asked.

He shrugged. "That's the plan. I took them last night and I've been squirting it out ever since."

Pablo asked, "How many did you use?"

"Five."

"Five!" Pablo and I shouted.

"Yeah. Do you think it was too many? I can't stop going. The only time I don't feel like taking a dump is when I'm taking a dump."

We both laughed and he dove on top of us.

"Uh oh, speaking of." Tex grabbed the back of his sweatpants.

"You gotta go now?" Pablo sat up. "Coach'll be here any second. It's two hundred push-ups if you're late."

"He ain't gonna be happy if I drop manure on his mat."

"Just get your butt out of here! We'll do the push-ups with you," I yelled.

If you were friends with a fellow wrestler, and stupid enough, you could serve his punishment with him.

Tex stuck out his tongue and scampered away. "Thanks, man."

Pablo asked, "We will?"

"Would you rather wrestle in Tex's turds?"

"Good point."

The whistle blew and I hustled to my spot for warm-ups.

****

During wrestle-offs I pinned my first two opponents. One within a minute, and the next guy in the second period. That meant I'd meet Hector in my battle royale. Pablo pinned each of his challengers in less than forty-five seconds.

We sat on the outskirts of the mat to watch the finals. Everyone respected their fellow wrestlers. Caring enough about the sport to spend a grueling week in gloomy Shultsville earned you a lot of admiration.

Pablo appeared totally at ease, and yelled advice to each guy. "Keep your hands in front, get lower, shoot"— that kind of thing.

Whenever I was nervous, my muscles tightened up, especially my calves, like someone crocheted little knots into them.

"I need to stretch." I stood and massaged them, spying Hector across the way. He laughed with some guys, looking way too confident.

Pablo flicked me a thumbs up.

To psyche up for a match, I jacked the volume on my walk-man to eleven. Ozzy was my favorite and he gets my blood pumping. I always began with side two of *Blizzard of Ozz*.

They had set up a mat in the back for warmups. Fifteen minutes later, I had a decent sweat going and felt loosened up. I flipped over the cassette and practiced a few moves. The ref called for the 134 pounders as *Crazy Train* finished.

"Let's go Luca!" Pablo yelled.

Someone tossed me an ancient set of headgear. I slipped it on and adjusted the straps while the camp director spent a couple minutes at the scorer's table. The ear pads were moist, and the chin guard had turned brown and damp from years of sweat and blood. A faint iron smell drifted into my nose. Most kids would get skeeved out, but wrestlers didn't care.

Pablo grabbed my arm, and whispered, "As soon as they blow the whistle, shoot at his legs. There's no way he's expecting it, and you'll catch him off guard."

"Are you sure that's the way to go?"

"Trust me, dude," he said.

I nodded and joined Hector at the center of the mat. Pablo definitely knew what he was doing but I wasn't sure it would work.

Hector glared at me. "I remember you. You're that pussy from John Marshall."

Total shock. "What?" I may have squinted. Not exactly my toughest look.

"Didn't I beat your ass at States last year?" He used a mocking tone of voice.

His trash-talking caught me off guard. Wrestlers didn't do that.

I was about to push him in the face with an open hand. A punch would get me thrown out of here. But the referee returned.

"All right gentlemen, shake hands," he ordered.

As I reached forward, Hector blew me a kiss. The ref didn't see it, otherwise he would have penalized him a point for unsportsmanlike conduct. That did it. My Italian blood boiled. I decided to follow Pablo's advice and immediately torpedo Hector's legs.

Like a fool, I played right into his plans. He totally expected it. In reality, he engineered it by knocking me off my game. As I shot forward, Hector threw the Cowboy hold around my neck and arm. He was on top of me with all his strength and force squeezing me into a headlock. He reeked like four-day-old body odor—the gross jerk.

I lay on my back, unable to do anything, except struggle to keep one shoulder a few inches off the mat, barely enough to stop the ref from calling a pin. Leverage was one hundred percent on his side. Nobody escaped the Cowboy.

His huge arms choked like a boa and his thick legs kept chugging toward my head.

It took all my focus, energy, and stamina, but I refused to get pinned by this moron. I may lose on points, but no way was he pinning me. After suffering through Hector's bone crushing power and heinous stench for two minutes, I heard the whistle blow. I survived the first period. But since he had scored the initial takedown and had me on my side and back the whole time, he racked up a ton of points and led 10-0.

Matches lasted for six minutes—three, two-minute periods. We were both so exhausted, the second and third periods went by with almost no scoring. Hector won 12 to 1, but as I returned to my corner of the mat I looked across and saw him throwing up—right down the back of some poor 108 pounder.

"What the heck?" The little guy screamed. He arched his body, spun around, and shoved Hector away. When he saw the chunks of spew running down his singlet, he sprinted for the showers.

It didn't make sense. Hector held the upper position the whole time. He should have been a lot less tired than me. What was his deal?

Losing sucked, no matter what, so I felt lousy—embarrassed too. No cool t-shirt for me. Plus, Piper knew about our wrestle-offs. I swallowed hard, imagining our conversation. She'd probably be excited when she asked me about it, assuming that I won. Then I could picture her shifting to her supportive voice and telling me that I'll do better next time. But it was going to feel like I let her down.

A bunch of guys came by. They shook my hand, patted my back, and congratulated me for avoiding the pin. That softened the blow a little, but I couldn't believe how Hector dominated me. I sat there with sagging shoulders, re-living what happened.

Pablo warmed up in the back, his match was coming up. It would have been nice to be consoled by my best friend, but it also stunk that he was so much better. Maybe I was a tiny bit jealous. I had hoped to win a state championship this year, too. Perhaps, a scholarship. But if I made it to the finals, I'd have to face Hector again.

This guy had my number. I didn't know how to beat the prick.

Chapter 5

First Day

On the first day of school, I didn't know what to feel.
Excited to be the big senior on campus? Eager for new
opportunities? Proud because I made it this far or
nostalgic because this was my last, first day of high
school?

None of those seemed like a big deal. Mainly, I was
bummed my girlfriend wasn't with me. Piper's classes
started a couple weeks ago, and she already had her
routine down. When we spoke on the phone last night,
she forgot school began today.

The last time I went to school was with Piper. Once
we started dating again, she picked me up in the
mornings. Every time I got in her '85 Buick Regal, we
kissed hello. It was never a simple peck on the lips. They
were long and passionate. I'd lean across the bench seat,
my hand would play with the back of her hair and unless
we were running super late, there'd be some tongue, too.
Butterflies would immediately dance in my stomach, and
I'd realize how lucky I was to be back together with her.
What a great way to start the day.

Since I still didn't own a car, now I bummed rides
from my friend, Jimmy, the biggest Billy Joel fan in Big
Dune's history. It was a gorgeous morning, eighty-one
degrees and sunny.

"How many times can we listen to *We Didn't Start the Fire*?" I asked.

"Dude, Billy Joel's awesome."

"I agree, and it was great the first ten times we heard it. But can we please put on something else?"

He stuck out his tongue, biting it, and cranked the tunes. I seriously considered taking the bus.

Two tractors mowed the grounds of John Marshall High, and we arrived five minutes before class. We both liked to sleep until the last minute, and Jimmy always timed things perfectly. After pulling into the parking lot and inhaling a bunch of secondhand smoke along the way, we strolled right to our classrooms. It would be a pain on the days I had to stop at my locker, but the extra two minutes of sleep was worth hustling before the bell or even risking the occasional tardy.

I had Mr. Richter for first period, U.S. History. He had the most easygoing personality of any teacher. I don't think he ever wrote a tardy in his career, so I didn't have much to worry about.

When we walked through the main doors a wall of sound hit me. Students shouted to each other, they tried to talk over the noise, and one particular girl squealed every time she recognized someone. Had to be a freshman.

I jogged up the stairs two at a time. But a slow-moving couple had their hands in each other's back pockets and clogged things into a jam. Those people were the worst. If karma was on the job, they'd dissect a bunch of frogs today.

Hugging the railing sideways, I tried sneaking by, but caught a spiral notebook to the face. At the top, I took a hard right turn, things finally loosened up and I could walk without being bumped into. I said hi to more people than I could count.

My thick black hair had almost dried from my morning shower. I wore a blue t-shirt from the mall, jeans, and white high tops. Toting my three-ring binder, I entered my classroom.

"Luca, over here."

"Porco." I waved with my notebook hand.

He sat in the last row, right next to the windows. He didn't play sports but was in the best shape of all of us—he had brown hair and looked like a bodybuilder. Making my way past the other desks, I snagged the seat in front of him and we high-fived.

"You need a haircut," I said.

"You're worse than my mother."

"Well, you look like a Muppet."

"Thanks." He spit a brown gob of dip into an old ginger ale can.

Secretly, I hoped Mr. Richter would make him throw it away. Dip skeezed me out. I tried it a couple times, but it tasted like ass. Plus, it never stayed balled up in my mouth. Little pieces always broke off and drifted around, which enhanced the ass flavor and made me nauseous. I didn't get the appeal.

"I want you to meet someone," he said. "This is Michael Chase."

I glanced up and down the row but, but there was no Michael anywhere. I stared at him like he was nuts. "Did you inhale a bunch of dip?" I asked.

The only person near us was a girl I'd never seen before. Her tight, raven-haired curls fell below her shoulders, and she had deep blue eyes. Pretty smokin'.

She extended her hand. "Porco thinks he's funny.

Hi, Luca, my name's pronounced Michael, but spelled M-Y-C-K-A-L."

Most girls didn't shake hands. Already, she was kind of rad.

"Myckal huh? There's got to be a story behind that," I said.

"My parents thought I was going to be a boy and wanted to name me after my grandfather. When I came out as a girl, they stuck with Myckal anyway."

"That makes sense." Was it my imagination, or had she held on to my hand longer than normal? Why was everyone doing that, lately? I tilted my head and smiled, trying to get a read on her, but she broke eye contact, and looked down.

I motioned at Porco. "How do you know this moron?"

He punched me in the shoulder and with his size, it really hurt. But I didn't flinch or let on, especially not in front of the new chick.

"Oh, I've known Porco a long time. We've been riding our bikes together for years," she said and bit her bottom lip.

Although I knew almost nothing about girls, I had learned one thing in seventeen years. They didn't *accidentally* bite their lips. So, was she was flirting with him, now? What gave?

"She lives on the same street as me," Porco said. "It's a mile long and she went to Alexander Hamilton until last year. But thanks to re-zoning, we'll have to deal with her annoying personality."

"Shut up." She drew out her words like they were old friends. She seemed cool. It's too bad he never mentioned her.

41

"When Porco says you're *annoying*, is that code for Canadian?" I asked.

She chuckled. "No, but do you have something against Canadians?"

"Not at all. It just popped into my head. Thought it'd be funny. So, is this horrible for you, starting a new school as a senior?"

"It's not as bad as it could be. If I moved here from another state, I'd be scared to death. But luckily, I have a few friends that go to John Marshall." She wore a light shade of pink lipstick and had a pretty mouth, full of white teeth. The type that probably sat in braces for the past four years and came out perfect.

"So, Myckal, Luca's one of the resident brains in our group. You'll meet Pablo later, he's the other one. They're the two to cheat off of," Porco said.

"Very funny," I said. "Porco obviously doesn't have a brain."

"Is that right? You're smart?" she asked.

That was a weird question to handle. Admitting I got good grades was embarrassing for some reason. It shouldn't be, and I didn't want to come off as stuck up and say, *Yeah, I am smart*, but I didn't want to say I was dumb either.

"Put it this way. In elementary school my teachers would arrange our desks by reading groups. I was always in the highest group, which meant I had to sit with a bunch of girls."

After pressing her hand over her mouth like she was mortally wounded, Myckal let it fall to her heart. "That must have been terrible for you."

"Hey, when you don't like girls yet, it was pure torture. But few people know what secrecy there is in the

42

young and the terror."

"Who said that?" she asked.

"It's Dickens from *Great Expectations*. I'm sure I didn't get it exactly right." I shrugged. It was cool that she knew I was quoting someone.

"Well, I happen to be one of those girls that put you in mortal terror. But it's not our fault that boys are dumb and don't know how to read. So, on behalf of the female population in top reading groups everywhere, let me formally apologize to you."

"Sorry. Can't accept it. The scars run too deep. You big bullies."

Her hands flew to her heart again. "Ahh."

We both grinned at each other.

"All right, let's talk survival skills," I said. "You may know this guy from the bike trails, but he's a different animal inside school. If you're going to sit next to Porco, you need to know a couple things."

She leaned forward, her chin on her hand. "Like what?"

"He'll borrow something almost every day. If you loan him a pen, you have to be the adult in the room and childproof it. Don't ever let him have the cap."

She gathered in her eyebrows. "Why's that?"

"As soon as he gets bored, he starts chewing on it. First, he puts the clip part in his mouth and immediately tongues it to a right angle."

"I'm surprised Porco knows what a right angle is," she teased.

"You're giving him too much credit. He's like a monkey nibbling on a chocolate protractor. As soon as the overhead projector clicks on, the whole thing goes in his mouth. At the end of the period all you get back is a mostly digested pen cap—soaking wet. Hopefully, no dip. I'm telling you, Myckal, Porco is gross."

She had an easy smile. Her face lit up when she giggled.

"Yeah, yeah, yeah," he said dismissively. "But don't you think she's the hottest Myckal you've ever seen?"

"Porco," she growled out his name, then leaned backed in her seat and clenched her jaw.

I tried coming to her rescue. "Yes, she is. I mean yes, you are. And didn't I already say he was an idiot?" The burning in my cheeks increased which meant I was blushing. I hated when it happened. The more I tried not to blush, the more embarrassed I got. Which made me blush even more. I didn't understand why. I've complimented girls a million times. What made her different?

"Thank you, Luca." Myckal used a peppy voice, then pointed at us. "And I think you're both incredibly hot. Except for Porco."

He gestured at me. "Don't waste your loyalty on this guy. Luca's got a serious girlfriend."

She kicked him in the shins, and he yelped in pain.

As I laughed, we made eye contact for the second time. Again, she peeked down and broke it off. I had to stop checking her out. Scoping out the freshmen at Albany seemed perfectly natural. But this girl gave me a twinge of guilt.

A bunch of shushing broke out. The teacher must have come in. I decided to concentrate on my actual girlfriend, who I loved like crazy. I put a pen cap in my mouth and tore out a piece of paper to write Piper a letter. Mr. Richter would think I was taking a ton of notes. It'd make his day.

My mouth fell open. I blinked rapidly, trying to process what was happening. Ever have a teacher that hated you for no reason? For me, that was Ms. Maroney. Why was she in here?

"Oh no, where's Mr. Richter?" I asked.

"Oh no yourself, Mr. ESPUZITO." She knew how to pronounce my name correctly and she knew that wasn't it. "Consider this your first and only warning. I will not tolerate any of your monkey business. The next one buys you a ticket to see Mrs. Wild."

The opening bell hadn't rung yet. She was already sticking it to me.

Chapter 6

Lunch

Last year, about ten of us sat together at lunch. The cafeteria had long rectangular tables and ours was tucked in the corner. Since this was the first day, not everyone established their territory yet. Battle lines were being drawn. The fifty minutes during lunch could be the most stressful of someone's existence. So far, six of us had arrived at the same spot. Pablo, Jimmy, me, and Garret Wu—and two girls, Nicole and Cheryl.

"I don't know what this is, but it ain't pizza," I said to our crowd.

"What's he complaining about?" Garret asked.

"Who knows, who listens *to him*?" Pablo said.

"It's just a square of greasy bread, with congealing cheese, and grody-looking pepperoni. What the heck was I thinking?"

"For someone who claims to be Italian, you'd think you'd know better than to order the pizza here," Pablo joked.

He was right. I got on the lunch line with Nicole and Cheryl. We'd been friends since seventh grade, so there were no romantic considerations between any of us, but waiting with the girls made me miss Piper.

Even though we each wrote a couple of letters and spoke almost every night on the phone, it's not the same as her being here. I must have been daydreaming when I grabbed my lunch.

"Hey, I heard pizza and reached for it like a gag reflex. Believe me, won't happen again," I said.

The cafeteria had filled up. Kids yelled and laughed, plates and trays hit the tables, and silverware was "accidentally" thrown out. It sounded like comfortable white noise.

"Speaking of gagging, does anyone know what's going on with Mr. Richter and Ms. Maroney? She was subbing for him this morning but wouldn't elaborate when someone asked where he was. Typical," I said.

Cheryl answered. "Didn't you hear? He has some mysterious disease and he'll be out a while. They're dividing up his classes. You must have one that she's taking over."

"That sucks. I guarantee you, one way or another, that lady is going to cause trouble for me."

"Stop being such a pussy," Pablo said. "You sound like a baby."

I tore off a piece of pepperoni and whipped it at his head like a frisbee, but he ducked underneath. It stuck to the wall like gum.

"Who's that with Porco?" Nicole asked.

We all turned to look. He had just come through the double swinging doors with a soda and a brunette.

I said, "That's Myckal Chase."

"Do you know her?" Nicole asked.

"He introduced us in first period. We have history together."

Cheryl leaned forward, a gleam in her eye. "Really, what kind of history?"

I sighed. "*U.S.* History."

"Oh, you're so boring." She scrunched her face and bit a chicken nugget in half.

"Sorry."

"That chick's hot," Garret said.

Nicole crinkled her nose. "You think so?"

"I do," Pablo said.

I didn't say anything, didn't want to get in trouble. Myckal wore a black denim mini skirt with a white V-neck t-shirt and black ankle boots. Her white socks peaked just above the boots and her legs were tanner than I realized.

"I remember her," Cheryl said. "We had gymnastics together in like, fifth grade. She always stood out because of her weird name. She was nice, but I thought she went to Ackerman."

"Hamilton, actually." I pushed the disgusting plate away, brought my hands to my throat, and made a gurgling noise.

"Hey, everybody, I want you to meet my good friend, Myckal." Porco took a half bow and motioned to her with both arms.

Cheryl spoke first. "Hi, Myckal."

"Hi, Cheryl." Myckal held her books in front of her and waved at the rest of us.

Porco went behind each person, placed his hands on their shoulders and introduced them. People replied with a mixture of head nods, heys, and what's ups.

After Myckal said hi back to everyone, she had a twinkle in her eye. "You're Pablo Salinas, aren't you?"

He glanced at her sideways. "How do you know that?"

"Oh my gosh, and you're the Luca Esposito that wrestled one-thirty-four last year, right?"

"Yeah?" I drew out the word as a question.

She smiled. "I knew, I knew who you were this morning. I was the wrestling manager for Alexander Hamilton last year. You're a really good wrestler, you know that?"

"Well—"

Before I could answer, she turned to Pablo. "But you're the best anyone's ever seen. Will it be your second state championship this year?"

Porco threw his arm over Pablo's shoulder. "Third, but who's counting, except Pablo."

"Shut up." His eyes sparkled. He tried pushing him away, but Porco had so many muscles, it was a challenge, even for Pablo. "You know our manager graduated last year. If you have any interest in the job, we're looking for someone good."

His voice had elevated three notes higher than normal, like when you're first dating a girl and she asks you to go to the mall. *Of course, I love shoe shopping. What's that, you want me to stand around at a kiosk while they teach you about makeup? Awesome. Sure, and why don't we try on expensive things we can't afford. That sounds super fun.*

Myckal beamed. "Really? That'd be amazing. I was hoping to do it again, but I figured you already had a manager."

"How about I take you over to meet Coach Slaz? He's probably in the teacher's lounge. We can set this up right now."

"Are you serious? I'd love it. But how can we go through the halls in between classes? Don't we need a pass or something?"

Garret piped in. "Pablo's the 'or something.' The

rules only apply to us mere mortals. He gets to go wherever he wants."

Myckal shrugged. "Sure, let's do it."

"Outstanding. It's right this way." He placed his hand on the small of her back and guided her toward the double doors. "So where are you from?" He turned around, stuck his tongue out at us, and flashed the double hang loose sign.

Porco gave him the finger. Garret and Jimmy watched her leave, tilting their heads—probably already in love with her.

"He moves pretty fast." Nicole took a bite of her sandwich. She raised her head to motion to me. "I didn't think he was over Jessica yet?"

I gave a small wave, indicating they should move in closer. "Here's the story, and not everyone knows this, so let's keep it on the down low." I slurped from my can of apple juice and set it on the table. They all nodded.

"So, Pablo and Jessica go to the prom together and she wins the queen title. They're having a great time at Jimmy's after party and sneak away downstairs. They were messing around on the couch, right between the beer ball and the laundry room. It was like springtime, but instead of roses, the smell of Tide and dryer sheets hung in the air. Unfortunately, Jessica's allergic to dryer sheets. They were making out, and her throat started closing up. She broke out in hives, *even in her lungs!*"

"Her lungs broke out in hives?" Nicole looked skeptical.

"I may be exaggerating, just go with it."

She sipped her chocolate milk. "Okay, continue."

"Well anyway, Jessica gets up, stumbles toward the dryer and throws up in her crown. But they don't know what caused it. The champagne, cheap beer, or the lint trap."

"Oh no. Is that why she left the party so early?" Cheryl asked.

"Yup. Too bad for Pablo. After that night, they tried a couple dates, but I think she was embarrassed. Plus, she was going off to college in a couple months, so she never let it get too serious."

"Poor Jessica and poor Pablo," she said.

"I know, stinks for him."

Actually, Jessica kept things from getting hot between them. Pablo really liked her, despite the puke and laundry issues. If he had his way, he'd be stressing over a long-distance relationship, too. He's hoping they get back together over winter break. He told me that last part in confidence. I wasn't about to announce it, even if we were all friends.

"How are things with you and Piper?" Cheryl asked.

"Real good. I'm going up this weekend. I'm dying to see her."

Chapter 7

Let Down

It only took two hours and forty-five minutes to drive to Albany. Forty minutes quicker than when I trailed behind Mr. Kraft's lame minivan. My radar detector remains the greatest thing I ever bought.

I meant to leave right after school, but my mom got home late and had a bunch of chores for me to do, including cutting the grass. I wanted to complain, but since I didn't have my own wheels and had to borrow her car, there wasn't much I could say.

By the time I took a shower and packed, it was already 5:45 p.m., so I didn't arrive at Piper's parking lot until almost 8:30 p.m. I stepped out of the car, stretched, and took a deep breath after the long ride. Some early crickets welcomed me onto campus. Twilight emerged and the outdoor lights turned on.

The charred scent of a nearby barbecue drifted over. A group of kids sat on a patch of grass and laughed while a small hibachi smoked in front of them. Two guys played hacky sack. I never understood the concept of kicking something that didn't bounce.

The Friday night buzz and energy that I pictured at college had shown up. Inside the dorm, kids wandered about, leaving in packs of twos, threes, and fours to begin their drunken evenings. A lonely TV played in the rec room. No one sat there watching.

I got off the elevator on the thirteenth floor with a duffel bag full of clothes slung over my shoulder. I had on a pair of jeans and a blue polo shirt. Handmade posters hung in the halls. BEAT ITHACA, in big blue letters ran the distance from one door to the next. Stereos blared inside their rooms.

A door opened and a wet girl wearing nothing but a cropped white cami, men's boxer shorts and flip flops banged into me. She had been peering back, talking to her friend and hadn't noticed me.

"Sorry about that." She smelled great, like a soap commercial. With a shower caddy in her left hand, her right hand scraped through her damp hair and tucked a strand behind an ear. Golden butterflies dangled from each of her perfect lobes.

"Please… um don't be. It was all my fault." I stumbled over those short sentences and froze solid in place.

When she didn't make a move to leave, my eyes dropped to her legs. An ankle bracelet clung to her moist skin and a drop of water trailed down and disappeared behind it. Next, I glanced at her exposed midriff, where a silver hoop pierced her belly button. I took in a sharp breath, afraid to look away. Her cami rose and fell with each deep inhale. I didn't know brown eyes could sparkle like that, but hers did. They were full of mischief, and I saw nothing but trouble behind them.

I knew I should take a step back to give her some space, but my legs refused to budge. A devious smile appeared on her lips, and it felt hotter in here.

Her equally showered friend came out of the bathroom, struggling to close her tiny silk robe. "Oops. I didn't expect anyone to be here. Come on, let's go," she said, and led her friend away by the elbow.

"But he's cute," Cami girl said.

They giggled down to their room and out of my life forever.

I shook my head and cupped the back of my neck. "I have a girlfriend. I have a girlfriend. I have a girlfriend." I kept repeating it down the hallway.

Eventually, I got to Piper's room, 1313. Blue construction paper was taped to the top half of their door, with white paper framing it. They had "t" in the middle, separating it into four quadrants as if you were looking through a window onto a pale blue sky. They used black paper to make a window box with pink, purple, yellow, and red flowers. The letters for ROBYN & PIPER were cut out of hot pink construction paper and stood out against the black background.

I pictured two goofy college girls acting like they were at some giant four-year camp, having fun with arts and crafts. Except, this camp came with sorority hazing, ladies' nights, chicken wings, and karaoke. As I tapped on her door, my fingers and toes tingled. We hadn't seen each other in three weeks. I was so excited.

"Come in," she yelled.

I peeked around the door and took a timid step. "Anybody home?"

"Luca!" she squealed and flew across the room.

Her face lit up, full of warmth and tenderness. It's why I drove up here and skipped a party back home. I didn't want to be away from her any longer than I had to be.

Leaping into my arms, she knocked me against the door, slamming it closed. And just like that, we were making out.

She was always the best at it, but this was more powerful and raw, like she'd been away at war for months and finally returned home. I forgot how much I craved her kisses. Her hands were all up and down my back, so I dropped my duffel and returned the favor, lingering in certain places longer than normal.

Her skin smelled tasty, like a jasmine and vanilla smoothie. My heartbeat pounded and a flash of heat spread from my belly outward. But it wasn't just physical. Having her hands on me and being so close with her again—it made everything right in the world, like things couldn't get better.

"Wow! Have I missed you," she said through the kissing.

My brain went fuzzy. I felt safe and whole with her. If someone asked me, I would've said emotions like that were only for girls, that guys didn't need them. And I would've been dead wrong.

She broke our kiss and pouted. "You're over an hour late."

Right away, I knew what that meant, and my shoulders sagged. I missed my chance to fool around with her. Damn those State Troopers—55 MPH sucks.

I tried pleading. "Sorry, my mom had me doing a million things—"

She shrugged. "Doesn't matter. We gotta go. Just leave your bag."

"Ugh. Where are we heading?" I asked, then made one final stab at teenage bliss. "I thought we might spend a little time alone together. Especially since Robyn isn't here and we have the whole place to ourselves. Did I mention how much I missed you?" I held both of her hands and tried leading her toward the bed.

She took two steps then tapped me on the nose. "Next time, don't be late." Piper smiled and went to her desk, grabbing her keys and I.D. "We're going over to Danny's dorm to party. Robyn's already there."

After exhaling an extremely disappointed breath, I did my best to sound upbeat. "Love the room."

"Thanks. I do, too."

All I could think about, was coming back here.

Standing on a hot pink rug, I stared at Robyn's side. It was like a pink, fuzzy hot pink, or purple monster had attacked. Even her string of lights was hot pink. She also had a poster of The Cure, a six-foot square of pictures with her and Danny, and a poster of four shirtless guys wearing jeans.

On the other hand, Piper's bedspread was blue and white, and her string of lights was white. She had a six-foot square with pictures of us, copied from Robyn, no doubt.

She pointed at a blank section of wall. "I still feel like I need to catch up with Robyn."

"Yeah, maybe add some pink."

"Funny," she said and made a face. "Ready to go?"

"Are you forgetting your purse?"

Chuckling at me, she slipped her I.D. into her back pocket. "No one carries purses in college."

I took one last glance at her bed. It seemed kind of thin, but for two nights, we could fit perfectly. Robyn was already at Danny's. Did that mean she'd be sleeping there? Was tonight possibly *the night*? I got a lump in my throat.

"Oh, that's right. I forgot. Purses are *so high school*," I teased. "So, let me get this straight. Your parents have paid thousands of dollars in tuition, thousands more in room and board. You've lived up here a couple weeks, and gone to a bunch of college classes and you *finally* learned that your jeans have pockets?"

She stuck out her tongue.

"How do you know purses are out? On the way to Psych 101 did a mean TA take you to the side and say, 'Look girly we can tell by that purse you're *just a freshman*. Up here you only carry a Student I.D., a room key, and two singles for chips and soda.'"

"You think you're so clever," she said and grinned.

"All right, let's try an experiment. Do you have any money on you?"

She patted all four pockets.

"Ha! You've never checked your pockets in your life. A couple weeks ago if I asked about money, you'd have searched your purse."

"So, what does that mean?" she asked.

"If I doubted you, you would have huffed and pulled your purse open on the sides like you were cracking a clam. Then said something snarky like, 'Do you want to see for yourself?'

"I would have been scared, then raised my hands, and backed away slowly. 'Everything's cool here, man. Just put the handbag down.'"

She shook her head. "Let's go." As we walked through the door, she pulled out a few bills.

"That's three singles, not two. What do you have to say about that, smarty-pants?"

I shrugged. "The extra one is for a candy bar."

After locking her room, she *very* deliberately slid the key into her back pocket, taking her time. Knowing my eyes were glued to her, she took it back out, flipped it over, and put it in again. I gulped.

She bit her bottom lip. "Are you done with the purse jokes?"

"I have one more."

Scrunching her face, she said, "Save it."

I tried being the attentive guy. "Cool door."

"Do you really like it?"

"I think it's a-door-able."

"Aww. You're the coolest boyfriend in the world." We started kissing again.

My imagination took over.

I pictured her reaching back, unlocking the door and saying, "You're right, but not about the candy. Why don't we take advantage of this empty room, after all?"

"Really? You mean it?" I'd ask.

She'd nod. "I've dreamed about this moment with you for a long time."

My pulse would race faster than ever. I'd pick her up and carry her over the threshold. Candles somehow replaced the strings of lights and flickered around the room. When I placed her gently on the bed, she stared up at me with those gorgeous green eyes, but mumbled something I couldn't make out.

"No. You're the one. Darling," I'd say.

Piper glared at me like I was nuts. "Darling? I'm the one? Darling? I said you need to press one for the lobby. What are you talking about? And since when do you call me that?"

We were in the elevator, heading to Danny's—not in her room playing out my fantasy. White, fluorescent lights nearly blinded me. I must have blanked and spaced out. I smacked both cheeks to clear out the fiction going through my mind. Our first time would have to wait a little longer.

"Oh, sorry about that. Darlin'." I never knew why I said that.

Chapter 8

Quarters

Danny lived in Colonial, one of the other towers, about a ten-minute walk across campus. Piper and I took the elevator to the fourteenth floor. Students came and went, although no beautiful mermaids emerged from the bathroom. We turned past two corners and at the absolute farthest door, she walked straight in without knocking—kind of surprising.

"Jailbait!" Robyn yelled and came over to hug me.

My eyes popped, then I tried to hide it. When we first met, she wore a baggy t-shirt and loose-fitting jeans. Apparently, that was just for move-in day and lugging around boxes. Tonight, she sported a hot pink miniskirt with a black zipper down the middle, black tights, a leather belt, a long sleeve fishnet shirt, with a black bra underneath, and boots. *Wow.*

"Robyn. I'm guessing yours is the pink side of the room." I knew she had curves but didn't realize she had the confidence to use them like this. When we went out later, how would Danny deal with every guy drooling over her?

She said to Piper, "I thought you were just keeping him around for his body. I forgot that he's smart, too."

Ignoring the jab, I shook Danny's hand. "Hey, dude."

"Let me introduce you to my roommate, Clive Jones."

Clive was as tall as Danny, with dirty blond hair, and in good shape.

"We just call him Jonesy." Robyn walked by, stroking her finger along the bottom of his chin. She smelled like cherry blossoms.

"Thanks for that," Clive said to her. "Here, Luca. Looks like you could use a beer."

"Batavian brand, huh? Thanks." I popped open the brown can.

"Have you had it?"

"First time, actually."

"The brewery's a couple hours north of here, so the price is low. Cheers."

We clinked cans and I took a sip. Tasted cheap, just the way I like it.

Piper came over to my side and put her arms around my waist. "I keep you around for more than your body."

"Glad you do," I replied, only slightly disappointed. I wouldn't mind if she kept me for my body. We kissed.

"Don't you two start already. You won't believe them, Jonesy, once they begin making out, they never stop. It's gross," Robyn teased.

"Cut 'em a break. They haven't seen each other in a long time. It's not easy having a long-distance relationship." He nodded at me, like he knew what it was like.

"Thanks, Clive." Piper kissed me again. Her tongue did a tiny dance with mine, re-awakening the butterflies in my stomach.

"Jonesy's just saying that because his girlfriend goes to Buffalo, and he misses her sooo much." Robyn blew a pucker at him.

"Did you guys know each other before coming to school?" I asked. They seemed way too familiar to have just met.

Danny said, "Clive's a year older, but we've been best friends since ninth grade. He's actually a sophomore and pledged Zeta Beta Chi last year. His old roommate moved into the frat house, and I moved in here."

"If you come up next year, Luca, you should think about pledging. It's a good bunch of guys." Clive's shirt sported the Greek letters ZBX. He seemed cool.

"He's too brainy for us. He's looking at Northwestern, same as my genius little sister."

"Don't pay any attention to her. She's jealous because her baby sister's the favorite." Danny pulled her close. "But don't worry baby, you're *my* favorite."

"Awww." Robyn kissed him.

"Now look who's gross." Clive stuck a finger down his throat and gagged. "So, what are we doing tonight? The party at ZBX doesn't get going until eleven. We've got a couple hours to kill."

Robyn broke her kiss with Danny. "How about we play quarters?"

Piper clapped. "Yes, quarters."

Yes, quarters? Did those words come out of my girlfriend's mouth? It was hard enough getting her to drink at a party, much less play quarters. Usually, the most I could accomplish was having her sit next to me. But now she was rooting for it? What else has she been doing up here?

Clive pointed at me. "Luca, can we agree that we're all ganging up on your girlfriend?"

"How's that, now?"

"She destroyed us last time."

I spun in a circle, checking behind me. Was I in the *Twilight Zone*? Had someone replaced Piper with a party girl and didn't tell me? Maybe this one would pay for dinners and movies.

"Why, Clive, are you afraid?" she joked.

"Actually, yes. I was quite hungover last week, thanks to you. I'm hoping Luca helps us get revenge." He grinned at me and held up his beer.

I raised my palms in an *I surrender* gesture. "I've learned not to tangle with Piper. You're on your own, bro."

Danny exclaimed, "Well, all right! Let's get this game going." He and Clive set up a small card table in the middle of the room. Robyn slid their desk chairs over. Then Danny went into the hall and returned with three more chairs. It all seemed very choreographed, as if they had played together—a lot.

As I sat down Piper bent over, kissed me on the ear, then used a soft voice. "Thanks for not saying anything. I'll explain later." Next, she made a big display of kissing me on the cheek and wiping off her lipstick. "There, honey, that's for luck. You're going to need it."

"Oooh hoo hoo," everyone cheered.

This ought to be good.

She grabbed a rolling office chair and zipped over, bumping into me. "I love you," she whispered.

Goosebumps tickled the back of my neck. "I love you, too." My hand went around her waist, then drifted lower.

"Not yet," she hummed in my ear and nibbled on the lobe while pulling my hand back up.

I kept moving it northward and tickled her ribs.

"Hey." She hopped out of her seat and smiled.

Even though she slammed on the brakes, it didn't mean my tingling did. I was racing the clock to get us back to her room.

"So, Luca, Piper tells us you're pretty good at quarters too," Robyn said.

"I'm all right. You already know I'm not as good as her, but I can usually hold my own." I held up the index finger of my beer hand. "Hey, do you guys ever run into that R.A., Jamie?"

Robyn and Piper looked at each other and giggled.

"What?" I asked.

Robyn said, "We wondered how long it would take you to bring him up. I said that you couldn't help yourself and you'd do it tonight. But your girlfriend claimed, 'No, Luca's not the jealous type. It'll probably be Saturday, if he does at all.'"

"Oh. I guess I screwed that up." I had threatened to beat up Jamie when he bragged that he'd sleep with Piper by Christmas.

"And on our first day, too. You should have trusted me to handle a jerk like him on my own. You don't always need to start a fight." Piper ran her fingers through my hair and kissed the side of my neck.

A hot flush drifted across my ears. Part of it came from embarrassment but the other part was her touch. I shrugged, smiled, and shivered.

Robyn said, "You should hear the horrible pick-up lines he uses to try to get girls to go back to his *single* room. As if that's a big deal."

I took a swig of beer, trying to cool down. "He told me freshmen girls fall for that all the time. You mean they don't?"

She lowered her voice, doing an impression of him. "Hey Robyn, would you like to see a picture of a beautiful girl? I've got a mirror in my *single room*." She waved a hand, dismissing the idea, then nodded at Piper. "Tell them the line he used on you."

Huh? Piper said she never talked with Jamie.

Her eyes widened. "No, we don't need to—"

"Come on," the other three exclaimed.

She looked at me, unsure of what to do.

I deflected. "Go ahead. It can't be worse than what he said to Robyn."

She shrugged and deepened her voice. "Hey Piper, I'm good at algebra. If you make Luca your X, you'll never need to figure out Y."

Everyone stared at me, waiting to see how I'd react. I burst out laughing and high-fived Danny. "Those are so idiotic. We can't even do anything about it."

Danny laughed. "I know, when Robyn told me her R.A. hit on her I wanted to straighten him out. But then she told me the line. I figured it'd be better to let him suffer in his own stupidity."

Clive chuckled. "I think we've given Luca a hard enough time. As our guest, why don't you start us off, man?"

Nodding, I raised my beer as a salute. I knew Jamie wasn't a threat, and I didn't want to suggest that Piper lied to me. I didn't want to be one of those possessive boyfriends that freaks when his girlfriend talks to other guys. But the whole thing seemed a little weird.

Meanwhile, Clive set out six glasses, one in front of each player, and filled them up. A community cup went in the middle.

I smacked the quarter off the table, and it missed,

slamming off my glass. The turn passed to Piper. She picked it up, holding the coin so it would hit edge-side down.

I put my arm around her. "First off, you're holding that all wr—"

She bounced it in my glass.

Robyn smiled coyly. "Let's see how fast you can chug."

I downed it quick and made a face at her.

"Impressive," Dan said.

Handing it back to Piper, I leaned over to whisper. "Before you go, let me show you the right techn—"

Bang, in again.

Was that a trick quarter? I tilted my head. Were they playing games with me? Guzzling the beer, I let the coin drift into my mouth, then bit it to find out. Hard as a rock, with that metallic money taste. I raised my eyebrows and gave it back to her.

Scooching closer, I tried to give her advice. "Okay, you were lucky with those first two but don't expec—"

She nailed it a third time and shot her arms in the air like she won a gold medal. "Woo hoo!"

Everyone was laughing. After finishing my drink, I didn't want to just pass it back. Three straight quarters deserved something special.

Glancing around Danny's room, I found a black tray on his desk and placed the coin on it. With a swoosh of my hand, I made believe we were at a jewelry store. "Look sweetheart, it's a three-karat quarter."

The beer wasn't enough to get me buzzed, but the haze and rush of alcohol drifted into my brain. A mix of pride and a stab of hurt flowed in afterward. She must have done a lot of practicing to become this talented. But why did she hide that from me? I would've been thrilled for her.

"That's three in a row. You get to make a rule," Clive said.

For a tiny second, Piper stuck her tongue out, and locked eyes with him. "Okay. I'm choosing my favorite one—"

"We know. You can't point with your finger," the other three chimed.

Piper had a favorite rule? And they all knew about it? That meant she was so good, she consistently sank three in a row. No easy feat.

"Should we just agree to her next rule right now? We all know it's coming," Clive joked.

"You can't say anyone's name. Otherwise, you take a penalty drink," Dan said.

My eyes darted across the table, trying to glean some information from one of them. But they all acted like this was a fact of life. Piper rocks at quarters, the moon is made of green cheese, and chewing gum stays in your stomach for seven years. What the frig?

I imagined her wearing a green transparent visor and a pinky ring, like a trick dealer in Vegas. With a cigarette dangling from her mouth, she'd say, *"Is this your card? No. Well, drink."*

She clanged a quarter in Dan's glass, then one in Clive's. Each time she used her fingers to fire imaginary guns at them. With Clive, she even blew the smoke off the top of her gun. Her sixth attempt flew into the community cup. Everyone scrambled for their beer. I finished first.

"You came in last, Piper. That means you have to drink the community one," Clive said.

"So do you. No names, dude," Dan proclaimed, catching Clive's mistake.

"Oh crap." Clive had a sly smile as he refilled his cup. He toasted Piper. "Cheers."

"Cheers." She clinked glasses but brought her fist up to her mouth, concealing a burp. She may have become a quarters superstar, but being able to drink fast and hold your booze only came with lots and lots of painful practice. She couldn't have accomplished that, yet. Half her beer spilled out the sides.

When she finished, we all applauded, and she bowed. Her eyes were red. With the quarter wedged between her teeth she muttered, "Come here, Luca. Come get this thing."

She grabbed my shirt and pulled me to her lips. We made out for a few seconds as she passed the cold quarter to me with her tongue. Some fluttery feelings came along with it.

"I've always wanted to do that." She laughed and put her glass down.

Robyn's eyes twinkled. "So, does Jailbait have the quarter?"

Grinning, I took it from between my teeth, and handed it to Piper. It was still her turn.

Dan had caught Robyn's mistake. "Hey, does that count as a name? You've been calling him that all night."

"Ohh." Robyn pouted. She didn't try to fight it— simply accepting Jailbait as my rightful name. That might be a bad thing.

"Plus, Piper said Luca's name before, too," Clive pointed out.

"Drink," came the chorus.

Clive's shoulders sagged, realizing his blunder. He

filled up everyone's glass. Dan and I leaned back and high-fived, watching the other three pound a beer.

Piper bounced her next quarter off the edge of my glass, finally missing. The turn passed to Robyn.

The game continued for another hour. As promised, they ganged up on her. It was great hanging around with these four, but I worried about how drunk Piper was becoming and her impending hangover. More importantly, I *so* wanted to fool around with her. We had never spent the whole night together. I, at least, hoped tonight would be *the* night.

Then she fell off her chair, laughing her tail off. Officially wasted.

"Are you okay, roomie?" Robyn asked, careful not to use her name.

"I'm shleww. Woo hoo." Piper smiled, holding her cup in the air.

"Here, let me take that. And maybe we should get you back to your room." I lifted her off the floor. She started to tumble back down, and I caught her.

She ran her palm across my cheek. "Noooo. I don't want to go. I wanna kick your cute little ass at quarters."

"I think that's done and done." My arm went under her shoulders, supporting her.

Clive asked, "You going to be all right getting her back? Do you want any help?"

I hoped his question was out of real concern, not because he's already carried my drunk girlfriend to her room. "We'll be good. But thanks." Has anyone else lugged her back?

"Bye," Piper said, with a cutesy wave.

Stumbling out, we rode the elevator down and began our drunken trek across campus. I had never seen her this bad off. She alternated between walking straight and falling into my arms like dead weight.

"Did I ever tell you how much I love you?" She slurred her words, then grabbed the back of my head and brought me in for a long kiss. She tasted like cheap beer, I probably did too. I had a good buzz on, but definitely wasn't drunk.

Piper pulled away. "Did I ever tell you how much I love you?"

I chuckled. "I think you just did—twice."

"Good, because I do." She staggered toward a garbage can, grabbed the sides and perched her head inside of it. "I think I'm gonna be sick."

I sighed, totally disappointed.

Instead of puking in the can, she decided to rolf on a centipede. "That's what you get for being nocturnal." Unfortunately, she wasn't done throwing up. She sniffled, placed her hands on her knees and spewed out beer like a fire hose. "Argh. The bug just slithered away. But first, it gave me the finger like fifty times."

I ran over and grabbed her hair, holding it back as she barfed out my chances of getting lucky. "I'm sure it did."

If she felt this bad now, there was no chance of her recovering before I left on Sunday.

Who had the stupid idea to play quarters, anyway?

Chapter 9

Struck Out at Lunch

Myckal became a regular at our lunch table. Along with Nicole and Cheryl that made three girls to go along with five guys, Pablo, Porco, Jimmy, Garret, and me. An occasional straggler or two would hang out.

I met Nicole at Gino's Café about two years ago. We both waited tables. They paid us off the books, so even though we were under twenty-one, no one cared that we served alcohol to the customers. Supposedly, Gino was a hot shot in town and always knew when the liquor inspectors popped in for a surprise visit. We'd get those nights off, and the forty-year-old wait staff worked.

We had casually known each other, then became good friends at work. She was a pretty Black girl, almost as tall as me.

Cheryl was cute, with dirty blonde hair. Everyone knew her since seventh grade. She and Nicole became best friends after Nicole started hanging with us last year.

We had a fairly diverse group of friends. Pablo was Puerto Rican, Garret was Chinese, and Porco and Jimmy were the other white guys. Other than me, no one at our table currently had a girlfriend, which was a little unusual. The girls were single, too.

Pablo had been the most popular kid in our grade for the past several years. Since we were now seniors, that

71

made him the most popular in school. For a little while, I thought he and Myckal might hit it off, but nothing materialized. Porco liked her, that was obvious. Maybe Pablo stepped aside to give him a chance? Not much seemed to be brewing there, either.

I was the last to arrive today. They all had their food in front of them. A heinous collection of hot dogs, chicken fingers, salads, burritos, and tacos surrounded me. Everyone's dessert contained a ton of raisins—pudding, brownies, cake, whatever, they put them in everything. Only the ice cream sandwiches were immune.

"Hi Luca, why are you late?" Myckal scooted over and made room for me.

Jimmy was on my other side.

"No big reason. I stayed after science to discuss an extra credit project."

I placed my double order of crinkle fries and grape soda on the greasy table. Before I plopped down, seven sets of tentacles attacked my fries. Only a few stragglers survived. Why did I even bother? I shook my head at the injustice of it all.

The extra credit would set me up in science, my weakest subject. I had a legitimate shot at Binghamton, the top state school in New York, Boston University, and Northwestern thanks to Mrs. Wild, the assistant principal. Last year she took an interest in me and said if I pulled straight A's, she'd not only help me get into a great school, she'd also find me scholarships. Of course, I had to rock the SATs too. My safety school was Albany. Or, depending on Piper, it might be my top choice.

Nicole raised her eyebrows. "I don't want to hear

about your silly science fair experiment. I want to know about your weekend alone with Piper." She sat across from me, right next to Cheryl.

Cheryl pursed her moist lips around a straw and sipped some chocolate milk. "That's right. You went to see her this weekend. How's she doing at college?"

"She gets along really well with her roommate, and they have a circle of friends to hang with. So far so good." I drowned a fry in ketchup and shoved it in my mouth. It tasted as oily as it smelled—half cooked. Maybe the thieves did me a favor.

Nicole looked at me sideways and the tip of her tongue parted her lips and teeth. "That's not what I mean, and you know it. Pablo told us you were going to be *doing it* with Piper. And it would be your first time, *ever*. So how was it?"

I scowled at Pablo. "He did, did he?"

He sat at the end of the table. If there were any side conversations going on, they came to an abrupt halt. They all wanted to know if I slept with Piper.

"That's not exactly how I put it, bro. And thanks for trying to get me in trouble, Nicole." Pablo bit off half a chicken nugget and threw the other piece at her. She and Cheryl put up their hands and ducked under. "I didn't suggest you were a virgin, and this would be your first time. But I might have said you were hoping that Robyn would clear out and give you and Piper a night alone."

"Oooh," a chorus rang out.

I took a slug of soda. "You guys suck. You know that."

Myckal came to my rescue. "Come on everybody. That's a private matter between him and Piper. He might not feel comfortable sharing something so intimate."

"Thank you, Myckal. I appreciate your maturity." I smiled at her, and she grinned right back. The table went silent for a few seconds.

"On the other hand. We're all dying to know, so you might as well tell us."

So much for Myckal being on my side.

"Yeah, spill it, dude," Porco said.

Jimmy added, "Let's hear the story, man."

I shook my head, but they complained so loud it sounded like a zoo.

People at other tables looked over to see what all the commotion was about. I put up my hands to calm my friends down. "All right, all right, all right. You really want to know what happened between us?"

"Yes," the group echoed.

"You're sure you want to know?"

"Yes!"

A mean, fifty-year-old lunch aide walked in our direction.

"Nothing happened!"

"No way," Garret frowned.

"He's lying," Nicole said.

"My ass." Porco chucked his napkin at me. The rest of them joined in with straw wrappers, balls of paper, and disgusting wads of hot dog.

Covering my face, I slouched into my shoulders, like a frightened turtle.

The lunch monitor strolled by with her hands behind her back, frowning at us. They were like parents. As long as the yelling had stopped, and things were at a normal volume, they didn't care what happened.

She seemed happy that I got pelted with my friends' left-over garbage. "You *will* clean that up before you leave."

"Absolutely. It'll be better than when we sat down."
Why was I the one who answered? I was the victim! My
stupid friends threw the junk.

She nodded and wandered away.

Pablo stood up with his long arms stretched wide.
"Hold on. Let's give the man a chance to explain why he
couldn't close the deal with his girlfriend that he's *so in
looove with.*"

They stared at me, totally quiet. Having to relive the
story brought back my frustrated memories. For pure
raging teenage hormone reasons, I wanted to hook up
with Piper. In my opinion, she was the prettiest girl in
school last year and was the hottest thing at Albany, way
more than that sexy roommate of hers. But Myckal hit
upon something. I wanted that intimate experience with
a person I was in love with. I probably desired that more
than just sex. But I would never admit that to this group.

"I know no one's going to believe this—because I
couldn't either—but when I got up there, about five of
us were hanging out. Someone asked what we were
doing. And Piper said we should play quarters."

"No way."

"That's a lie."

"Since when does Piper play quarters?" Cheryl
asked.

None of them had ever seen her play.

"Since she got up there, I guess? And not only that,
but she's really good at it, too."

Garret was our resident champ. You couldn't afford
to get on his bad side during a game. He'd destroy you.
"How did this happen?" he asked.

I shrugged. "Apparently, she's been practicing like

crazy. She said she tried to surprise me and get good at it. She was too. Her friends bragged at how deadly she was."

While Piper cried and suffered through the depths of her hangover, she confessed her plan. She tried acting like she was more popular in high school than she really was and hoped being a quarters pro might give her that. If she was decent at a drinking game, Robyn and Danny might think she'd been to a lot of parties and had lots of friends.

I'd never been away at college before, who was I to fault her?

"So, what does this have to do with you two hooking up?" Nicole asked with a lilt to her voice.

"Everything, unfortunately. She did great at the beginning. Piper was even making up rules. Then the beer started flowing too fast for her. She's still a lightweight and can't handle more than two or three drinks. We were having so much fun, I didn't notice how sloppy drunk she was getting."

"Oh, no. The chunderdragon didn't show up, did it?" Cheryl brought her hands to her face, with real concern for Piper.

We all snorted out a laugh and I asked, "What's a chunderdragon?"

She glanced around the table. "You know, when you're throwing up in the bathroom. It kinda sounds like that."

"Okaaay. And yeah, it did show up. Pretty soon she's yakking her brains out and promising to become a nun if the pain would go away."

Pablo said, "She might not keep that deal."

"Better not," I answered. "Any hope I had of

hooking up with her disappeared down that porcelain god."

"Why do we always have to worship a guy while we we're puking?" Nicole asked.

"Fine, she knelt at the feet of a porcelain goddess. Better?"

"Thank you." She smirked.

Jimmy punched me in the shoulder. "That sucks, man."

"She was so hungover, there was no chance of anything happening between us. No matter how *in looove* we are. But I did get to perform one very important boyfriend role."

Myckal asked, "What was that?"

"I got to hold her hair out of the toilet all weekend." All I could smell right now was Piper's puke. And cleaning it up when she missed.

All three girls crossed their hands over their hearts and tilted their heads. "Ahh."

"She finally stopped throwing up late Saturday, around four. But she felt so nauseous and headachey, she just wanted to sleep. So, she told me to drive home then barely rolled over."

Myckal and I locked eyes for a second. An expression crossed her face that I wondered about. It almost looked like relief. I must have imagined it.

Pablo asked, "So when are you going back up?"

I turned toward him. "A couple weeks. My parents are giving me a hard time about borrowing the car again."

"Too bad you don't have your own car," Garret said.

"Yeah, too bad."

Chapter 10

Piper's Birthday Present

Piper's birthday fell on Sunday, October seventh—definitely a weekend visit. Driving up that Friday night, I lucked out on the timing. The green mountain leaves had changed into a brilliant yellow, red, and orange, like it was art class, and the paint was still wet.

The weather had turned a little nippy. My summer shorts were sadly packed away for another year. On my walk from the parking lot to her dorm, it felt cooler than in Big Dune, but that didn't mean I brought anything warmer than a sweatshirt.

Robyn was in the shower, down the hall. She'd be back any minute.

"Mmm, you taste good," Piper purred as we made out in her room.

"I can't believe how much I missed you," I answered between kisses. "I don't think I fully realized it, until just now."

"That's sweet. But less talking and more kissing. We don't have much time."

No need to tell me twice. There's nothing like making out with Piper. The way she lilted her tongue with mine, exploring, tasting, and discovering—it sent tingles everywhere. She tugged on the front of my shirt and pulled me in close. Her hands traced over my

78

shoulder muscles, tickled down my spine, and frolicked into my back pockets.

Each time she squeezed those fingers my legs tensed up and twitched. Thirty seconds later the door opened.

"Jailbait, you're here!" Robyn entered wearing nothing but a towel, flip flops, and a shower caddy. The pink fabric struggled to stay cinched on the side, scantily covering her curves. Water droplets clung to her tan skin and her black hair hung past her shoulders.

She held out her arms for me. How did I get this lucky? Making out with my girlfriend one second and hugging her stunning, wet roommate the next. She smelled like tropical flowers.

Gulping when we parted, I hoped neither of them noticed. I was pretty sure Robyn had. Her smile remained a little more sly than normal. She clutched the towel's knot, and stood there, dripping on her hot pink rug. I turned to Piper, trying to keep Robyn out of my field of vision. "So, what are we doing tonight?"

That bed still mocked me from last time. I had hoped to share its thin frame, cuddling up to Piper's body. Instead, I slept on the hard, cold floor, forced to pop up when she puked from drinking way too much beer.

"Jailbait. You're going down the hall and waiting in the lounge while your girlfriend and I get ready." Robyn playfully jabbed my chest, forcing me toward the door.

"What's happening after that?"

She wagged her finger in my face, then pointed. "We're meeting Dan and Jonesy in a little while. Now, out."

"You sure you guys don't want me to stay? If you need, I can be your fashion consultant."

They both stopped and placed their hands on their

hips. An *Are you kidding?* look passed over their faces.

I shrugged. "All right. All right. Have it your way." After closing the door, I leaned against it and exhaled deeply, wishing I could have taken a movie of Robyn in her short towel. Not that I'd ever choose her over Piper, but my friends would never comprehend how hot this girl was without seeing her. There was nobody like her in our hometown.

An hour later, the three of us were hanging out behind their building. No one else was around. The temperature had dropped to the mid-fifties, not cold enough to see your breath, but damp and chilly. The smell of burning leaves drifted by, one of my favorite things about the fall. We had a crescent moon with a ton of stars in the sky. "Hey look, there's Venus," I pointed out.

"Hey look, there's Dan and Jonesy." Robyn ran into Dan's waiting arms. She planted a big, wet smooch on him.

"Whoa, what was that for?" he asked.

"After watching Piper and Jailbait make out. I got a little horny and felt like defiling my boyfriend. Just wait until later." Robyn trailed a seductive finger across her cheek. She let it come to rest on her full lips while maintaining eye contact with Dan.

Piper pushed Robyn. "Shut up." They giggled together.

I said hi and shook hands with Dan and Clive, but I refused to call him Jonesy.

Everyone had jeans and jackets on, except for me in my sweatshirt. To warm up, I stood behind Piper, hugging her. She shimmied her hips against mine, allowing me to envelop her in my arms. Too bad her coat was so bulky. This could've been a really intimate moment, and a lot warmer.

"So, who's got the joint?" Clive asked.

"You gave it to me." Piper answered.

If I was surprised at learning how great she had become at quarters, it was nothing like hearing those mind-blowing words. She reached into her front pocket and sure enough, a fat joint popped out. If I wasn't holding onto her, I might have fallen over in shock.

"Who's got the lighter?" she asked.

"Here you go." Clive ran his thumb across the wheel. A flame appeared, and he held it in front of her.

She placed the joint in her mouth, put her hand on his to steady the lighter, and sparked it up like a pro.

Instinct told me to take a step closer and warn Clive off. But he hadn't really done anything. Besides, Piper'd be pissed if I did. She'd accuse me of making a fool of myself. Was I overreacting? Probably. I hadn't seen her in weeks and missed her like crazy. So, I put on a happy face and buried my suspicion.

She sucked in a deep toke. Holding her breath, she mumbled out, "Here, Clive." A few seconds later she blew out a lengthy trail of smoke.

"Luca, you want any?" He squinted while taking a long drag.

At Jimmy's after-prom party, Piper had tried pot for the first time. She claimed she didn't like the way it made her feel. Apparently, things had changed.

I merely nodded. Clive spit out half a cough and passed it to me. I took a huge drag then handed it to Dan.

"Oh, I'm sorry, baby," Piper said. "I should have given you the first hit after me. It's just that it was from Clive's stash. Can you ever forgive me?" She snuggled her body up to mine, keeping her hands at her sides and kissing me with the sweet, skunky flavor of marijuana.

Stash? When did she start talking like a *Grateful Dead* follower? But instead of questioning her about it, I was happy to return her affection.

"Actually, that's your weed," Clive said.

Pulling back, she angled up her eyebrows. "Oh, yeah." Then took another hit. When she couldn't hold it in very long, she burst out laughing.

"Are you stoned already?" I asked.

"Shh." She placed a finger on my lips.

Leading her away by the elbow a few steps, I whispered, "Since when do you smoke? And you have your own pot, too?"

The others formed a mini circle and passed the joint among themselves.

"So, what if I'm stoned?" She shrugged one shoulder. "I'm a lightweight. And don't be mad. I thought you'd be happy. Now, we can do it together." Raising her gaze to meet mine, she pouted and looked extremely cute.

Like a lot of people who first experiment with marijuana, it didn't take much to get high. From the looks of her glassy emerald eyes, Piper was baked.

"I'm not mad. Just surprised. But what's going on between you and Clive?" There, I touched on it. Let's see how she reacts.

"What do you mean?" She rubbed the base of her neck.

That was one of her tells. She was deflecting.

"I don't know. You two sharing joints. Other stuff, too. You guys seem awfully chummy."

She put her arms around my waist. "I like that it

makes you a tiny bit jealous. Seeing me talk to another guy."

My stomach clenched and a slow smile built up. "Me, jealous?"

"I've had to put up with other girls flirting with you. Now, that the tables are turned, it's a little sexy that you're insecure."

"It is?" Did she mean Robyn toying around with me in that towel? Maybe I shouldn't have enjoyed it so much. I didn't know if the pot was making me paranoid, but she ducked my question about Clive.

"Hmm mmm. Makes me wonder what you'll do to keep me." She tilted her head and gave me a long, delicious kiss.

My senses went fuzzy. The combination of the weed, her confidence, and that amazing kiss had me puzzled. "Anything you want," I said. She definitely knew how to handle me.

A stinging breeze swept by. The smoke floated over and smelled awesome.

Biting her bottom lip, she looked at me with doe eyes. "Promise?"

"Always. So, you knew we were getting high tonight."

She slowly nodded at me. "If I remember right, it lowers your inhibitions and turns you on a little. Doesn't it?"

"Sometimes." I peered at her sideways.

She poked me in the chest. "Good. Because I have another surprise for you. But you have to wait here."

Before I could object, she sprinted away.

I rejoined the group and took a few more hits, but the joint was getting pretty small. It was good stuff, the conversation became goofy, and we laughed our tails off.

"We should grab a couple beers," I said.

"It's been a little while." Robyn looked at her watch. "Piper should have been back with your surprise by now. Why don't you head upstairs and check on her?"

"What is it? Will I ruin it if I cruise up there?"

"I'm not telling you anything." She shrugged, then blew her smoke in my face. It blended with her perfume. "Should be all right if you go help her."

After thinking about it for a few seconds, I said, "Okay." Then jogged away.

"Bring back wings! There's a bunch left in Robby's fridge!" Dan yelled.

"All right!"

"And don't forget the ranch!"

"No way, I hate ranch!"

I rode the elevator to the thirteenth floor. The harsh fluorescent lights worked against the dope and sobered me a smidge. At room 1313 I knocked on the door.

"Come in, Luca," Piper called.

My jaw almost hit the floor. There had to be twenty candles blazing in here. They rested on every surface, except for Piper's bed. The dark room flickered, perfectly romantic. *Open Arms* by Journey played softly on her CD player.

That's not what shocked me. Piper stood on the other side of the room, more stunning than I'd ever seen her. One leg was wrapped behind the other. She slowly brought the back one forward with her knee bent toward me. She had on glossy, silk, black lingerie with black panties, and nothing else.

"Surprise." Her voice pitched higher than normal, and she clasped and unclasped her hands several times.

Frozen in place, I recognized the full force of that moment, and my pulse spiked a million points.

"How about closing the door?" she said.

I didn't know it was still open. At that point, I couldn't have told you my name. I slowly leaned back and banged it shut with my shoulders, barely able to move.

"Why don't you lock it, too. Robyn's staying at Dan's tonight."

"She is?" I reached behind, fumbling for the doorknob.

"Uh huh. Aren't you going to say anything?"

Rendered speechless, my gaze wandered over her entire body, not knowing where to let it settle. I stroked my throat, willing my voice to answer. "What's that called? What's that called that you're wearing?" Stupid question. But my brain hadn't found a way to start working. How could two tiny pieces of clothing intimidate me so much?

"It's a nighty. Robyn and I went shopping together. Do you like it?" She nibbled her finger and watched my reaction with hungry eyes.

My mouth felt dry as sandpaper and I found it impossible to breathe. "I love it. And Holy Cow, Piper, you're like *goddess level* beautiful. I mean… Just… Wow! Did I ever tell you how much I desperately love you? I think I have, but rational thought left me the instant I opened the door and saw how gorgeous you are."

She crossed the room and my eyes never left her, afraid to blink. Each step skyrocketed my blood pressure. When I stumbled backward, a chuckle curled her mouth upward. She took my hands, went up on her toes, gently kissed me, then brushed her tongue over my lips. One of her favorite moves.

My skin prickled with thousands of goosebumps and my heart hammered so hard I was sure she could hear it.

Her chest rose and fell with deep breaths. It happened when she was nervous. Glad to know I wasn't the only one.

"I've thought about this night for so long," she said, her lips pressing against my hands. "I want my first time to be with someone I'm in love with. I'm glad it's your first time, too." She lifted her gaze to meet mine.

Nodding slowly, I wished I said something equally as special. But that last part felt like a question. Teen bravado made it difficult to cop to my virginity, even though she knew the truth.

She turned and held onto my fingers with both hands, leading me to the bed.

I got my first view of her from behind, how her toned legs rose up to that nighty. Her perfect curves and flowing hair forced me to take shaky breaths. I tried to walk in a straight line but swayed along the way.

Right before the bed, she stopped and placed both arms around my neck. Her fingers played in my hair, sending shivers down my legs. When we started making out again, it was like she poured burning oil on a red-hot flame.

I thought I was prepared for this moment. Now that it was here, I was scared to death. Was Piper?

My hands drifted to her back, gliding along the silky fabric. Then they moved lower, travelling over her panties. My knees hitched and I actually lost my balance for a second, which broke our kiss.

"What's wrong?" Piper asked, concern in her eyes.

"I know this is going to sound totally lame." I exhaled deeply. "But when I touched you, it felt so incredible, my legs literally gave out."

She chuckled and her eyes lit up, looking a little devious and flattered.

"I don't think that's lame at all." She pulled off my sweatshirt. My t-shirt came for the ride, and she threw them on Robyn's bed. She kissed my chest, then my abs. My muscles twitched so hard, it felt like I pulled one. When she reached for my belt, I thought I might pass out.

They say the first time a couple is together, things are clumsy and awkward. I can honestly admit, we were clumsy and awkward—and fast. But rounds two and three were pure magic.

The next morning, waking up with Piper's leg draped over me and her head on my chest, was the best moment of my life.

Chapter 11

Best Offer So Far

Driving home last night, it's a wonder I didn't crash. It was one of those rides where your head is in the clouds and you can't remember making one turn.

The school day finished twenty minutes ago and I was waiting around for Pablo. A few other students lingered in the near empty halls. In between periods you never noticed the sound of a locker door slamming. It's too packed and there's way too much going on.

Three classrooms away, some kid flipped his closed and took off in the other direction. The clanging really echoed off the walls.

Today was awesome. I didn't learn a darn thing. During every subject, I'd sit down, and Piper filled all the tiny spaces in my mind. Teachers would teach, friends would talk, but out of nowhere I'd laugh over a memory, smiling and just feeling so happy. It was like being radioactive.

I never had a day like it before—I couldn't concentrate on anything but her. I was lucky there were no tests. Picturing everything as a movie, suspended in time, I relived the weekend scene by scene—the candles, the nighty, the music, the intensity.

Like the grinch, my heart grew three sizes and pumped gallons of hot blood through my veins. I walked around with goosebumps all day. In the cramped and crowded halls, I noticed about seventeen different perfume fragrances. They all reminded me of Piper's.

Honestly, I didn't know why girls used all those floral and spicy scents. If they really wanted to attract a teenage boy, they'd spray on something like, *Chocolate Chip Cookies Baking in The Oven.* They'd have us running at them like zombies.

I imagined two girls sitting in one of their bedrooms, gossiping. *"How did you land Chip Stephens as a prom date?"*

Her friend would say, *"Well, I was wearing Sugar Cookie and three varsity baseball players asked me. It wasn't until I switched to Warm Cinnamon Buns that I lured him in like a largemouth bass."*

"What's up loser?" Pablo smashed a punch into my kidney.

"Dude." It's all I had the energy for. He caught me staring into my locker, still in the middle of that goofy daydream. It hurt a lot, but I wasn't admitting it.

"Come on, we got to hit it," he said.

A janitor began mopping in our way. We scooched to the side, balancing on the edges of our sneakers, trying to avoid his lemon-scented, disinfectant streaks.

"So, where are we going?" I asked.

"Why, you got some place better to be?" He shoved a forearm into my side. I slid toward the middle of the wet floor, tracking in footprints, then tip toed out like a ballerina.

"Hey, watch it," the janitor's gravelly voice called. He had a half-smoked, unlit cigar in his mouth, and smelled like three-day old beer.

"Sorry about that." I punched Pablo in the shoulder.

The janitor turned his back and re-mopped his ruined work. "Punks."

We both cracked up.

"Seriously, punk, where are we going?" I asked Pablo. "I have to work at five o'clock."

Instead of answering, he took off in a full sprint. What choice did I have? I bolted after him. It was cool running through a deserted hallway.

We arrived at the gym, then ducked into the locker room, laughing. I caught up with him at the end. Football and soccer players marched by in their cleats, leaving mud and grass behind.

He finally told me. "Coach Slaz wants to see us right after school."

"About what?"

"No idea."

Travelling down a long, dark corridor, then scooting past the boiler, we ended up at the Wrestling Office— Pablo knocked.

"Come in."

Our coach stood behind his desk. He and another gentleman shared a laugh.

"Fellas, thanks for coming. I'd like you to meet Dan Flanholtz. Head coach of Northwestern."

He wore a purple shirt, looked cut, and had the unmistakable sign of a former college wrestler— cauliflowered ears.

My eyes blinked like crazy, and my mouth filled with saliva. Trying to slow my breathing, my stomach quivered with nervous energy. I had never been visited by a college coach before. To Pablo, it'd become a regular occurrence, especially after his second state championship. If someone was interested in me, I would have thought it'd be a state school or even a community college—never this.

Coach Dan shook both of our hands and crushed mine with the most powerful handshake ever. "Since you're a little bigger I'm guessing you're Pablo Salinas, and you're the one hundred and thirty-four pounder, Luca Es-Poh-sito."

He pronounced my name correctly.

I was impressed already. "Nice to meet you."

"Hi Coach," Pablo said.

"Take a seat, guys."

Slaz sat behind his dented, antique gray metal desk. Coach Dan perched on its front corner and crossed his huge forearms. A chalky blackboard hung behind them.

Northwestern was my dream school. I couldn't believe he was here. My GPA rested on the bottom cusp of meeting their high standards.

I never seriously considered wrestling beyond high school. I didn't love the sport or the lifestyle that college wrestlers endured. Year-round training and dieting, waking up at 6:00 a.m. to run. Then practice, go to class, hit the weight room, then more practice, then mandatory study hall. And a lifetime of deformed ears. I didn't think it was for me.

My goal was to major in English, then head to Wall Street. The train to Manhattan was only ten minutes from my house. But a top-notch school meant I could begin my career at a big-time firm.

I figured he was here to offer Pablo a full ride. But what did he want with me? I was a pretty good wrestler, but nowhere near Pablo's caliber.

"Actually, gentlemen," Coach Dan said. "I would have recognized each one of you. Your coach sent me a lot of tape to review, and I have to tell you that I'm very impressed. Pablo, let's start with you. A two-time state champ can pretty much decide where he wants to go to college. And unless something unforeseen happens, you'll be a three-time champion.

"Have you ever considered Northwestern? At this point, we'd love to be included in one of your premier schools."

"To be honest, Coach, I haven't. Not that there's anything wrong with the Wildcats, but I've had my eye on Iowa and Penn State. When I get to college I want to wrestle with the best, and from what I hear, those two are it."

It must be nice to be Pablo. If I had a school drooling over me, I'd sign up right now. My leg started to twitch. I placed a hand on my thigh to stop it and pretended to smooth out my jeans. I still didn't understand what I was doing here.

"Well, Pablo all three of our colleges are in the Big Ten. And I can tell you from personal experience there's one thing better than wrestling with the best," Coach Dan said.

Pablo crinkled his eyebrows. His acne problems were a thing of the past, although, he still had some scarring. "What's that?"

"Beating the best. If you come to Northwestern, you'll have a chance to wrestle against those guys and kick their asses each year."

We let out an awkward laugh. He said, *asses*. Slaz never cursed.

"I'm not looking for a commitment today," he continued. "We'd need to have your parents involved if we were at that step. I just wanted to meet you and get you to start factoring us in. Is that fair?"

"Yes, sir. It is."

"Good to know, now to you, Luca. Have you ever thought about Northwestern?"

"Oh, definitely." My voice vibrated a couple octaves higher than normal, like I was training a puppy. I had to get myself under control. "It's actually my number one school."

"That's great to hear. I've looked at your grades and they're impressive, straight A's so far this year. But as you know, we only take top students. You scored a 1,410 on your SATs. Are you taking them again? You're probably still on the low side."

"The test is in two months. I've been studying like crazy." Actually, I barely cracked the books.

"I tell you what. If you score closer to 1,500 and bring home a state championship, I think we can get you in. We might have to do it as a combination of athletic and academic scholarships. Again, no commitments on either of our parts, but what do you think?"

"Yes, sir. That'd be amazing." I loved every word out of his mouth. Maybe, I *would be* wrestling next year. "Well, I—"

Pablo tried to interrupt. "You know—"

Coach Dan held up his hands. "How about this? Why don't we set up a campus tour? Bring you guys out, put you up for a weekend, and have you meet some of the other coaches and wrestlers."

Pablo and I looked at each other with big grins. It occurred to me that Coach Dan was using me to get to Pablo. If his best friend was going to Northwestern, it might persuade Pablo to go there. But if it got me a scholarship, too, I'd be thrilled.

He was their first choice, so I motioned for him to do the talking.

"Sure. That'd be great," Pablo said, but his voice lacked enthusiasm.

Hopefully, they didn't pick up on it. I didn't want anything derailing this opportunity. Wait until I told Piper!

Coach Dan slapped his hands together. "Excellent. I'll have one of my assistants get in touch and we'll set it up. Gentlemen, it was a pleasure meeting you both."

We stood and shook hands. He pulverized mine again.

After we left the office, Pablo patted me on the shoulder. "So, what are you thinking?"

With a serious expression, I nodded for him to follow me down the corridor. "Dude, you gotta do me the biggest favor in the world."

"Anything for you, bro."

"Drive me to the drug store. Help me buy some rubbers."

Chapter 12

Sucker

Pigeons scattered as Pablo pulled into a parking space with the sound of pebbles grinding in a pothole. We opened our doors and I stepped into a deep puddle. I guarantee he planned that. A smirk crossed his face. The birds returned as soon as I was out of their way. An open bag of potato chips lay nearby.

Pablo walked faster than anyone I knew, and we hustled through the lot. This strip mall contained the Everhard Pharmacy. We passed three other drug stores to get here.

"So, why did we have to come all the way to Everhard's?" he asked.

Big Dune was a small town. Mr. Everhard had coached my Little League team and was my first-grade teacher. His wife, Vicky, was the pharmacist. Who wouldn't want a teacher named Mr. Everhard?

He claimed it was an English name and his relatives modified it from Eberherd when they immigrated here. Seriously, none of them went to middle school? Nobody thought to run the name change past a thirteen-year-old boy?

They could've said, *"Come here kid. We'd like to switch Eberherd and make it Everhard. What do you think?"*

As soon as he snickered, that should have been the end of it. And after the first Everhards got made fun of a million times, why stick with it? You're in America, you can change it to anything. Boner, Cornfoot, even Cockburn was out there. Why cling to Everhard?

"Steve Platis is working today," I said.

"And?" Pablo lifted his arms to his sides.

"And he told me he's working at the cash register. I need to buy a box of rubbers, and I don't want to get them from some little old lady cashier."

"You're such a wimp. What are you afraid of?"

I held out my cash. "How about I give you the money and you buy them for me?"

"Not a friggin' chance. Even at Everhard's, it's way too embarrassing. But since I'm here as moral support, I will stand off to the side and watch. I might even ask, 'Is this kid old enough to buy rubbers?'"

"Please don't." He was joking but my face flushed hot and feverish. I wiped my hands down my pant legs to dry them. I had never bought any before and honestly didn't know if there was an age limit, like with beer and cigarettes.

He walked into the store first. "You're such a baby."

The Everhard Pharmacy used to be the Wang Pharmacy. When Vicky Wang married Mr. Everhard, she changed the name of the store.

I wondered if she debated hyphenating her name. Actually, I hoped her parents had a long conversation with her about it. *We've worked hard to make the Wang name really big. If you must take your husband's name, stick it in the middle. The Everhard-Wang Pharmacy has a nice ring.*

We had shopped here since I was a kid and I used to

love it because they had video games up front. If my mom gave me a dollar's worth of quarters, I wouldn't bug her while she browsed.

I heard the ding of the bell and turned toward the front of the store, making eye contact with Steve. He nodded and gave me a thumbs up. Earlier in the day I told him what I needed. His shift ran until 6:00 p.m.

"So, what have you been using for protection?" Pablo asked.

On the way over, I confided that Piper and I had our first time over the weekend. He already heard about it from three other people. So much for Myckal and Porco keeping a secret.

"Piper kept going over to Robyn's top dresser drawer. Apparently, she has a stash of condoms," I said.

"You mean hot Robyn has her own box of condoms?"

"I mean super-hot Robyn has a *king-size* box! They must have ordered them through the mail or something."

"When am I going to see this chick?" he asked. "She can't be as gorgeous as you claim."

"Dude, you would not have believed her in that towel. Come up with me one weekend. You'll see."

Pablo shrugged. "We'll plan a road trip soon. In the meantime, why not just keep using their rubbers?"

After wandering around a few seconds, we found the right aisle, with a huge rack of condoms.

"I don't know. I kinda feel like a tool always copping one from Dan. Plus, I'd like to be able to have sex with Piper someplace besides her dorm room. Like, maybe when she comes home from college."

Pablo shoved me in the shoulder. "I bet Dan's are too big for you anyway."

"Too small, maybe."

"Speaking of small. Here's a box of minis for you."

A stern-faced mother passed behind me. She saw us in front of the condoms and gave me the evil eye. Her daughter looked about five. A green sucker spilled out of the kid's mouth, tumbling down her fuzzy pink jacket, gathering frizz along the way, before landing on the floor. She shrugged and took another one from her pocket. That wrapper hit the ground, too.

I pointed at her and mouthed, *pick that up.* The brat stuck her tongue out.

When they had safely turned the corner, I stared at the display and scrunched my face. "There's so many different kinds. Latex, non-latex, extra thin. What do we do?"

"To tell you the truth, buddy, I have no idea."

"What do you mean you have no idea? You've had sex before, right?"

He glanced over his shoulder. "Whisper, you idiot. Yes, I've had sex. Once with Jessica and two times with Nicole DeMayo. *They* always brought condoms. So, no. I've never bought any, either."

"All right. This looks like a regular box. I'll just buy these."

Pablo handed me a much bigger box. "We're not going through this again. You need to buy a ton of them now."

"Good idea. But I feel like a freak going up to Steve with *just* a box of rubbers."

Pablo crinkled his eyelids together. "Let's pick out some other stuff. Like the rubbers are just one thing on your list."

I nodded. "What else should we get?"

He snagged an empty hand basket and chucked it to me. "Ooh, here's vaseline, put that in there. And let's get a porno mag, too."

Before I knew it, all three items landed in the basket. "Really? Condoms, vaseline, and a porno mag. What is this, Saturday night at your house?"

Neither of us had ever bought a girly magazine before. Once, when we were fourteen, we were walking through the woods and we came across a blue tarp that looked like it had been buried for a long time. A couple of the ends poked through the leaves. When we turned it over, there must have been twenty magazines under there. We scooped them up, found a much better hiding place, and that became our supply.

Pablo glared at me. "Okay, screw you. What do you want to get?"

"I don't know. Let's walk up and down the aisles and pick out a few things."

"I'll put the vaseline back, but you're keeping the porno mag. Steve'll let you buy it. That's my charge for driving you here today."

Flipping the magazine over, I hid the rubbers underneath. "Whatever."

Pablo stuck out his tongue and pointed at me. "I have a thought. How about we buy a bunch of awkward stuff and then the condoms will fit right in."

"Like what?"

He cracked a smug grin and tossed me a pink box.

Turning it over in my hand, I held it up. "Menstrual cramps?"

"Exactly. Plus, we'll get some maxi-pads, wart medicine, yeast infection cream, lice shampoo, and some anti-fungal stuff. That'll be for you."

"You're a moron, do you know that? Why did I even bring you?"

"Um, because you're such a loser, and you still don't have a car."

After putting the cramp medicine back, we spent ten minutes picking out more reasonable products. I grabbed a razor, toothbrush, shaving cream, travel toothpaste, deodorant, two cans of soda, two candy bars, baby powder, and mouthwash.

"That's all I can afford," I said. "There's one customer at the register. Let's hurry before someone else goes up there." As Steve rang in the guy's stuff, I kept peering over my shoulder. I didn't want that mom with her kid getting in line behind me. In fact, I didn't want anyone in line behind me. My foot tapped and I pulled on my shirt collar. The guy paid and walked away.

"What's up, man?" I said to Steve.

He grinned and looked around for his boss. "Did you get them?"

I used a soft voice. "Yeah, they're at the bottom of the basket." As cool and nonchalant as possible, I bit my bottom lip and passed it to him.

"Excellent. Nice job," he said. "Hey, Pablo."

"How's it going, Steve?" He stood just behind my left shoulder.

Steve gave us a double thumbs up and got to work. He flipped over the toothpaste, searching for the price tag, when my worst nightmare happened.

Mr. Everhard slapped him on the back. "Steve, I'll take over here. Vicky needs help with some of the inventory in the rear of the store. Give her a hand for me, will you?"

Steve's face turned white, and his eyes bulged. "Oh.

Okay, sure. But I'm already halfway through this order. How about I finish it, first?"

"Nonsense. I've known Luca and Pablo since they were young lads. It'll give us a chance to catch up."

Steve shrugged and mouthed "sorry" as he walked away.

Not half as sorry as me.

With a cheery smile he rang up the baby powder and deodorant. "How are you boys?" Only the toothbrush stood between me and impending doom.

"Hi Mr. Everhard," we chorused together. Pablo's voice sounded distant as if he had slid closer to the door. I was on my own.

"Actually, it's Deacon Everhard now." His smile widened as he keyed in the toothbrush.

Oh come on! I wanted to yell. Instead, I muttered, "Huh?" Things had begun moving too fast for me to process.

"Didn't your mother tell you? I saw her just the other day. I've been ordained a deacon at the Big Dune Baptist Church."

My toes curled in my sneakers. "Of course, you were."

He cocked his head. "How's that?"

"I mean, congratulations." I closed my eyes, fighting off a panic attack. I heard the magazine pages rustle and listened for the keys, typing it into the cash register. That sound never came. When I opened them, his lips pressed tight into a grimace, and he shook his head.

"If my math is correct, you're not old enough to buy this magazine, are you?"

My birthday was November fourth. The cutoff for

school years in our district was November fifth. That made me the youngest kid in class every year. So, I'd only be turning seventeen soon. Pablo was eighteen already. I could claim it was his.

But when I spun around, he had slunk away, pretending to watch some ten-year-old play a video game. The jerk.

My chin dropped to my chest, and I used a timid voice. "I didn't know how old you had to be."

The deacon huffed. "Eighteen, Luca. Care to show me your license or should I return this to the shelf?"

Time slowed to a crawl. Maybe, it stopped altogether. "You can return it," I mumbled.

He squinched his face. "I can't say that I'm not a little—Whoa! What is this now? Prophylactics too, young man?"

My stomach cramped. Deacon Everhard ran into my mother all the time. He had the power to destroy my life.

He probably noticed the terror on my face and took mercy on me.

"I can't say that I approve of this behavior. But as your pharmacist I have to be satisfied that you're engaging in safe sex. Between the AIDS epidemic and unwanted pregnancies, I'm glad you're making appropriate decisions. But I am including a brochure on abstinence too. I'll place that in your bag."

I swallowed. "Thank you. Mr. Everhard. I mean Deacon Everhard."

He exhaled. "And don't worry. I was young once, too. I won't share this with your parents. The veil of privacy between pharmacist and client extends to your transactions."

All I could do was nod. Thank goodness he wouldn't

tell on me.

"What the fudge? There's no price tag on these. Did you notice how much the prophylactics cost?"

"I didn't." I placed my cash on the counter and took a step back. "But here, you can charge me whatever you want."

A little voice cried out behind me. "Why *can't* I have fake eyelashes?"

"Because I said so!"

The mother and daughter got in line. I clutched my stomach.

"Don't be silly. I would never overcharge you." He motioned to one of his employees. "Marge, will you come over here, please."

She turned out to be a little old lady with gray curly hair and bad posture. She wore a hand-knit white sweater over her misbuttoned shirt. Her nametag read, *Mrs. Flanagan.*

The door dinged and two smokin' hot cheerleaders came in. They each wore a school jacket, and their short uniform skirts fell at the top of their tan legs.

"Faith. Hope. What are you guys doing here?" Naturally, Pablo would run into someone he knew, and it would have to be twins.

"Us," one of them said. I could never tell which was which. "We live in this part of town. What are *you* doing here?"

He pointed at me. "I came with Luca. He's buying a box of condoms."

Glancing my way, they both giggled. Hopefully, they assumed it was a joke.

My brain screamed, *Are you kidding me?* I nodded to them, and my ribs squeezed tighter.

"Marge, can you put this pornographic magazine back in the rack? Then amble over to aisle five and get a price check on this box of condoms, please. Our optimistic young lad here selected the jumbo quantity and I believe they're on sale."

"*Luca,*" the other twin emphasized my name, and they strolled to the rear of the store.

My face burned red.

Clutching the magazine with two fingers, Marge held it as far from her as possible. Everyone could see it was a porno. She winced at the condoms, like they were infested with yeast. Out of the corner of my eye, the mother pushed her daughter behind her body, shielding her from me.

Marge's voice boomed across the store. "I can't find a price sticker on the rubbers, Deacon! Do you mind coming here and giving me a hand?"

Sneaking over, Pablo whispered in my ear. "Did she just call them rubbers?"

From the side of my mouth, I hissed, "Shut up. This is a disaster."

I heard the twins laugh.

"For Pete's sake," the deacon exclaimed.

For the first time, I noticed he had a knee brace on and limped with an aluminum cane.

Marge and Deacon Everhard bent over at the same time, rummaging for a price. "Steve, you didn't tag the condoms properly," he called to the rear of the store.

Steve peeked around the corner. "Sure did. I put them on the end." He saw Faith and Hope smiling and he ducked away.

"A sucker!" the deacon screamed, slipping on the little girl's candy. He momentarily lost his balance, then stiffly regained it—not before clunking heads with Marge.

She stumbled backward into the condom display. Her arms splayed to the sides, and she landed on a shelf. It kept her from going down. Rubber boxes cascaded around her, as if she were trapped beneath a waterfall.

"Son of a bitch!" Marge yelled.

The sticky little girl cowered to the other side of her mom.

Pablo couldn't take it any longer. He staggered behind the sunglasses, laughing his ass off. I buried my face in my hands.

The only way this could have gone worse is if my mother walked in right now—the door opened. And Myckal entered with her dad. She came right over, all smiles.

"What are you two shopping for?"

I wanted to throw up. "Please don't ask."

Chapter 13

Afternoon Delight

My thirteen-year-old brother, Vic, kicked my bedroom door open and stuck his head inside. "It's time to get up jerk face, someone's here to see you."

There was a football on the bed next to me. I whipped it at his head. "Get out of here, you little twerp."

Dropping to his knees, he managed to duck under, just in time. "I'm telling that you won't get up." He turned and stalked out of the room.

A few minutes later, my mother called from upstairs. "Luca, time to rise and shine!"

I rolled over. "It's Saturday. Let me sleep!" The window shade was pulled down, but it was so old, sunlight poured through rips on the sides and radiated through the yellowed middle. I squeezed my eyes tighter.

We lived in a split-level house. When you enter the front door, you can either walk up the stairs or down. My bedroom was downstairs, right next to the laundry room.

A thin door led from my room to the garage. The builders probably had a left-over closet door and stuck the cheap thing there. Whenever my mom warmed up her car, deadly carbon monoxide would leach under it like a Bond villain trying to poison me. I'd end up smoking the equivalent of eleven cigarettes.

The wall didn't have insulation either, so I froze my

tail off during the winter. Sometimes mice would sneak in and join me. We'd talk about starting a campfire together, but they always left, complaining the garage was warmer. It wasn't the greatest room in the world, but it was away from everyone else.

"You have a guest in the living room!" My mother's voice echoed off the blue paneling. My father wouldn't let me drive nails or tacks into it, so anything I put up had to be done with tape. An E.T. poster hung in a corner since I was little. A couple years ago I added a classic Farah, then I found an amazing Cindy Crawford at the mall.

"Whoever it is, tell him to go away. It's only eleven-thirty!" Which one of my idiot friends would be up so early? And why were they at my house already? My only guess was Pablo. Wrestling season wasn't that far off. Maybe he came over to go jogging before our 2:00 p.m. workout. I flipped onto my stomach and yanked the covers over my head.

"No. Get up here and do it yourself."

Why was she being so insistent? Why couldn't she tell him to come back later? I waited tables at Gino's Café until 2:30 last night. Sixty-seven bucks sat on my dresser—not bad.

"Now!"

"All right." I threw off the blankets, yawned and glanced in the mirror. My hair went in every direction except down. I wasn't combing it for Pablo, I wasn't getting dressed for that schmo either.

Yesterday, the only clean pair of boxers in my dresser was a novelty gift from Christmas—cartoon aliens eating pizza. I slept in them and nothing else. I scratched my chest, and pounded my heavy feet on the stairs, hoping he'd get the hint of my displeasure. Waking up at this unholy hour was not my version of fun. On the way to the kitchen, I rubbed my eyes; they hadn't focused yet. "Why are you in my house so early, moron?"

Since he didn't answer, I poured a tall glass of apple juice and didn't offer him any. I wandered into the living room, plopped on the couch, slung one leg over the arm and exhaled an exhausted breath.

"Aww, don't you look cute in the morning."

Instead of a deep gruff voice, I had heard Piper's sweet lilt.

"Holy cow!" I jumped out of my seat, spilling the juice on my chest and soaking a piece of pepperoni. My mother sat right next to her, each of them in an armchair, otherwise I would have let a curse fly. They both thought I was the funniest thing either had seen in a while.

"Mom, why didn't you say something?" I demanded.

"Like what?"

"Like *Piper's* here."

Piper toasted me with her glass of O.J. "Don't blame your mother. She tried waking you up peacefully. You're the cranky one."

My eyes danced around the room and landed on a small blanket. I wrapped it around my waist. "What are you doing here?"

When she stopped giggling, Piper said, "I wanted to surprise you. So. Surprise."

"How long are you here for?" I didn't know what to ask. My brain desperately tried to process how my girlfriend ended up in my house.

My mom interrupted. "Luca, I'd prefer you to be

halfway dressed for this conversation."

"Oh, yeah. I'll be right back." I threw the blanket to Piper and bounded down the stairs, taking them three at a time.

"Good. I'll take you to lunch." She caught it and laughed.

****

Piper drove her blue Buick, the big engine droning us forward. It used to be her mother's car, but when she got a new one, this coupe became Piper's.

"What restaurant do you want to go to?" I asked.

"It's a surprise." She raised her eyebrows and bit her bottom lip.

"A mystery." That was fine with me. But nothing could top this morning's shocker.

There were two decent radio stations in town. One pop, and the other classic rock. An oldie from the seventies—*Afternoon Delight* by Starland came through her speakers. We turned off the highway and traveled on back roads. The gray woods sped by at sixty-five miles per hour, even though we were in a forty zone. She drove much faster than me. My body often stayed at a forty-five-degree angle as I slammed my foot against an imaginary brake pedal. My butt rarely remained on the seat.

"So, did your parents know you were coming home this weekend?" I wiped a nervous bead of sweat off my forehead. She hated when I complained about her driving. Hopefully, she didn't notice.

"Yeah. I told them Clive was visiting his cousin and could give me a ride here and back to school."

I was thrilled that she came home, but the idea of her driving three hours in a car with Clive didn't sit right. It bothered me more than it should.

"Where does his cousin live?"

"About an hour south of here, somewhere in Westchester."

I decided to put him out of my mind. I'd rather spend my energy on Piper. Besides, she looked great. Ever since she saw me in my underwear, she was beaming her beautiful smile. She wore a pale blue mini skirt, a white cropped t-shirt, and white tennis sneakers. Her hair was in a high ponytail.

I tugged on her shirt. "You look awesome. Is this outfit new?"

"Uh huh. Robyn and I went shopping last week and she helped me pick out a few things. I'm glad you like it."

"Well, I do." Her legs retained their summer tan. I pictured her and Robyn laying out by the school fountains, but I kept my imagination on Piper in a bikini. I watched her toned legs maneuver the car's clutch.

She shifted gears effortlessly then wriggled while smoothing out her skirt. I reached over and gently massaged her neck. As always, she let out an adorable moan of pleasure.

That little bit of touching shot my heart rate to the moon. "Wait a minute. There's no restaurant up here. Why are we heading toward your house?"

Without answering, Piper pulled into her driveway and turned off the car. She lived in a big place overlooking the Hudson River. She got out with a devious grin, then started for the front door. A carpet of green grass with orange flowers lined each side of a curving walkway. A white wrought iron table with two chairs sat on the lawn.

I ran ahead of her and stopped. "Please tell me you didn't bring me here to have lunch with your parents. Because I skipped a root canal this afternoon. I could probably still make it."

She kept smiling then snuggled her body up to mine. Her arms slipped around my shoulders and her fingernails raked through my hair. "My parents are at a wedding in the city all day. They won't be home until after midnight."

For a second, I stood there with a vacant expression. We had the house to ourselves for twelve hours, what could we possibly do in all that time?

"Do you still want to find a restaurant?" Her eyes glowed with a twinkle of mischief. She giggled, parted her lips, and kissed me deeply. We ended up making out on her front lawn.

As her hands traveled across my shoulders they went downward, ending under my t-shirt. She ran them over my lower back, causing it to arch and my skin to tingle.

A new perfume tickled my nose—one that I never tasted. It made her neck irresistible. My lips grazed the side of her, I inhaled deeply, and my knees weakened. My stomach fluttered as her bare legs brushed forward against mine. That same moan escaped her again. I took it as my cue. My hands drifted over the back of her skirt.

Her hug strengthened, and she raised on tippy toes. "I guess that's a no to a restaurant." She chuckled. "But there is something I want to try with you."

I was dying to find out what, but she started making out again. I was powerless to cut things short and ask questions. You'd need something really powerful to separate us, like a bulldozer. Or she could say "no." But

Piper was saying an encouraging "yes." She deepened our kiss with every stroke of her tongue. It felt like she was going to pull my shirt over my head—then she hesitated.

I swallowed and pulled back a step, holding up my hand and trying to catch my breath. "Okay, what do you want to try?"

"I want to take a shower with you."

Those eight words hung in the air, as if I could reach up and touch them.

"How's a...what did you just say?"

She found her soft voice. "Cosmo says it's incredibly sensuous with your boyfriend. I've thought about it for a couple weeks. I've never done that with anyone, have you?"

Considering Piper knew exactly how many girls I had been with—one, and she was it—she knew my answer. But for some reason she felt the need to ask.

"Hmm, let me think." I looked at the sky and counted on my fingers, making believe I had showered with a bunch of girls.

She didn't buy it and glared at me like I was an idiot.

"Umm, no. I haven't. But I love your idea. How about we go...now?" I took her hand and ran toward the house.

A couple weeks ago, when she had surprised me with our first time, I was scared out of my mind, not that I'd ever admit it. But this was the opposite emotion—totally intense. My body was quaking with excitement, like a fantasy coming true. Plus, I loved that she'd been thinking about this for weeks.

Luckily, the door was open, and her parents were *not* inside. That would have ruined my weekend real quick.

She giggled behind me, and we hustled up the stairs to the guest bathroom.

"Okay. What do we do? What do we do?" I hopped up and down, super eager.

"Easy, tiger." She kissed me and locked the door behind us. "How about we start by turning on the water?"

She bent toward the faucet and stayed like that a few seconds, adjusting the temperature. Her skirt pulled a little tight and I studied her form. One leg remained on the floor, the other curled backward, a smidge in the air. Her curves were perfect.

Tilting my head, I watched the water roll off her arm. When she had it just right, she wrung out her hand, getting rid of the last drops and leaving me breathless.

She caught me staring at her and stood straight up. "What?" she said, a little bashful and playful.

"You just look so beautiful right now. The sun is shining through that window, and it cast you in this amazing light. I'm so psyched you came home this weekend. I really love you, Piper."

"*Lucaaaa*." Her soft lips pressed against mine.

While she's up at school it's like half of me is on fire, going crazy because I'm not touching her. Then she does something incredible like this, and I'm loving life. The mirror steamed up. The shower hummed through the pipes and sprayed against the tub and wall. It's all I heard.

"Now, let's get you in there," she said. This time, she did take my shirt off.

Chapter 14

Say Uncle

"Wow! Nothing in my life *ever* compared to that."

"Wow yourself, mister."

After making sure we were *really* toweled off, especially Piper, we tossed the wet towels in the hamper and put on plush, warm ones. We left the upstairs bathroom and turned right. She led me by the hand to her bedroom—two doors down and across the hall. There was a white four poster bed, with a light pink bedspread. A white, metal bookshelf stood next to it with fake ivy dangling off. Artificial flowers adorned the shelves, along with books and several framed pictures of us.

She turned on the stereo. For some reason, we kept our towels on when we got under the covers. We laid on our sides, face to face and I stared into her deep green eyes.

"Your hair is still wet." I slowly brushed my hand through it.

"Yeah, that's the *one place* on my body you forgot to dry."

"Oops."

She toyed with the heart necklace I gave her for her birthday. We kissed each other. No tongue or Frenching yet, but affectionate ones that lingered. At any moment, the passionate stuff would start, that was a given, but I wanted to savor this feeling and enjoy being with her.

The rest of the world got tuned out. Everything I wished to concentrate on, was right in front of me. My stomach fluttered like crazy. Being this close to Piper brought it on, no matter what she was wearing. Of course, a comfy towel multiplied things by a billion.

My hand drifted to her shoulder. Moisture from her hair caused some friction as I stroked up and down her arm. I switched to the back of my fingers. She smelled like strawberry conditioner. My toes curled and she shivered.

Piper wiggled closer and bit her bottom lip. "Are you ready to get rid of these towels?"

"Dying to. How about on the count of three? We'll do it together."

"Okay. You count."

My pulse zoomed like a rocket. "Here goes. One, two—"

"Did you hear that?" She sat straight up, clutching the blanket over her and staring at the bedroom window.

My brow furrowed but I remained laying down. "Three."

"Shh." She placed a hand over my mouth. "A truck's coming up the driveway."

"I don't hear anything." I mumbled through her fingers.

"Trust me. I know the crunching sounds. You hear it before you see it." Leaning over me, she looked out the window.

Even now, in the grip of a mini panic attack, her back was incredibly sexy. She still had a slight tan, along with bikini tan lines. I once explained to her that guys love tan lines on a girl. She thought I was nuts. Her skin stretched over her toned muscles and her hair hung straight and low. My fingers traced small figure eights on her.

I wasn't nervous about anyone pulling into her house. As long as it wasn't her parents, we had nothing to worry about. Besides, they would have called to say they were leaving the wedding early. That heads up would give us two and a half hours.

Her blinking increased and she took in a sharp breath. "Someone's definitely here."

"But we were counting to three."

She shook her head and halfway smirked.

Finally, I heard the tires grinding across their white gravel. "Do you want me to see who it is? I could check the answering machine, too. Find out if your parents left a message."

"Oh frig. Frig! Frig! Frig!" She leapt out of bed. With lightning speed, she threw on a pair of gym shorts, a t-shirt, and pulled her wet hair into a sloppy ponytail.

"Who is it?" I sat up but stayed halfway under the quilt. Our afternoon could *not* be over already. We didn't even officially do it yet. The shower was truly amazing, but we were waiting until we got into bed. The idea was to spend the next few hours in here.

"My uncle!" She hopped on her left foot, trying to put on a sneaker. Her frightened eyes swept the room, searching for its mate. She dove under the bed.

"Your uncle!" Now I was up, but still in my towel. "I thought it was a family wedding. Why isn't he there?"

She reached all the way under, then popped up with the sneaker. A big vehicle stopped in front of the house, it rumbled like a tow truck.

"He's my father's best friend and works for him. We

call him Uncle Jack but technically we're not related."

"What do you think he wants?"

"No idea. Probably something from my dad's office. Wait here. I'll get rid of him, and then we can get back to… you know." Her panicky voice had been downgraded to nervous. Her face relaxed and brimmed confidence.

The doorbell rang and she gave me a short kiss. "Stay right there and don't make a noise. And don't you *dare* take off that towel. I may have plans involving it." When she broke away, she reached for the towel, pretending to tug it off.

I playfully slapped at her hand. "Cut it out, Delilah."

"And when I get back, *I'll* finish the counting." She blew me a kiss and ran out of the room—her feet speeding down the staircase.

Even though we were interrupted and might be in a jam, I couldn't stop smiling and my chest beat nothing but warm rhythms. I was so totally in love with her.

Sneaking to the window, I pulled back the sheer curtain. We were on the second floor, just to the left of the front door. A red pick-up sat in the driveway. *Kraft Cement Company* blazed in yellow letters.

Her uncle was huge, with a brutish, rough appearance. The type you get from working with cement all day, not sitting in an office like her dad.

He glanced in my direction, and I leaned backward. No way he could see me.

The front door opened. "Uncle Jack!"

"Sweetheart. It's been way too long. I hear you're the big college kid now and smarter than Einstein."

"Yup, Albany," she said. "It's going great so far."

"What are you taking up?"

"English. I really like it."

"English? That's odd. The other day your father said you were taking up time and space."

She snickered. "That's such a dad joke, Uncle Jack. But my parents aren't here. They're at my cousin's wedding in Manhattan. Someplace fancy off the park, so no kids. Too expensive, I guess. It's just me at home."

Feeling foolish in this thick, orange towel, I spun around like I was on the teacups, scanning for my clothes. Then I remembered, they were still in the bathroom. That was stupid.

I stuck my head outside her bedroom door to listen in better, but it didn't matter. Sound echoed off their high ceilings and traveled up here. One time, her father was in the kitchen, trashing me left and right—no problem.

"That's actually why I came by." His voice took on a more serious tone. "Your dad was worried about you being home all alone. He asked me to stop over to make sure you're all right."

That sounded bad. I bet it ticked her off.

"Uncle Jack, I'm a big girl," she growled sarcastically. "I go to college and I'm *your* babysitter. I *think* I can take care of myself."

This guy wasn't leaving any time soon. Waves of fear trickled down my spine.

"I hate to come off like the bad guy, but that's what your dad's worried about."

I needed my clothes. What was I thinking, leaving them down there? I knew exactly what I was thinking—about showering with my really hot girlfriend and the greatest afternoon ever. I didn't imagine giants coming by to pound my bones into cement and mix my body into someone's tennis court.

Unfortunately, the bathroom was just off the main staircase. It wasn't visible from the front door, but if he saw a shadow move, I was as good as dead.

"What does that mean?" She used her annoyed tone.

Uncle Jack let out a deep breath. "He's worried that you *are* a big girl and that your boyfriend might be upstairs right now. He called me a few minutes ago. If you were alone, I was supposed to see if Lucas was here, too."

"It's Luca and absolutely not!" She was losing her temper.

"I don't think your dad likes him very much," he joked, but it fell flat. When she didn't respond he continued. "Look, sweetheart, I'm sorry. I don't want to do this anymore than you want me to. Do you mind if I take a quick peek inside and I'll be on my way? When he calls back, I can honestly say I didn't find anyone here. Then you can get back to Loverboy."

"Uncle Jack! What are you suggesting?"

"Oh, no, no, no. I don't mean Lucas," he sounded apologetic. "You must have the radio on. *Working for the Weekend* by Loverboy's playing."

Did he do that gag on purpose? A silent scream boiled up from my chest like I was in a haunted house. What other surprises could he have for us, scary clowns with machetes?

When my heart re-started, I cringed and began my slow walk down the hall. I shimmied with my back to the wall, like I was on the ledge of a building and afraid of heights. Her father once threatened to throw me into a vat of wet cement. This guy looked like his enforcer.

Her voice shrilled. "Actually, I do mind. I can't believe my father asked you to spy on me?"

I made it to the bathroom. As quietly as I could, I gently put on my jeans and t-shirt. I didn't bother with the socks and boxers, just slipped them into my pockets. I couldn't stay in here. With my luck, Uncle Jack needed to go to the bathroom.

Would he think it was weird that the room was fogged up? I opened the window to let the steam out.

Cracking the door, I tiptoed into the hallway, sneakers in hand. Three more steps and I'd be back in Piper's room, safely under her bed. Even if she let him up, there's no way he'd search underneath.

But Murphy's Law was working overtime, and the wind gusted. With the window open as well as the front door, a mini vacuum slammed the bathroom door shut.

His voice boomed. "What was that?"

I darted into Piper's room. Decision time loomed— under her bed or out the window. In that microsecond it occurred to me, a door slamming warranted a hard target search under the bed.

My first leg went over the windowsill and I glanced at the ground. It felt like the top of the Empire State Building. An evergreen bush lurked below, the kind with spikey needles. After a deep breath, my head ducked through the window, and I pushed off the outside wall, hoping to clear the bush. With any luck I'd land like a sprinter to absorb the impact, and bolt away like an Olympian, never to be seen by Uncle Jack.

But I didn't land like that. Instead, my back foot caught on the window frame, and I yelled, "William Shatner's nuts!" Tumbling head over heels straight into the bush, I splashed upside down. My mouth was full of those little red berries your parents say are poisonous. They didn't taste half-bad. I tried spitting them out, but a gob dribbled into my nostrils, magnifying their deadly toxins. "Flomebody shelp me," I mumbled.

My head and neck rested on the base of the roots. The evergreen needles dug into my skin like frigging daggers. I performed the worst somersault out of there, landing hard on my back. Slowly, stumbling up and twirling around, I scanned for my sneakers. Bees swarmed around my head. A hive must have been growing in the bush.

Swatting at them, I ducked low, and zig zagged like a rabbit dodging a wolf. Why didn't her father get rid of the nest? Hopefully, the queen targets his ass tonight.

I was covered with bloody scratches and my clothes were stained with those stupid berries. No stings yet. "Son of a monkey!" Spoke too soon.

A bee nailed me on the wrist. At least the little turd would be dead soon. Whirling around I sucked on the sting, trying to get the bug venom out. My wrist tasted like a pine tree air freshener.

The sneakers materialized on the lawn. I grabbed them but didn't dare put them on. I dashed across her gravel driveway on the back of my heels and dove into the tree line, ending up in a patch of poison ivy.

Was mixing a bee sting, berry slime, and poison ivy dangerous? If I passed out soon, I'd have my answer. I reached into my pocket and pulled out two nickels. There was a convenience store at the bottom of the hill. I could call her from the payphone—find out if it was safe to come back.

I refused to let this special day be over. Who knew when a moment like it would come around again?

A bunch of squeaking trilled next to me, and I ended up face to face with a mother groundhog. "Ugh!" I popped up and ran for my life.

The little turd chased me right back toward Piper's house. Uncle Jack sat in a wrought iron chair, smoking a cigarette. Piper was in the other one, one elbow on a table, with her chin in her hand. When the groundhog saw them, it bolted in the opposite direction. I stopped in my tracks but must have dropped my coins. The stupid thing owed me a dime.

What was going on here?

"This is the guy your father's worried about?" Uncle Jack casually flicked off an ash.

"Luca's not usually so clumsy." Piper shook her head and shrugged. "Sometimes he uses the front door."

Chapter 15

Assembly Required: Tuesday, October 23, 1990

A few minutes ago, the assistant principal, Mrs. Wild, made an announcement throughout the school. Everyone had to come to an assembly. The halls went rowdier than normal as people tried guessing the topic. *Selling oregano that looks like weed, buying oregano that looks like weed, or why can't boys use better aim in the bathroom?*

We were supposed to go straight there, and not stop at our lockers first. Naturally, I went to mine then met Pablo at his. I was telling him the Uncle Jack adventure.

"I don't get it," he said. "It sounded like Uncle Jack was about to bounce upstairs and find you cowering in her room."

"That's what I thought. It's why I dove out the window."

"So, what happened?"

"It turns out Uncle Jack was a pretty cool guy. Since her father is his boss, he felt obligated to ask to snoop around and look for me, but he told Piper he was never going to do it. He didn't really care if we were fooling around or not. So, when she told him no, he asked her to hang out on the front lawn while he smoked a cigarette. It'd give them a chance to catch up. Apparently, they're old buddies since she was a kid."

"Really. Then what was Piper thinking when she saw you climb out the window?"

"*Climb* is putting it generously. It's more like I fell out. She said if I didn't make such a spectacle of myself, she would have been really embarrassed. Up to that point, she was still denying I was there. But when I came tumbling out, it looked so crazy, she ended up cracking up."

"Why did you dive out, anyway? What did you think he was going to do?"

"Dude, I was in panic mode. I wasn't thinking straight. When you're wearing a towel in your girlfriend's bedroom, you lose all ability to process rational thought. Only two things go through your mind. The first is, please don't ever let this end."

"Oh yeah, what's the second?"

"Please don't ever let this end."

"You're an idiot." He punched me in the shoulder. We ran into a traffic jam in the hall and things came to a crawl. Too many kids all going one place. The scent of cigarettes hung in the air. "All right, keep going with the story."

"Anyway, I didn't hear anything after the stupid bathroom door slammed shut. If I had been able to listen in a few more seconds, I would've heard Piper and Uncle Jack joking around and knew everything was chill. Instead, I figured he was about to throw me in the back of the pickup and haul my ass to the cement factory."

"You have some imagination." He drew in his eyebrows.

"Oh yeah, let's see how clearly you're thinking the next time you almost get caught."

"Even if he saw you, he's an adult and you're just a

kid. He couldn't have done anything. You know that."

"Doesn't matter. My brain melted the instant I stepped into the shower with Piper. When I thought he was coming for me, my mind was still in the towel zone. It's a good thing they don't have a law against it. I could've gotten a DWIT. Driving While In Towels."

Pablo shook his head, grinning.

I shrugged "I couldn't help it. My biggest fear loomed in front of me. I pictured Uncle Jack and her dad dressing up like freaky clowns and chasing after me with giraffe balloons."

Passing through the large doors, we entered the theater. With a grant from some rich alumni, they rebuilt it last year. It used to be musty, now it smelled like new furniture. Supposedly a thousand people could fit in here. Pablo pointed and we saw Garret, Nicole, and Myckal at the end of a crowded row, halfway to the stage.

"You've seen too many movies," he said. "What is it with you and clowns?"

"Who knows? It's kinda like you and jellyfish. You pussy." I tilted my head and smirked. "But Piper claims Uncle Jack is the biggest teddy bear in the world. At most, he would have told me to leave. We could have made believe Piper was driving me home, then turned right around and come back."

The auditorium buzzed with excitement. We had to walk single file to get past a bunch of students.

"Wait, wait, wait. That means you jumped out that window for no reason and all these cuts and scratches were because you overreacted. So, after your little drama, did he take off and give you and Piper some one-on-one time?"

I let out a huge, frustrated sigh. "No, that's the worst

part. Right after she introduced me to Uncle Jack, her best friend, Stephanie, and Eric pulled into the driveway."

"What stupid luck." He slapped me on the back as we walked down the sloping aisleway. "That means you and Piper never—"

"Can you please take your seats." Ms. Maroney stood on the stage speaking into a microphone. She drowned out the rest of his question, but he could figure out the answer.

Last year, Eric fought with the wrestlers against the football players at the prom. He went to our rival school, so he could have stayed on the sidelines. That's what Stephanie encouraged him to do. But he was a cool guy, and helped us out, big time. I felt like I owed him. So, even though I was dying to be alone with Piper, we spent the rest of Saturday night playing board games.

We hung out with them the following day, too. Although, that wasn't a big deal, since Piper's parents were back home.

Pablo and I scooted past a couple stoners and found our friends.

"Hey Myckal." I sat down next to her.

She slid over so Pablo could be on one side and me on the other. Our legs ended up touching and she felt really warm. There was a lot of room between her and Pablo, however.

"Hi Luca. Any idea what this is all about?" She wore a pretty perfume, something like lavender and honey.

"Not at all."

"Have they ever done this at John Marshall before?"

I thought about it for a second. "I'm not sure. I don't ever remember an impromptu assembly."

Ms. Maroney barked at us from the stage. "This is the second time I'm asking you. Please settle yourselves and come to attention. If I have to ask a third time, my fellow teachers will start handing out detention slips."

Nothing like some arm twisting to get a bunch of students to quiet down. A little sporadic chatter continued but pretty soon, the room had gone silent. I scrunched my face. Myckal and I smiled at each other. She knew my low opinion of Maroney.

"Very well then," Ms. Maroney said. "Let me introduce you to our new school principal, Mrs. Wild."

Pablo looked at me, surprise on both of our expressions. Some murmuring began as she walked onto the stage.

She raised her arms, and the talking stopped. "Thank you. I'm sure you're all very curious as to why we're here. I'll explain things in detail and at the end, I'll answer a few questions. First, many of you know that Principal Wehbe has been taking quite a bit of time off these past two months. Unfortunately, his illness has progressed, and he won't be returning."

Mr. Wehbe was a cool dude. He let the assistant principals dole out the punishments, so no one had a reason to dislike him. He came to almost all of the sporting events, concerts, and plays and was the school's biggest cheerleader. When they announced him at graduations, he always received the biggest applause.

"Please everyone, please," Mrs. Wild continued. "I'll be assuming his duties as principal for the remainder of the term, but that's not why I've called you here today." She paused and glanced around the huge crowd.

"This isn't easy to say. Recently, our school was discovered to have a fire retardant in the ceilings known

127

as asbestos. Its properties are so powerful that it has been estimated to have saved thousands of lives from fires that otherwise would have started and spread.

"However, as I'm sure you'll read about and hear on the local news, asbestos is also carcinogenic."

People whispered, asking what that meant. Myckal glanced at me and shrugged.

"It causes cancer," I said.

Mrs. Wild held up her hands to calm us down. "Although, the experts say that our building is not in any immediate danger, because of the potential cancerous agents, the school will close on December thirty-first. After that, a removal company will eliminate every last trace of it. They anticipate John Marshall being completely cleaned out and ready to re-open by next September."

We piped up again and started asking questions among ourselves. It took longer this time, but Mrs. Wild eventually regained order.

"Here's how things are going to work. Beginning next Monday, the school day will still start at eight a.m., but it will go until six p.m. This will essentially give us two school days in one. There will be no more vacation time for the rest of the year. Thanksgiving and Christmas will be the only two days off.

"Final exams have to be completed by December thirty-first. Now, let's discuss sports. I know a lot of you have concerns. Most of the schools in the district have asbestos and will shut down as well. Here's what the school superintendent has determined to be the fairest course. Remember, your safety is our highest priority. Fall sports going on right now, like football and soccer will continue their normal schedule. Winter sports like wrestling and basketball will begin next week. Spring sports are cancelled."

People in the theater vented their frustration, complaining and yelling, trying to figure what all of it meant. Pablo and I locked eyes and nodded. We'd been working out hard since camp. We'd be ready for the early start of the season.

When Mrs. Wild resumed control of things, she asked for questions. Our student body president, Elaina DeGregorio raised her hand. "Are we still having a prom?"

The room went very quiet.

"Yes, but it will have to be in the beginning of December. We don't want it to interfere with finals."

The room erupted.

Chapter 16

Wrestling Update

I sat in the corner of the gym, waiting for our wrestling coach to come out and tell us how the season would run. A painful sigh escaped my lungs. The assembly ended a few hours ago. How could the school close in two months? We didn't even have homecoming yet. Would we still have one? Dances throughout the year were gone, except for the prom. Parties, pep rallies, grad night, they were all up in the air.

Silly things were in jeopardy too—passing notes in class, flirting, hanging out in the parking lot, and smoking in the boy's room. Not that I smoked, but my chance to get caught and suspended was slipping away.

Everything we had taken for granted was at risk. Would we have a yearbook? Not that I was in any clubs, but what happened to them? Most would probably be out of luck. Then there were band and orchestra nights, plus plays in the theater. They might be cancelled too.

What about graduation? Was there going to be a ceremony this year? Nobody knew anything—so frustrating. My throat choked up and I pursed my lips.

Most of all, it was going to kill me to lose time with my friends. The school year usually lasted until mid-June. If we ended in December, that'd be six months without seeing them every day. Sure, I'd get together with my closest friends on the weekends, but what about people like Nicole, Cheryl, Myckal, or even guys like Steve Platis who helped out at the drug store? We'd never get the time back we should have had together. All because of something incredibly stupid that none of us ever heard of before—asbestos. I hated it.

What about the prom? Last year's was the most insane day of my life but it brought Piper and me back together. I could still picture her at Pablo's house. She arrived after me, wearing a little black dress and an awesome waterfall braid in her hair. It was the most beautiful I'd ever seen her. It was the most beautiful I'd ever seen any girl. What would this year's be like?

My chin dipped slightly, lost in the past and dwelling on her. A whistle blew, pulling me back to reality.

"Everyone grab a seat." Coach Slaz was decked out in his singlet. Thank goodness he had a t-shirt underneath. *We* look stupid enough wearing them. Forty-year-old men should be arrested.

He peered at his clipboard but looked as dejected as the rest of us. Normally, we had our first informational meeting in the cafeteria. But almost every club in school was there. The boys' and girls' basketball teams were on separate ends of the main gym.

We were stuck in the wrestling team's small practice gym. That wouldn't be so bad, except the mats hadn't been unrolled in a year and stunk like old liverwurst. It takes a week for my nose to adjust to our gross B.O.

Unrolling day was always the worst. The bacteria that decayed inside stayed moist until we freed them—then they floated away like smoke. People swore you could see the germ clouds and feel them nibble on your skin. Some of the toughest wrestlers puked their guts out.

There wasn't enough room for everyone to sit on the rolled-up mat. Pablo tapped me and a couple other veterans on the shoulder. "Let's take the floor fellas." He turned toward the new recruits. "Rookies, you guys can have the good seats." That was the type of guy Pablo was, and why we loved him as captain.

Coach Slaz began. "We're in a whole new world, gentlemen. Quite frankly, we're lucky they didn't cancel the season. A lot of people thought they should. So, what I'm going to explain to you isn't ideal, and it's not written in stone. Things are probably going to change, and there won't be anything to do about it. But it's all we're going to get, so there's isn't any point complaining.

"We need to stay flexible and overcome every obstacle thrown our way. And there's going to be a lot of them. Most of the time they won't be fair. This whole situation with the asbestos isn't fair to any of you, especially our seniors. Remember, you can't control what happens in life. All you can control is how you react to it."

He paused to let that settle in. Slaz liked inspiring us—when he could.

But this sucked big time. I shook my head. The state championship may not happen this year. Did Coach Flanholtz at Northwestern know, yet? Would the asbestos crap affect the scholarship?

Slaz paced in front of us. "Wrestling practice will begin next Monday, October twenty-ninth. Normally, there's several weeks before our opening match. We usually have two or three scrimmages against other schools to prepare for the season. Not this year. Our first match is eleven days from now, on Saturday, November third."

The veterans grumbled. The rookies didn't know enough to understand how crazy our world had become. A sophomore directly behind me raised his hand. I'd seen him around school. He was small with red hair and a pale, angular face. If he made the team, he'd probably wrestle at 103 or 109. Coach Slaz wouldn't be thrilled about him interrupting.

"What's your name, son?"

"Francis, Coach. Can I ask a question?" He sounded upbeat.

"Normally, I only take questions at the end. But this is a strange day. Go ahead." He crossed his muscular arms over his barrel chest and clipboard.

"This doesn't seem fair."

Groans echoed throughout the gym. He was already straining the coach's patience.

"What did I just say?" Slaz used his *you-can't-be-this-stupid-voice.*

"Normally, you take questions at the end. But this is a strange day." Francis'd be lucky to survive the meeting.

Coach Slaz took a deep breath, then gave him a death stare. "Not that part, Francis. I said that this isn't fair but there's no point complaining about it. Now, can I get back to things?"

Francis shrugged. That might fly for today, but normally Slaz would never accept such a casual response to his question.

He turned back to his clipboard. "The regular season will only run for four weeks. The fifth week will be the county championships and then States. Right now, we don't know whether all of New York is adhering to this schedule. It doesn't look like the upstate schools have an asbestos problem. But we're confident we'll have some sort of state championship. Maybe there will be one for asbestos schools and one for non-asbestos schools. Who knows?"

Francis's hand went back in the air. I turned and stared up at him, shaking my head, hoping he'd get the hint to stay quiet. He didn't.

"Yes, Francis."

"I do."

"You do, what?" Coach asked.

"I know. You asked who knows. I know."

"What is it you think you know?"

"My dad works for the Health Department. He said the upstate schools haven't been tested yet. They won't be tested until next year. So, they won't be competing in our state championship."

"I appreciate that your father works for the Health Department, Francis." It was never good when Coach Slaz kept using your name. Wind sprints usually followed. If we ended up running tonight because of this dude, I was going to kill him.

"But does your father know how the State of New York will be holding their varsity wrestling championship in this shortened season?"

Francis shrugged again.

Coach Slaz's eyes tightened to slits. "In this gym, Francis, we don't say that something is a fact, without knowing it's a fact. It's okay to ask questions. But get your facts straight before you make declarative statements. Is that fair, *Francis?*"

This time Francis nodded and shrugged. I knew that

look on Coach's face. If Francis made another assertion, we'd all be dead. No way was I letting that happen.

Slaz continued. "Hopefully, you guys have stayed in shape on your own. We won't have much time to do it for you. Most likely, the fellas you wrestle against won't be in great condition, either, but you never know. Remember, there are three things that make up a great team."

Holding up his fingers, he ticked them off. "Determination, mental toughness, training, and a spirit of brotherhood. Now, are there any other questions?"

Francis stood and raised his arm.

Pablo nudged me in the ribs. "We have to save this kid from himself."

"I know." Since Francis was behind me, I grabbed his legs and took him down. His hands flailed in mid-flight. He was short and didn't have far to fall. Slaz walked to the other side of the room, pretending not to notice.

Diving on top, Pablo covered Francis's mouth with his hand, and whispered. "Francis, you don't realize it but I'm rescuing you. If you tell Slaz that he just said four things instead of three, then at our first practice, these guys are going to put Ben-Gay in your underwear. You don't want that, do you?"

His eyes bulged and he shook his head.

Pablo allowed him to sit up but kept his arm around his shoulder. "I like you, Francis. You're a cool kid. You're going to make a good teammate, and I won't let anything happen to you. But stay down here and hang out with Luca and me. All right?"

I reached over and shook Francis's hand. He smiled back. I placed my finger over my lips and gave him a thumbs up. He returned it and looked happy to be with us.

A ton of other hands went up. I tuned their questions out. Luckily, I was friends with Pablo. He was one of the insane ones who work out like mad all year and come into the season in top physical form. For the first time I had a legitimate shot at a state championship, so I'd been working out with him since we attended wrestling camp this summer.

Except for the times I visited Piper, or when she surprised me, he and I have either been at the gym or running almost every day. Maybe that'll give me a leg up.

Plus, the biggest obstacle in my way has always been Hector. But he goes to school upstate. If they're not participating in our bizarre season, I won't have to face him. If I can win the county championship, and then States, that should get me into Northwestern. Asbestos may solve my Hector problem.

Chapter 17

Last Saturday of Freedom

Pablo and I drove up to Albany—our last free weekend to party. Once the wrestling schedule came out, we'd face two schools every Saturday. One in the afternoon and after a short rest, one in the evening— probably two or three during the week, too.

Not to mention all the insane studying we'd have to do once our teachers figured out how to cram six months' worth of material into sixty days. Somehow, I'd have to manage straight A's to keep the dream of Northwestern alive. If we were going to visit Piper this semester, it had to be now. Plus, Pablo was dying to see if Robyn was as hot as I claimed.

None of my friends had girlfriends in college, so they jumped on anything I said about dorm life. Without her ever knowing it, the legend of this gorgeous Korean girl had grown throughout Big Dune.

Garret even lent Pablo his Polaroid—they all wanted pictures.

We ended up at the ZBX house, Clive's fraternity. They were throwing a huge party, maybe a ten kegger. A wall of hot steam floated out when we opened the door to enter.

"A lot of bodies must be in there," I said.

It cost us three dollars to get in, which bought us a

red plastic cup. After that, it was all the Batavian Beer we could drink. In case an undercover cop tried to sneak in and bust them for serving alcohol to minors, the fraternity brothers were *supposed to be* carding people at the door. In reality, they were already wasted and flirting with every girl in line.

Since they knew Piper, they didn't ask to see our licenses. It felt cool getting into a college party without being proofed, but we had paid a lot for our fake I.D.s.

As we strolled in, Clive spotted us. "Hey guys, I'm glad you're here. Give me your jackets and I'll drop them in my friend's room." He took them and disappeared up a side staircase.

We weren't allowed on the second floor, but at least our coats were. Most people had taken theirs off and held them at their sides. They looked like they were roasting in the Bermuda Triangle.

There had to be over a hundred people in here, maybe closer to two hundred. We followed Piper to the bar. Kids mobbed it. Standing five deep, they hoisted their empty plastic cups high in the air, like baby birds praying their mother would feed them.

"Let me have your cups," Piper yelled. She took them, scooted around the crowd, ducked under some guy with four full ones, and approached the bar from the side. One of the bartenders nodded to her and filled ours up.

When she returned; Pablo toasted her. "Here's to coming a party with a cute girl."

We clinked cups and she led us into another room. It said Parlor above the doorway. The window frames looked craggily, like they'd been painted over a hundred times. Old couches lined the perimeter and fraternity composites hung on the walls. A mushy, hardwood floor squished beneath our feet.

A band played in the other room which only made it louder. We hung in the Parlor for a while, long enough for Piper to make another beer run.

She and Pablo ended up in a conversation. "That sucks. How long is the wrestling season, normally?" she asked.

"Usually, from November to March. We have twenty matches during those five months, about once a week. We have no idea how many we'll have this year. Just trying to figure things out."

Piper wore a jean jacket over a short-sleeved dress with floral print. She told me it was called a baby doll. I told her I loved the name. Her sandy blonde hair had a butterfly clip on the side, and she also had on white socks and a pair of black boots. I wouldn't exactly call them combat boots, but they were close.

"Aren't you dying in this?" I tugged on her sleeve.

In more ways than one, she looked hot. "Yeah, wait here. I'll go find Jonesy. We'll head upstairs and I'll drop this jacket off with our coats. It's boiling and too loud down here, anyway. Plus, he said he'd give you guys a tour."

She planted a quick peck on my cheek. Her skin felt slick with sweat, reminding me of our shower. My stomach did a full summersault.

Holding her beer over her head like a pro at navigating large, crowded parties, she vanished into a formless ocean.

"Who's Jonesy?" Pablo asked.

My eyes shifted back and forth. "Clive's last name is Jones."

"She calls him Jonesy?" He arched his eyebrows.

"She didn't always." I sipped my brew and my stomach hardened. It bothered me that she started using his nickname.

Pablo and I shrugged at each other. We gave up trying to talk over the noise.

After finishing half of our beers, he shouted, "Let's go check out the kitchen."

Anything was better than nursing our drinks and fighting our way back to the bar, so we made the trek.

"Ugh, it has to be ten degrees cooler in here," Pablo said.

The kitchen was huge, with an old stove, a stainless-steel sink, and a slippery floor. Everything smelled like grease, and I literally felt it seeping into my pores. A couple tables, manned by pledges blocked us from their refrigerators and pantry. Probably making sure their food didn't disappear. About twenty people were hanging out.

"Let's stay here until Piper and Clive find us." I tugged on my shirt collar, hoping she'd be back by now.

"Sounds good, but what happens when we finish our drinks?"

"Jello shots," some pledge called. He placed three trays of plastic shot glasses on one of the tables. Green, red, and orange flavors shimmied in front of us, no doubt mixed with vodka.

"Forget what I asked," he said.

"Here you guys go. Enjoy." A college kid handed them over. PLEDGE was written with red magic marker on his white t-shirt.

"Thanks, man." I turned to Pablo. "Cheers."

We stayed by the tables. The only people who knew about the shots were in this room. It remained our little secret. Nobody wanted to share the vodka.

After sampling each of the colors, we were finally able to exhale and relax a little. My buzz had kicked in and judging by Pablo's eyes, so had his. Two cute girls stumbled out of the hallway and into our little oasis. They weren't carrying coats—they must know some big shot living in the house.

"What's going on in here?" The taller one asked. She was almost as tall as me. Neither of them wore Greek letters.

"Ladies, may I interest you in some Jello shots?" Pablo asked.

"Sure." They looked at each other and smiled.

He grabbed four cups off the tray. "Can I offer you something in a red? I find it a little sweet, however, aged perfectly. Whereas the orange is tart, but with a nice contrast. And while the green is sublime, it coats your tongue a lovely shade of lime. So, how about we start with the red?"

They giggled, and he passed around the shots.

"What should we toast?" the taller one asked.

"Yeah, Luca. What should we drink to?" Pablo asked.

All three of them stared at me, hoping for something profound.

"Okay. I know." I lifted my cup.

Pablo interrupted, "And it better not be something lame like, *Here's to the University of Albany.*"

I gave him a dirty look.

"Or something even worse like, *let's salute the brothers of Zeta Beta Chi.*"

My sneer deepened. "I wasn't going to." Crap. He stole both of my ideas. Now I had nothing to say and no time to come up with anything. I rubbed the back of my neck, a little nervous from being put on the spot and tried stalling. "Can I do my toast now, please?"

"Go right ahead."

I hoisted my cup and blew out a sputtering breath. "Here's to that long straight piece in Tetris."

"What?" the shorter girl asked. They both squinted and looked at me like I had two heads.

Pablo let out short laugh. "That was the dumbest thing I ever heard in my life. You'll have to excuse my friend. He may have already had one too many."

"You think you can do better?" I challenged.

"Couldn't be worse." He scoffed. "Give me a second." He held up his finger and lowered his head, as if pondering a deep thought. An instant later he came up with an idea. "All right. You know what, I *have* got one."

Pablo cleared his throat, and his cup went high in the air. The rest of the kitchen partiers chose this moment to look over. The room fell silent.

"Uh oh. This better be good." His eyes shifted back and forth, realizing what happened.

The girls chuckled nervously.

I've often said he's the life of the party. A metal chair sat next to the table of shots. Without hesitating, he jumped on top of it. Everyone focused on him. He raised his cup again and yelled.

"Here's to a long life and a merry one!" The room started to woohoo for him.

"A quick ending and a happy one." His voice grew brasher, so did the cheering.

"A good girl and a pretty one." He toasted to our two new friends, going louder.

"Aww," they both said with big grins. The rest of the room laughed.

"And here's to a cold Jello shot and another one!" That time he yelled the loudest.

Everybody in the kitchen elevated their cups. "And another one!" They toasted back, downed their shots, and cheered for Pablo. He thrust a hand in triumph and hopped down. He grabbed four greens along the way and passed them to us.

"So, which one am I?" the tall chick asked him. "The good girl or the pretty one?"

He clinked her cup. "Who do you want to be?"

She slurped her shot and bit her bottom lip. "Not the good girl."

Chapter 18

Brothers Only

Just like that, Pablo and the tall girl were making out in the corner. The band played *Shooting Star* by Bad Company. They had a pretty good rendition going. All the shots were gone.

"So, what's your name," her friend asked me.

"I'm Luca, how about you?"

"Andrea. How come I've never seen you before?" She spoke loudly, with a slight drunken slur. We shook hands.

"This is my first Zeta Beta Chi party," I said. "How about you?"

The tall girl had her back to me with Pablo pressed against the wall. He opened his eyes for a second and flashed me a thumbs up. I didn't dare return it. Andrea might not appreciate it and I refused to do anything to hurt his chances.

She leaned in close, one hand going on my right arm and staying there. "We love these guys. We're here all the time. You think you might pledge one day?" She bit half of her bottom lip, then smiled.

Switching my beer to my right hand, I raised it to my mouth and took a short swig. It made her let go of me. I was uncomfortable with her coming on so hard, but I didn't walk away. I was Pablo's wingman and firmly committed to the role.

Now that we had switched to shots, I felt pretty buzzed, and wondered about a hangover. Piper's hangover after the quarters game ruined that weekend for us. No way did I want that happening again.

How did the saying go? *Liquor before beer, never sicker. Beer before liquor never fear.* That sounded right, but I might have it backward. Either way, I didn't need any more alcohol for a while. Milking my warm beer was the right choice. Besides, if I finished it, I'd be obligated to head to into the other room and suffer through the crowd for a refill.

"Do you know Clive Jones?" I asked her. "He invited me to pledge, so maybe. We'll see what happens. Are you in a sorority?"

"Us, no. But a lot of Zeta guys live in our dorm, including your buddy, Clive. What year are you?" Andrea stepped closer. Every time she took a sip of beer, she made strong, hungry eye contact. When she found out Clive invited me to pledge, she started nibbling on her cup. Thoughts of having a ZBX boyfriend probably drifted through her plastered mind.

Boy, was I on thin ice? I desperately needed Piper to come through that door and save me.

"We're seniors," I announced. Not a lie, but probably not the way she imagined. "What year are you?" I took another nursing taste, needing to do something with my hands. Beads of sweat appeared on my forehead, the first since entering the cooler kitchen.

She closed the distance again. Right answer for her, I guess. If I wasn't going out with Piper, thoughts of what could happen flew through my mind. Not to mention the stories that Pablo and I would tell for years to come—

that we made out with two cute friends at the same fraternity party. We'd return to John Marshall as conquering heroes. A lot of girls never understood that about guys. Almost everything we did, revolved around the stories we could tell.

However, that's not why I drove up here. I wanted to spend time with my hot girlfriend, instead of playing second fiddle to Pablo—again. Whether in wrestling, getting good grades, or flirting with girls, everything came so easy to him.

Unfortunately, his expertise at picking up tall girls could get me into big trouble. If I blew off Andrea, she might want to leave. She'd grab her friend away from Pablo and I'd be the worst wingman ever. On the other hand, if she kept touching my bicep, Piper might walk in and get the wrong idea. Not likely—we didn't have that kind of insecure relationship. We trusted each other.

"We're sophomores." When Andrea leaned in this time, she stumbled into my arms, spilling beer on me.

"Whoa. You, okay?"

It took her a second to regain her footing and she gave me a peck on the cheek. She smelled like cherry body spray, cigarettes, and a Batavian Brewery.

Sliding a quick step away from her, I slipped my free hand into my pocket, wishing she hadn't kissed me. A guilty quiver invaded my throat and stomach.

"Wow. You have strong arms. Hey wait a minute. How can you be a senior if you're thinking about pledging next year?"

I blew that rap. Somehow, buzzed Andrea saw through my level of BS. I leaned in to whisper directly into her ear. She smiled as I approached. Her star-shaped earrings dangled near my face. I had no desire for the rest of the kitchen to hear my next admission.

"Actually, we're seniors in high school."

"High school?!" she yelled. "Oh, that's gross."

Before I could react, she hustled over, and peeled her tall friend off Pablo.

"Come on Jenny, let's go. These two are still in high school."

Jenny frowned and shook her head. She looked pissed for being ripped away. "What?" she slurred. "What's going on?"

Andrea grabbed Jenny's hand and led her toward the kitchen door. "They're too young for us."

"Huh?" She wormed out of Andrea's clutch. Her other hand reached for Pablo, and he stepped closer.

Andrea shook Jenny by the shoulders. "They're in high school. They're jailbait! Let's get out of here."

As they left the kitchen, they bumped into two other girls. It turned out to be Piper and Robyn. Piper had taken off her jean jacket. She looked great in her short dress. But she had her arms crossed, and her eyes shot daggers at me.

"Jailbait!" Robyn ran over and hugged me. She wore a black miniskirt with a cropped, hot pink t-shirt and boots. She whispered, "We saw Andrea give you a kiss."

Crap! Piper was still scowling.

"Pablo, meet Robyn. And Robyn, this is my friend, Pablo."

His jaw dropped when he saw her. I motioned for them to shake hands, but my voice lost much of its power.

Piper turned and bolted into the crowded hallway.

"Oh, no way," I called and fled after her. "Please, wait."

There were so many drunk college kids between us she made it to the front door before I could catch up. She was smaller and navigated her way better than I did. I was afraid she was going to run outside. At the last second, she turned right.

Reaching out, I latched onto her arm, it was slippery with sweat.

"Piper, it's not what you think. Why are you so mad?" We stopped at the bottom of a thin, winding staircase. Two fraternity brothers stood a third of the way up, talking to sorority girls.

She pulled away. "Why am I so mad? Are you frigging kidding me?"

Several people looked over.

"Can you please not yell? And no, I'm not kidding. I don't understand what I did wrong."

Her green eyes glared at me. "I leave for five minutes, to find Clive to take *you* on a tour of the house, and when I get back, Andrea's kissing you."

My heart clanged so deep in my chest, I felt it in my throat. I knew this was bad but couldn't bring myself to admit it.

"First off, you were not gone for five minutes. It was more like a half hour. And second, I didn't kiss her. I was just talking to her for Pablo's sake. Did you notice him in the corner—making out with her friend?"

She shook her head. Her glare actually deepened. "Of course, I saw Pablo with Jenny. They're the two biggest sluts in Clive's dorm. They're known as A.J. as in, *have you slept with A.J. yet?* They're ZBX groupies and have been with half the brothers in this house. By the looks of it, Andrea had her hooks into you, and you didn't seem to be fighting her off."

"Oh, was that her name, Jenny?" I chuckled. What a dumb thing to do. As soon as I said it, Piper turned and took a few steps up the staircase.

I caught up to her. "Look, I'm sorry. I didn't know them. Pablo started talking to a girl and then a few minutes later, he's kissing her. The only reason I talked to Andrea was to be a good wingman."

"I guess we know what's important to you." She spun and sped up the stairs. The fraternity brothers nodded at her like she had the run of the place.

That comment hurt. A sudden coldness hit my core. I couldn't think straight, but I knew I screwed up. I should have found a way to politely cut loose from Andrea. My muscles felt frozen, and I didn't react until Piper went halfway up. When I tried following, the two goons stepped toward each other blocking my path.

"Sorry, man. Brothers only," the larger one said.

I pointed at her. "But that's my girlfriend."

She stopped and looked down, but didn't reply.

"Piper, tell them."

The smaller one held his hand on my chest, preventing me from going farther. He looked in her direction. "Is that true, Piper? Is this guy with you?"

I raised my arms in an *are you kidding me?* gesture. My mind raced, searching for answers. Where did she get the authority to dictate who went upstairs? A deep hole developed in my chest. Wasn't our relationship stronger than this?

She turned her nose up. "Never seen him before."

Chapter 19

Something Got in My Eye

Ever since Piper ran upstairs, Pablo and I had nothing to do except drink. When did she become so jealous?

A fraternity brother went from room to room, announcing some bad news. "Party's over, everyone. It's midnight, time to clear out." It took about twenty minutes for the place to empty. Besides the guys in ZBX shirts, there were maybe ten of us left. But I wasn't going anywhere without Piper. I'd camp on their lawn if I had to.

Wavering between disbelief and hurt, I wished the night had turned out so different. I wished I spent the whole time with Piper. Did I lose her? My scalp prickled with fear and my whole body felt heavy, like somebody chained a hippo to me. "Let's take another lap," I said to Pablo. "Otherwise, they're gonna kick us out, too."

He put his arm around me. "All right, listen up dummy. Since the party's over, Piper's going to come down any minute. Apologize the second you see her and beg for mercy."

"Dude, I still don't know what I did—"

"Stop. Do you want to prove that you were right, and she was wrong? Or do you want to sleep with your girlfriend? You can't do both."

Replaying everything in my mind, I fumed at the way she ran off and left me. It was so embarrassing. Right after it happened, I wanted to be proved right more than anything. Piper had no reason to overreact like that. I would never try to pick up Andrea. I would never risk what we had to be with *any* girl. She should know that.

I kept Andrea company to let Pablo put the moves on Jenny. That was all. I couldn't believe the way Piper jumped down my throat.

Pablo and I trudged into the center hall. A puddle of muddy beer sat in the middle of the floor. Piper came walking down the main staircase, step by agonizing step. She had one hand on the railing, a high chin and cold eyes.

I cocked my head to the side, put on a silly grin and mouthed, "I love you." Her tough veneer cracked, and tears formed in the corner of her eyes. I waited at the bottom, and she ran into my arms. Her momentum almost knocked me over.

"I'm so sorry, Piper. I'm so sorry," I said through kisses. Her hot cheeks felt wet on mine. We ended up making out in ZBX's hallway. Unfortunately, that's all I got that weekend.

Robyn stayed over at Dan's place. But when we got back to her room, Pablo, Piper, and I stayed up talking for a couple hours. He eventually fell asleep in Robyn's bed, and I got under the covers with Piper. Relief flooded through me, traveling from head to toe. I almost lost her tonight.

A strand of hair dangled across her cheek, and I brushed it behind her ear. "I was incredibly stupid. I shouldn't have prioritized helping Pablo hook up with some random girl over spending time with you. I am so totally, absolutely, and painfully in love with you. I'll never make that mistake again."

What an awesome kiss she planted on me, but with Pablo snoring his head off, nothing more was going to happen. The jerk.

****

On the following Saturday, we had two wrestling matches. The first one was against Myckal's old school, Alexander Hamilton. She knew almost everyone on the team. They joked and called her traitor a million times, but she laughed it off and gave it back just as good.

I pinned my challenger in the first period. I may have taken out some repressed anger on him. Poor bastard never stood a chance.

Our second meet was going on right now. We faced Ackerman, our rival school.

A vein in my neck twitched and my blood boiled. It happened before all my matches. I hit myself in the side of my head gear as the 128-pound match ended. My friend Pete defeated his Ackerman counterpart, six points to three.

I was next. Last year I beat this same opponent ten points to two. Basically, a blowout. The only question was if I'd pin him today or destroy him on points.

The referee called us to the center of the mat, and I shook hands with the Ackerman dude. The whistle blew. We circled each other a couple times. He shot at my legs but slow and sloppy. I pancaked my body on his head and smashed my forearm into the back of his neck, keeping him stuck in that position. When I spiraled behind him, the ref awarded my two points for a takedown.

It took about thirty seconds to drive him flat onto his

stomach. After that, I flipped him forty-five degrees over, but he felt stronger than I remembered, and I couldn't pin him. He worked his way out of my hold, and fought back to his stomach. When I regained control, I almost pinned him again, but he escaped at the last second. It earned me a ton of points.

The referee tweeted his whistle ending the first period. I let go of the Ackerman kid and we both stood up.

"Where do you want to start?" the ref asked me.

"I'll take down." I won the coin toss earlier, so I got to choose, up or down.

That meant I'd begin on all fours. When instructed, the Ackerman kid would kneel next to me. His right hand would grip my right elbow and his left arm would wrap around my body and end up on my stomach.

Feeling energized, and not at all tired, I stole a glance at my competitor. He had his hands on his hips, almost doubled over, and completely exhausted. He'd be out of gas soon.

I had a simple plan. As soon as the period began, I'd hook his right elbow with mine and use leverage to flip him on his back. Quick and powerful, I'd wrap his head in my arms, drive my chin into the side of his shoulder and pin him, putting him out of his misery. The whole thing shouldn't take more than twenty seconds.

The ref pointed at me, indicating I should get into position. Wanting to intimidate the kid, I hustled onto my knees, then placed my hands on the mat, my muscles vibrating with purpose. I stared straight ahead and had a perfect view of Myckal's legs. *Holy crap,* they were gorgeous!

As the team's manager, she had a seat at the scorer's

table, maybe fifteen feet away. She sat diagonally at the left end of it with her legs crossed. I didn't realize how tan and toned they were. I was on all fours, and they were *right* in front of me. Even with a chin strap on, my jaw dropped.

Her gray skirt, blue button-down shirt, and white cami looked amazing on her. Not that I was trying, but I could almost see up her… No, I wouldn't do it. No way. No way. No way. We were good friends. No way, dude.

I needed a distraction, otherwise my eyes might drift to no man's land. I never wanted the ref to blow the whistle so bad in my life. But this Ackerman idiot dragged things out, tying his shoe. I knew I had to turn away. But my hormonal brain refused to cooperate. With all the strength I could muster, I forced my attention northward and away from the dangerous view.

Her thick, black curly hair was down with a white scrunchy, high on top. Her upper leg started to bounce. It wasn't always bouncing, was it? No, I was sure it wasn't. It just started and pulled my gaze back to where it didn't belong.

Shaking my head, I tried purging my locker-room thoughts. There was something I needed to do, but I was afraid of the consequences. Straining, I glimpsed up. Sure enough, her dazzling blue eyes locked onto mine. She had been watching me the whole time. Of course, she was. *Oh, crud!*

Did she think I was trying to peek where I shouldn't? Because I wasn't. I swear. I wasn't. Geography made me do it. Did she know that?

Beads of sweat developed on my forehead and my face blushed, but it probably looked red from the match. She tilted her head and smiled, then gave me a double thumbs up, cheering me on.

The whistle finally blew. Instead of hooking my challenger's elbow and flipping him over, I froze, unable to tear my eyes from hers. She crinkled her brow and frowned.

The Ackerman wrestler didn't totally suck. When he saw that I didn't react, he hit me with a cross face. You can't use your fist, but you can take the side of your hand and drive it into your opponent's face, then keep going and smack him with your bicep, which is what he did—really hard. I saw stars, not the *Bugs Bunny* type, but red and blue pin pricks flooded my vision.

Before I knew it, he had me flat on my stomach and *he* tried to heave me over for the pin.

"What the hell are you doing, Luca?!" Coach Slaz's voice boomed throughout the gym.

That snapped me out of my Myckal induced fog. In no time, I got back to my knees, then escaped to my feet, earning another point. My breathing and heartbeat sped up. Adrenaline kicked in and so did my appetite to attack. I felt like a moron for letting him get the better of me. With lightning speed, I dove at his legs, and took him down, scoring two more points.

"Ugh," he groaned. Any fight he had left melted away, and I immediately pinned him.

After the ref raised my hand in victory, I headed back to the team to get my congratulations and a bunch of high-fives. The blue and red stars had disappeared.

Coach Slaz grabbed me by the arm. "What happened to you back there, Esposito?"

Myckal stood next to him, listening.

"Sorry about that, Coach. Something got in my eye."

She grinned and chuckled. Slaz saw her and

narrowed his glare. She put her head down and went back to the scorer's table, biting her bottom lip.

Chapter 20

In Your Dreams

Several hours later the team ended up at Jimmy's house. He wasn't a wrestler. He just happened to be throwing a party. His mother traveled a lot on business. If he didn't trash the place, she didn't mind if he threw the occasional bash. About forty people showed up.

Everyone chipped in four bucks, and he bought a bunch of beer and a few wine coolers. A game of quarters broke out in the kitchen. After my latest fight with Piper, I didn't want to participate in anything that reminded me of it. I wandered around the house. Billy Joel's voice came out of the stereo. A small group huddled in the living room, arm in arm, and singing along to *Piano Man*.

The laundry room had a solid cement floor, and he kept the beer down there—he didn't want to ruin the carpeting. I went downstairs to grab one out of the cooler, saying hi to some friends sitting on the staircase. The lighting seemed dimmer down here.

Jimmy and Cheryl hung out in the basement with six other kids, playing truth or dare. They invited me to join in, but I didn't feel like sharing tonight. Everybody knew I dated a college girl and they always picked on me to share some juicy truths.

Nicole was in the next room making out with some

dude on the couch, but I couldn't tell who. She must have sensed me and opened her eyes. I gave her a *who's that?* expression. She waved me away and went back to Frenching him.

Peering out a snow caked window, I noticed four people standing around the fire pit. I grabbed my jacket and took my beer with me. Pablo, Porco, Garret, and Steve Platis stood around drinking and sharing stories. Nobody sat on the frosty lawn furniture. Strong flames licked at a thick log. It smelled like Halloween time.

"Hey, what's up, Luca?" Garret said. "Happy Birthday, by the way."

"It's your birthday?" Porco asked.

"Tomorrow, actually. Seventeen."

Everyone raised their beer. "Happy Birthday."

"Thanks gents." I zipped up the whole way and blew into my non-beer hand. A crisp wind swept by, and the cold bottle stung my fingers. The fire jumped at the sudden gust of oxygen. The heat felt nice, but somehow, the smoke always followed me, no matter where I moved.

Garret pointed at me. "Pablo just told us how you both pinned your opponents today. Nice going, man." He held up his beer and we all clinked together.

I'd have to thank Jimmy for buying bottles instead of cans. It tasted so much better out of a glass bottle, especially an icy one.

"Here's to two state championships this year." Porco lifted his beer this time. Bottles sounded better when you clanked them too.

Taking a big swig, I already finished half. Most of them had their hands in their pockets and held onto their beer with a loop formed by their thumb and index finger.

"So, what happened in your second match today?" Pablo asked.

"What do you mean?"

"I don't know. You were beating the heck out of your guy. He hadn't scored a point. Then suddenly, he has your face against the mat, and he came close to slamming you on your back. No one's ever done that to you before, except Hector. What gives?"

None of these other guys wrestled, so they weren't there. A loud pop snapped. We laughed as sparks flew in Porco's direction. He threw another log into the pit and spit out some dip. Burning embers shot high in the night air like orange fireworks.

"Thanks, douche bag, for reminding me of him." Actually, Hector had been on my mind a lot lately. We didn't know anything new about the state championship. But I wanted to avoid him at all costs. With my straight A's, the only thing that could derail Northwestern was Hector. I still didn't know how I could beat him. My best bet was never having to wrestle him.

"Shut up. You know what I mean. So, are you going to tell us or not?" Pablo demanded.

I motioned for them to move closer to the fire. It wasn't something I wished the world to know. "All right. I'll tell you what happened. But you have to swear you won't repeat it. I can't have this getting back to Myckal."

Enquiring dudes wanted to know. They nodded, then Pablo spoke up. "What could your match have to do with her? I thought you were going to say you didn't want it getting back to Piper."

"Oh yeah, her too. Now that you mention it, especially not Piper." I scanned the faces in front of me—they looked really curious. "Did any of you see

Myckal tonight?"

"Yeah. She's inside. Why?" Porco said.

"Did anyone notice what she was *wearing*?"

With scrunching faces, they gazed into their brains, trying to remember what Myckal had on and how it could possibly affect my match. Eventually, they all shook their heads.

"Okay. The first period ends and I'm way ahead on points. At the beginning of the second period, I get into the down position, on my hands and knees."

"And?" Pablo moved his hand in a circle, trying to get me to tell it faster.

"And I found myself staring straight at Myckal's legs. She totally hypnotized me."

"What?" Porco asked.

"Dude, I'm telling you. She has on this short skirt and from that angle, she has the sweetest pair of legs I've ever seen. It distracted the hell out of me. One second, I'm concentrating on pinning this Ackerman schmuck, and after one look at her, he's got me face down on the mat."

They cracked up.

A girl's voice jingled behind us. "Who has the sweetest pair of legs you've ever seen?"

Appearing out of nowhere, Myckal stood with her hands in her pockets, smiling in her winter coat. Everyone turned in her direction. They all cocked their heads, checking out her legs.

"Good luck, Luca." Garret patted me on the shoulder and walked off with the others. They snickered and hiked up Jimmy's red deck stairs, opened the sliding glass door on the second floor, and stepped into the kitchen. Shrieking and hysterics from the quarter's game blasted out.

Myckal squinted and watched them leave. "Was it something I said? I don't usually drive boys away that easily."

"How much of that did you overhear?" I took another gulp of beer and closed my eyes, praying it was zero.

Striding closer to the fire, she bounced and flexed her knees, almost like a cute dance move. She had changed out of her shoes and into a pair of thick white socks and fur lined ankle boots, turned down at the top. Her legs had to be freezing but they looked even better now.

"Why, what *didn't* you want me to overhear?"

A strong desire to run home and not look back swept over me. Instead, I shook my head and cleared my throat. "They asked what happened in my Ackerman match. They wanted to know how he hit me with that cross face at the beginning of the second period."

"What did you tell them?"

"Exactly what you heard me saying. That someone with a gorgeous pair of legs caused me to lose focus."

Her breath came out and disappeared at a much quicker pace, but she maintained her cool. With a sly smile, she licked her lips. "And you're blaming me?"

"Are you doing that hot girl thing to me right now?" I chuckled and shivered.

"What hot girl thing?"

"You know the one I mean. It's when certain chicks automatically know how to intimidate a guy. You probably learned it on day one of junior high. I can picture everything in my mind. You're in the girl's locker room. The cheerleading coach pirouettes in and

161

explains the finer points of driving guys crazy. *'Don't ever give a boy a straight response. Just rephrase whatever he says and answer a question with a question. That'll keep him guessing.'"*

"You think I'm hot, Luca?" Her voice got softer and deeper.

The ability to swallow had become increasingly difficult. My legs got a little weak, too. "You realize in my version of this, you're all in your underwear."

She smiled. "What exactly am I wearing?"

"Huh?"

Her head tilted and she leaned forward. "Are they lacy, boyshorts, bikinis? What are you picturing me in?"

There's no way I was answering that. The cold beer in my hand nipped at my fingers—I finished it in one final guzzle and placed the bottle on the side of the pit. "We're friends, me and you, right? I mean, you know I have a serious girlfriend in college. Even though you've never met her."

She nodded slowly and we locked eyes. The last time we did, I was on all fours, gazing up at her baby blues. Except now, I didn't feel like she caught me doing anything wrong.

This situation had become totally intense. Before we crossed a dangerous line, I had to break her grip over me. I hadn't felt this kind of stirring in a long time. Where if you let it take root, something incredible could happen. I would never let things get that far, but man, oh man, if I didn't have a girlfriend…

My demeanor and the pitch of my voice raised to the teasing level. "Excellent. Then as your good friend I can admit that you're hot, Myckal. You're one of the hottest girls in school. And yes, you've got an incredibly sweet pair of legs!" I smiled—relieved that I could joke around with her.

"I do?"

"Shut up," I said and punched her in the arm, playful.

She grinned back.

Now that my hands were empty, I blew into them to warm up. "You know what the crazy thing is? If I was trying to get you to go out with me, I'd never have the courage to admit all this."

"You wouldn't?"

I smirked and grunted at her. "Let's go inside and get another beer. It's freezing out. Besides, I need to talk to a guy for a while. Finally get some straight answers."

"Are you sure you didn't get any from me?" She laughed, bright-eyed.

This girl was so much fun. I threw one arm around her shoulder. Boy, did she feel nice and warm—and her curly hair smelled coconutty. She was shorter than Piper, but not by much. We started walking in. "And one more thing. During my match I was *not* trying to peek up your... well, you know. I promise, I wasn't."

She stopped in her tracks and pointed. "Is that what you were doing? I knew it. I knew I caught you stealing a look, Luca Esposito."

"Yeah, you wish," I said as we strolled up the deck stairs. "But you have to do me a huge favor."

"What's that?"

"If you're going to sit at the scorer's table, you can't wear skirts anymore. I'll never win another match. From now on, *please*—jeans only."

She elbowed me in the ribs. "*In your dreams.*"

Chapter 21

After Piper's Night Out

It was Sunday, November eleventh. I wrestled twice yesterday, winning both matches on points. My record stood at an impressive 6-0. As a reward, my parents loaned me the car. I left for Albany at nine in the morning with the condition that I make it home by eight. It didn't leave much time to spend with Piper, but I'd take what I could get.

Earlier this week, Mrs. Wild announced the prom would be on Friday, December fourteenth, just over a month away. They couldn't find a catering hall on such short notice so it would be held in the gym. Fine by me. It's where I thought they should always have it. We made our memories in the school. Why shouldn't our most significant night be there?

Piper and I had a date to go dress shopping today. Luckily, her parents agreed to pay for it. Her mom was still mad at me from last year. Since I waited until prom day to ask Piper, that robbed them of the opportunity to go shopping together. When I mentioned that Mrs. Kraft could take her this year, Piper chuckled.

The laugh meant one thing. Her parents hoped Piper would have broken up with me by now. Her mom had no intention of participating in this year's prom, since it was mine.

I didn't mind, they were bailing me out. After draining my account to bankroll last year's prom, I had only saved a few hundred dollars. There's no way I could have afforded everything again.

When we spoke on the phone, I offered to leave at seven in the morning.

"That's too early. I won't be able to wake up before eleven," she had told me.

"Why not? It's our only chance to see each other for a while."

"Umm, Dan and Jonesy know this bar called The Shack. It's a little farther off campus but the band that played at the ZBX party is performing there. A couple guys from his fraternity are in it, so we want to check them out."

"But we just heard them. They weren't that great." Actually, they were pretty good. But since she was giving me a hard time, I didn't want to admit it.

"That was at the house. They don't have a good sound system."

"And how are you getting into a bar, Miss Nineteen-Year-Old?" If she noticed my annoyed tone, she didn't let on.

"Jonesy gave me his ex-girlfriend's license. We look a lot alike. Anyway, they close at two and by the time we stop for wings, I won't get to bed until three-thirty at the earliest."

"Wings?" I'd never seen her eat a wing in her life.

"I'll probably just have a slice. The boys will order wings, I'm sure. But I don't want to be hung over when you get here. Besides, the dress shops don't open until noon."

After losing that debate, I left at nine, and pulled into

her parking lot at twelve. The frost had burned off on my drive up and the green grass had turned an ugly shade of gray, mirroring the cement buildings, and overcast sky.

The guy on the radio said it might snow a couple inches tonight. Good thing my parents didn't hear that tidbit.

When I went through the lobby three kids were laid out on couches watching football. Their hair spiked in all directions—probably slept there last night. Old, crumpled boxes formed a leaning tower of pizza in the corner.

The silver elevator doors opened, and it smelled like someone got sick inside. I squeezed my nose and stepped on for the ride. In the hallways, not a creature stirred, not even a pledge. The construction paper with flowers and windowpanes on Piper's door were gone. The only thing left was a white board that said, *Robyn and Piper's Room. Caution—Hot Plate and Toaster Hidden Under Bed. Don't Tell the R.A.* I knocked and stuck my head in.

"Jailbait," Robyn's voice cracked, sounding husky and subdued. Normally she shouted her greeting at me, but not today. She was still in her pajamas with no make-up. For her, that was a huge deal. I'd never seen her without any.

"Hey, Robyn. Rough night last night?"

We hugged but she didn't move from her chair. Piper wasn't in the room.

Placing a finger on my lips, she whispered, "Shh. Or I might have to kill you." A huge glass of orange juice sat on the desk along with five aspirin tablets. "Ugh." She downed them, crept to her bed, sat cross legged, and stared into space.

"Hey babe." Piper came in and kissed me, but it

166

barely rated a peck on the lips. Our first kiss was usually long and passionate, especially if we hadn't seen each other in weeks. She tasted like peppermint toothpaste.

"Hmm, minty." I hid my disappointment and raised my eyebrows. "You look good. Much better than Robyn."

She nudged her shower caddy under the bed and they both smirked at me. At least Piper was dressed—she wore jeans, boots, and an oversized, blue Albany sweatshirt.

"You ready to go? We only have five hours before I need to leave."

Piper scanned the room, trying not to move fast. Her hands went out to her sides, like an unsteady gymnast on a balance beam. She grabbed her wallet, I.D., and keys. "I can't believe your parents are being such pains."

"Tell me about it. By the way, did I just see Clive stumbling out of here?"

A quick sheet of white blanked over Robyn's face and her eyes bulged. Scrunching her brows together, she tried to recover. "Stumbled out of where?" Her tone sounded deep, squeaking, and nervous.

Piper kept her back to me.

I squinted between those two. "Downstairs, leaving your dorm. I saw him when I parked. He had a ZBX jacket on."

"Are you sure it was him?" Piper glanced over her shoulder.

"I don't know what he looks like from fifty yards away. But I thought it was Clive. What's the big deal? Weren't you hanging out with him last night?"

Robyn shook her head. "No biggie. We split up after midnight. It looked like he was going home with a girl.

Maybe he got lucky." Her cheeks puffed out like a chipmunk, her fist went in front of her mouth, and something unholy barked out of her lungs. "Yuck. I think I need to lay down."

Taking a step back, I waved a hand in front of my face.

"Shut up. You didn't smell anything. *Did you?*" She looked toward the heavens and sniffed at the surrounding air, then took a couple imaginary bites.

I frowned like I inhaled something putrid. "No. I didn't."

"Your boyfriend's a real jerk. I may hate his guts." With a fake pout Robyn threw a pink bear at me.

After catching it in the air, I tossed it back to her. "So, who did Clive score with? Jenny?"

Piper snorted and covered her mouth. "Sorry, but no. Jonesy wouldn't touch a tramp like her."

Robyn's bed was still unmade from last night, she curled into the fetal position and pulled a pink comforter over her body. "Besides, a lot of Zeta brothers live in this dorm. If he struck out, he might have crashed in one of their rooms."

I wasn't a suspicious guy, but these two were acting weird.

"I've got everything. You ready to go?" Piper headed toward the door.

"Something about this scene isn't right."

With wide eyes Piper looked at Robyn, then at me. "What do you mean?"

"It's like twenty degrees out. How about your coat?"

"Oh, yeah." She laughed and went to the closet.

"Why wouldn't Clive hook up with Jenny? You told me she slept with half of the ZBX house and Andrea slept with the other half."

Letting out a huge sigh, she wrapped her arms around my neck. "How about we stop obsessing about who Clive may or may not have had sex with last night? I have big plans for *you* today. Do you remember what happened when we went shopping for a prom dress last year?" She tilted her head and kissed me.

"Mmm, still minty. Yes, I do. I remember you modeling quite a few dresses for me. Right before you sexually assaulted me in the changing room."

"Wait. What?" Robyn exclaimed, sitting up way too fast. "I never heard this story. I want details, now." She pointed at us with a weak, trembling finger and her face contorted in a lot of pain.

"No, you haven't heard it and you're not going to." Piper grabbed my hand and led me out of the room.

"Oh, come on. I want to know how you attacked poor Jailbait, you hussy!"

Piper smiled and slammed the door.

Chapter 22

All's Forgiven

We drove in my mother's silver Plymouth Fury, a sporty two door coupe with red interior. The wind kicked up, flurries dusted the road, and spiraled away with the speeding traffic. Unfortunately, Piper's mood turned as gray as the weather.

The inside of the car was ice cold. We could still see our breath.

"Do you think Robyn and Dan will last forever?" I asked.

She glanced at the floor, brought her right foot up on the seat, and shrugged one shoulder. "I don't know. Forever's a long time."

That comment hung in the air a few minutes. Not wanting to deal with silence, I turned on the radio, but static droned through the speakers. None of my stations came in up here. "Can you see if there's a cassette in the glove box?"

She sighed and banged it open like I asked her to work in the salt mines. Instead of popping one in, she handed it to me without looking. "Boston."

"Thanks." I stole a quick glance in the tiny cassette window. There was a ton of tape on side A. When I slid it into the player, *More Than a Feeling* came on.

"Would you know if Robyn was cheating on Dan?"

I asked.

"She's not cheating." Her face scrunched like she popped a lemon candy in her mouth.

"But if she hid it really well, how could you tell?"

Piper did a double-take, and her hands flew to her cheeks. "What?! Do you know something I don't?"

Normally, I'd sneak peeks at her when we had a conversation, but not now. "Me? How would I?"

Our four-lane highway contained a couple strip malls, and gas stations, but mainly lots of snowy woods.

"Why would you even think that?" She squinted, her jaw tightened, and her voice sounded as constricted as her posture.

"I don't really care if she is or not. It doesn't make any difference to me." I decided to match her tone.

"I don't understand where this coming from." She crossed her arms then pointed at the road. "Get off at this exit, behind those trucks."

The car finally warmed up and I lowered the heat. "She acted kinda nervous when I asked about Clive. I thought maybe she decided to cheat on her boyfriend."

"With his *best friend*? I don't think so. I'm surprised you have such a low opinion of her."

My chest tightened. *Taking this awful personal.* I wish I said that, but I didn't want to keep arguing about Robyn and Dan. This wasn't really about them. "I'm just making conversation. I know you've become good friends with her this semester, but I don't know anything about her, except what you tell me. It wouldn't be the first time a girl slept with her boyfriend's best friend. I didn't mean to upset you."

She studied me for what seemed like forever, then let out a deep breath. "You didn't. I may have jumped down your throat because I'm a little hungover. That's all." Piper angled her body my way. With a gleam in her eye, she put her hand on my knee and brightened her tone. "How about you let me make it up to you?"

Our exit took us into the heart of Albany. If you've ever been to New York City, you judge every other town against it, fair or not. Tough luck rest of the world. These buildings weren't Manhattan tall, but we entered a concrete jungle with five and ten story structures.

I smiled at her and raised my eyebrows. "All depends. What'd you have in mind?" My shoulders loosened up, which helped settle my nerves. I hated this tension between us.

Today was supposed to be a lot of fun and make up for last year. Shopping for a dress and tux at the last minute may have turned into a great adventure, but it wasn't the way she wished it happened. I wanted to make everything perfect for her this time.

The sound of her seat belt clicked and unbuckled. She slid across the seat and pinned the side of her body against mine.

"Wait. You meant, now? What are you doing?" I asked.

"What does it look like I'm doing?"

Knowing exactly what drove me crazy, she puckered up and blew a tiny puff of air into my ear. She ran her hands through my hair and long slow kisses lingered on my neck. Chills and goosebumps broke out. With all my might, I fought the temptation to twitch my shoulder. I didn't want to risk dislodging her lips—what if it made her stop?

Her fingernails went under my shirt, tickling the back of my shoulders. They went from relaxed and mellow, to sparked with a bolt of electricity. Her right hand landed on my thigh. She kissed the outside of my ear and her tongue danced inside, realizing it would blast my pulse to lightspeed.

"This is me, saying sorry for being such a bitch to you."

"You weren't a..." The most incredible tingling engulfed my body. No girl had ever done this to me while driving. "Whoa... Piper if you keep this up, I might crash the car." I arched my back and took my foot off the gas, afraid to go fast. Several cars honked.

Her voice softened. "Ignore them. Just think about what I did to you in Bartelli's last year."

She kept pressing her kisses on my neck. My stomach fluttered while she clenched and unclenched my jeans in her fist.

Barely able to speak, and picturing her in the little yellow dress, I muttered, "Okaaay. I am."

"Because that was nothing." She looked out the window. "This is the place. Pull into a space on the right."

After hitting the accelerator way too hard, we smacked into the parking bump, and I slammed on the brakes. Our bodies lunged forward and back with the car's momentum. I threw it into park and turned it off. She giggled and we made out. In no time at all, the windows fogged over.

"I love you so much," I said through the kissing.

"Hmm. Good boy. I love you, too."

A bunch of guys walked by. "Woo hoo. Get a room." Some of them clapped.

I swear, the whole Albany football team strolled right past my car.

"Ignore them too." I begged. "*Please.*"

"Uh-uh. Let's go. We're here." Piper pulled back, grinning.

Before I could appeal for more time, she opened the door and stepped onto the sidewalk. The coldest wind ever whipped inside. I let it cool me off before moving a muscle. A few of the remaining football goons commented on their way. She laughed. Finally, I joined her.

"So, am I forgiven?" She hugged me and planted another long kiss.

"I don't know. Everything went blurry there for a while. Were we fighting?"

She bit her bottom lip. "That *was* the idea." Grabbing my hand, she guided me up the block.

I exhaled deeply, my breath visible in the grim cold. The snow still flurried, but was getting stronger. "Is there a department store on this avenue?"

She had a skip to her step. "I don't think there's one in town. But here's where I wanted to bring you." Toma's Dress Shop.

It was all fancy stuff for proms, weddings, and parties. About seven other people were inside. An older couple, a mom and a daughter, and three college girls.

"I loved the little black dress I wore at my prom, but if we had the time to shop around, I would've liked a floor length pink one. You know, kind of what a princess would wear."

"Is that what you want this time?"

"Maybe, if we find one. But it doesn't have to be. We'll see what they have."

"Should we make believe that we're both picking out dresses for you? Or do you want to do it all yourself?"

"We don't need to pretend you know what you're doing," she said. "But I tell you what. There's a bar down the street. Do you think your fake I.D. will work? You can grab a beer while I find a few dresses. By the time you're done I should be ready to catwalk them for you." She pulled herself closer, threw her arm around my neck, and kissed me.

Last year, we shopped on prom day at Bartelli's Department Store. Piper suggested that we each select three dresses. They had a huge changing room with a bench in front of a three paneled mirror for guys to sit on while wives or girlfriends modeled for them. With a crinkle of her nose, the saleslady rejected my choices before I even showed them to Piper. So, what if I took them out of the clearance rack?

We had that room all to ourselves. Piper tried on two dresses, one hunter green and the other navy blue. I never enjoyed looking at her as much as I did that day. She said she had one more for me. A couple minutes later she came out in this tiny yellow dress meant for the clubs, not the prom—totally sleazy. She shocked me with it— not her style at all. Then she straddled me on the bench and we started making out. As a guy, I enjoyed having this hot girl do those things to me, but it was so out of character at the time; she blew my mind.

After we started dating again, she admitted that was her goal. A little bit of revenge for me waiting until the last second to ask her, and a way for her to regain some control over the situation.

"Sounds like a plan," I said. "See you in one beer's time."

Being dismissed didn't bother me, but I couldn't

wait to see what she picked out. She waved goodbye and turned toward the racks.

Venturing out in the cold, I found the bar in no time. The Albany football team had taken up most of the tables. Since it was Sunday, pro games were on the TVs. The scent of stale beer, dirty mop water and disinfectant caused my eyes to water.

Grabbing a seat at the bar, I ordered a Batavia draft, figuring I had a better chance of being served with the local brew. But the bartender didn't card me. Maybe she thought I played football. She gave it to me in a frosty mug, I took a sip and settled in to enjoy the games.

For about twenty minutes I milked my drink, battling my desire to run back over and be with her. My imagination drifted between our car ride and Piper posing for me. Maybe I was wrong about seeing Clive walk out of her dorm. A lot of guys wore ZBX jackets. Bringing it up might have been stupid. Why risk what we had?

The beer cost two dollars and I left a buck for a tip. The cute bartender waved thanks. The snow had progressed beyond the flurrying stage. Could a storm be on the way?

Chapter 23

Toma's Dress Shop

I found Piper in the rear of the store, browsing by a neon pink sign—*Fitting Rooms*.

"There you are. I've got three dresses to show you." She approached, pressed her body against mine and played with the snow on my shoulder.

Somehow, I found that very provocative.

"Unfortunately, boys aren't allowed in the changing room. There's no bench in there. But don't worry, I have a plan. You'll have to wait out here for now." She pursed her lips in a fake pout and batted her lashes.

My shoulders sagged at the disappointment, but the excitement level amped up, and I wondered what she had in mind. *That was nothing.* That's what she said in the car about our incredible escapades in Bartelli's Dressing Room. The adrenaline that reminds you you're alive and about to experience something great made me bounce from foot to foot and my mouth go dry.

The first dress she tried on was sparkly, baby blue, and cut low in the front with wide straps. It was ankle length with a leg slit just above the knee. The straps crisscrossed in the back, then tied into a knot, displaying Piper's fantastic shape.

Her second choice was hot pink and strapless. Some frilly ruffles circled it in a diagonal pattern. Floor length, but this leg slit began at mid-thigh, which I greatly appreciated. So far, both dresses were spectacular.

The final one was my favorite. "What color is that? Is it dark maroon?"

Could someone experience love at first sight, all over again? Because that's how it felt, and my pulse jumped about fifty million points.

She grinned at my ignorance. "No, it's black and red."

Seemed maroon to me, but totally cool. A dark red fabric with little black flowers scattered throughout the whole dress. It looked satiny, or maybe like silk. I could never tell the difference. Low cut again, with spaghetti straps. Ankle length, but with the highest leg slit of them all. Yum. Three straps traveled across her back, parallel to each other.

"I love them all. But you gotta get this one. I've never seen anything like it. You look so amazing. Elegant, breath-taking, I don't even know how to describe you." My heart pounded in my chest like a crazy cartoon character's. I hadn't seen her dressed to kill since her prom—the day we both admitted we were falling in love. "And wow, look at the way it makes the green in your eyes pop."

"I think you're right—but about the dress." Piper turned in the mirror and admired her figure from all angles, especially behind.

I scratched at my temple and pointed to her feet. "Were you always wearing socks?"

"What?" She chuckled, kept popping up and down on her tiptoes, and peered at herself over both shoulders.

"I just noticed you have white socks on."

"It's too much of a pain to take my boots on and off

with each dress. Wait. Did you think I modeled the other two for you, barefoot?"

Unlike last year, I didn't have to make believe I wasn't checking her out. Walking over, I approached her from behind, adoring her curves. My hands fell on her hips. Slowly they inched forward, all the way around until my fingers interlaced on her toned abs. The material felt cool on my bare forearms, and I gave her neck a tiny nibble. "Somehow, other parts of your body distracted me from your feet."

She let out a tiny moan. "When I have my hair done, I'll probably wear it up this time. Last year I had it down in that waterfall braid. Remember?"

My voice caught in my throat. "As if I could forget. You were so gorgeous." Plus, her stylist charged me two hundred dollars, with a tip.

She placed her arms on top of mine and we gazed in the mirror. She leaned her head on my shoulder, and I kissed it. Her hair smelled like a Pina Colada. We stayed like that for a minute, swaying to the store's music, then she took my hand.

"Come on. Let's go." She beelined to the fitting room. Dutifully, I followed.

The lighting was soft and neutral. Piper opened the door, and I scanned the area. The coast was clear. She pulled me inside and locked it.

"What are we doing *in here*?" I've asked dumb questions before, but never that dumb.

Throwing her arms around my shoulders, she began kissing me with quick passionate tastes. "What does it look like? Haven't you ever wanted to do it someplace fun?"

Without taking my lips off her, I tried answering and

my voice came out muffled. "You mean like in the changing room in a dress shop?" The smooth silky feel of her dress was sexier than straight skin. And I loved her skin.

"Exactly." She ripped my jacket off and threw it on the small seat. Unfortunately, they didn't design this room for two. She pushed me against the door. It caused the line of changing rooms to shake and bang much louder than expected. Her hands rushed under my shirt, pulling it toward my head.

"Hey, what's going on down there?" an older woman's voice called out.

Talk about a buzz kill. "Shh," we both said and placed a finger on each other's lips. We went completely still. Time froze. The only sound came from Piper's deep breathing. I stole a peek at her chest, rising and falling in that awesome dress. She caught me, glanced down, and smiled—her tongue grazed along her teeth.

A knock rapped on our door. One of the worst sounds I've ever heard. "Excuse me," came a shrill voice. "Are there two people in this room?"

Piper's eyes went wide, the white showing around her beautiful green irises—her muscles tight and clenched. I held up a finger, praying that whoever loomed outside would go away. For a lot of reasons, my blood pressure had elevated, fear and craving among them.

"I can see two pairs of legs. This is Mrs. Toma. I don't allow this type of thing in my store."

Waves of terror slammed into my body. The thought of walking out that door and seeing Mrs. Toma was a worst-case scenario. I closed my eyes so hard it gave me a headache. All I pictured was my mother's judgmental face being snippy at me. *See, Luca. I told you the little vixen was only after one thing.*

I exhaled deeply, grabbed my coat, and motioned for Piper to remain behind. How would I get out of this mess?

Opening the door, I shimmied through, trying to keep her hidden. "Oh, hello Mrs. Toma. My name's Luca, I don't think I met you earlier." Piper yanked it closed, spoiling that idea. It startled me. I wanted to run back in and hide.

Mrs. Toma, a stylish Black woman crossed her arms and tapped her foot like the meanest teacher ever.

"What was going on in there, Luca?"

Could I admit what we were doing? Could we get in trouble for it? Was it illegal, in a dressing room? In Albany? Was I going to jail?

My mind went blank, as if it stopped working. I had to say something. Mrs. Toma's death glare weakened my resistance, like I couldn't get enough oxygen. But I refused to admit the truth—that my girlfriend lured me in there. Instead, I went with a crazier version of the truth.

"Look, I'll tell you what happened." I glanced around like a secret agent searching for spies who are about to reveal the nuclear launch codes. "I was out here, innocently browsing for a prom dress and minding my own business when this crazy girl sneaks over, twists my arm up behind me, and throws me headfirst into your changing room. Did you hear the crash?"

Puzzling over the idea, she tipped her head to one side.

"Anyway, I tried fighting her off, but you don't have security. As a guy, I hate to admit this next part. She overpowered me with a bunch of punches and kicks. She must have some kind of karate training. Thank goodness you heard me calling for help. That is why you knocked on the door, right? You were saving me from this insane attacker?"

Her foot drummed quicker. She nodded as I told my story, and her eyes darted between me and the dressing room.

"So, your attacker is the young lady I helped earlier? We selected three dresses for a prom in Big Dune." She reached out, pressed down on my jacket, lowering it to reveal a *Property of Big Dune* sweatshirt.

"Oh, I didn't realize you knew that psycho nut bar in there. Thank goodness you came along. She might have killed me."

"Are you suggesting your girlfriend overwhelmed you? Or are you saying you enjoyed it?"

"Enjoyed it?" I asked, my voice pitching higher.

"Some people like the danger of forbidden places. Like on an airplane." Mrs. Toma arched her eyebrows.

"Hey now," I joked.

She squinted and pressed her lips into a tight, crass expression. We stared at each other a few seconds. I had no idea how to respond to the silence.

At a leisurely and confident pace, she strolled to the front of the store with a sly smile. "And you can follow me up here—while I call the police."

"What?!" My hands shook—instantly clammy and sweaty. I rubbed them together to hide it. Taking tiny steps, a horrible, painful tingling began in my shoulder blades and flashed at warp speed to my extremities.

A gray telephone phone sat next to the register, and she picked up the receiver. "Sure. Let's have her arrested."

My eyes bulged and my jaw dropped.

Her head cocked to one side, amused like the Cheshire Cat. "Or, if you're buying one of the dresses…"

"Holy cow! Don't ever do that to me again. Of course, we'll take the maroon one." My palm shot to my heart.

Her eyes brightened. "Sorry, I couldn't help myself. I had to get even after your tall tale."

Placing my hands on my knees, I took a few breaths to prevent hyperventilating, then stood up. "We were going to buy it anyway. Piper was *sooo stunning* in it. Would you call it maroon? It looks maroon to me."

"It's red and black," Mrs. Toma said.

"Yeah, but as a kid if you mixed red and black crayons together, they made maroon, right?"

She shook her head. "In the meantime, I'll protect you from your girlfriend, who I assume will *truly* want to attack you after that story."

Piper's voice rang out. "I'm going to kill you, Luca."

"I think that's a good idea," I said.

When we left the dress shop, the snow had picked up strength, coming down fast and slanting diagonally. We stopped at her dorm room, with the hope of continuing our extracurricular activity, but it was dark inside. Robyn was still curled up in bed, sleeping off her hangover.

With no other place to go, we decided I should hit the road. If the storm got worse, I might be stuck up here. With my bizarre class schedule, I had two tests tomorrow, and a wrestling match after school. I'd be in big trouble if I missed any days.

But I couldn't wait to see Piper in that dress again.

Chapter 24

Friends to the End

Our main crew sat around the lunch table. "What are we going to do about the prom?" Garret asked.

In the center of the room a chair crashed to the floor. The whole cafeteria turned to look. A kid stood up at a freshman table a little too quickly. He slammed his tray then ran away, zigzagging through the lunchroom. His red headed nerdy friend chased after him.

"Go get 'em," somebody yelled from the other side of the room.

"Hey, slow down!" a lunch monitor's voice boomed.

The first kid looked back at his pursuer with a toothy, braces-filled smile. The second kid laughed, both enjoying being the center of attention.

Too bad it was pudding day, and they didn't notice the huge spill on the floor. Earlier, when Jimmy dumped his tray in the garbage, his double-dessert fell off. He shrugged at the time and sat back down.

Geek Number One's foot found it, he slipped, flew into the air, and landed on his back.

Geek Number Two chased too close behind. He tried leaping over his buddy, but his sneaker caught on Number One's shoulder. He sailed over, hands outstretched and splattered into the garbage can. Today was also Gross Italian Food Day. Plates of spaghetti, lasagna, pudding, and chicken parm lifted into the air at ludicrous speed, paused in mid-flight, and like Dark Helmet in *Spaceballs*, smashed down on both of them.

The place became absolutely quiet for three seconds, then broke out in wild applause. Two lunch monitors gathered up the nerds and tried wiping garbage off them. Suddenly, all four slipped and fell. They tried helping each other up, but their feet kept treadmilling away, slipping in muddy pudding. Finally, more monitors and teachers appeared. Joining their hands and legs together, they formed a human bridge—rescuing the adults first, then the kids.

Pudding covered monitors led them out of the cafeteria, presumably to the assistant principal's office for a couple of detentions.

"Good one, jerk offs," someone yelled. A lot of people laughed and booed.

Eventually, the room quieted to its normal dull roar.

"Jimmy, wasn't that your pudding blob?" Cheryl slowly placed a straw in her mouth and sipped some milk, her pretty eyes batting at him.

"Was it?" A smile crept across his face.

"Can we get back to my question? What are we going to do about the prom?" Garret raised his arms and huffed.

"What exactly are you asking, dude? There's a lot of ways someone could take that," Porco said.

"December fourteenth is almost a month away. How are we all going to find prom dates in that short time? The only person here with a girlfriend is Luca. And who knows if she's even coming home for the prom."

That caught my attention. "Whoa. What are you

talking about? Why wouldn't she?"

All the heads turned from me back to Garret.

"I don't know. Pablo said you guys fought a lot when you were up there a couple weeks ago."

"Oh, he did, did he?" I glared at Pablo.

Pablo grabbed a fry and threw it at me. "First off, quit shooting those death rays out of your eyes. And second, you two did fight a lot. She ran upstairs and left us to fend for ourselves, if I remember."

"You didn't seem to mind. Not with Jenny's tongue down your throat all night."

"Oooh," the table snickered.

He raised his hands to quiet them down. "It was not all night. It was only for a little while, until you blew it by telling her drunk friend that we were still in high school—you schmuck. Besides, we were making out before you and Piper got into your big fight. But none of that matters now. Are you two still going to the prom together?"

That stung. It sucked having to defend our relationship. Usually, we were the couple everyone looked at as being rock solid.

"Of course. In fact, I drove up last Sunday and we went dress shopping."

"Already?" Nicole asked. "What color did she pick out?"

I tapped my foot under the table, excited over the prospect of seeing Piper in her dress again. "It's really cool. It's maroon and—"

"*Maroon?*" Nicole, Cheryl, and Myckal chorused together, sounding skeeved.

I ran my hands through my hair, slightly embarrassed. "Well, maybe it's not exactly maroon. Mrs.

Toma called it red and black."

"Who's Mrs. Toma?" Myckal asked.

"She owns the dress shop in Albany. And she's the one who caught me and Piper *hooking up* in the dressing room."

"Woo hoo."

"All right, Luca."

"Way to go."

Standing up, I took a slight bow. "Now, let's settle down you morons. I only told you guys so that you'll stop doubting that Piper's coming. So, how about we get off me, and we figure out how each of you losers is going to find a date?"

"Boo," they groaned, throwing straw wrappers and pudding napkins at me.

Porco pointed in my direction. "So, forget about our whipped friend over here. Does anyone else have a legitimate shot at scoring a prom date? You probably need to have one lined up by December first, which is two weeks before the prom. Otherwise, you risk waiting until the last minute and asking your date on prom day, like some idiot we know and love."

I gave him the finger, he ignored it.

Pablo raised his hand. "I'm thinking about asking Stacey Lampert."

Stacey had long brown hair and brown eyes that sucked you in if you talked to her for too long. She was the type of girl I'd expect him to go out with anyway. We didn't know if we'd be having a prom king and queen this year, but if we did, everyone expected Pablo to sail to an easy victory. There was no clear front runner for prom queen, but Stacey would probably be in the mix.

"Oh, she's pretty," Nicole said.

"I'll probably ask her this week."

The others looked around, but no one else piped up with a possible date.

"Here's my idea," Porco said. "That leaves six of us without dates, three boys and three girls. The rest of us have a couple weeks to try to find someone. On December first if there are still any of us without dates, then what if those people go as friends?"

"How would that work?" Myckal asked.

"Let's make believe none of us finds a date. We'll pair off and go as couples," Porco said.

"Yeah, but who would go with who?" Cheryl asked.

"Why? Are you afraid to get stuck with Jimmy?" Porco asked.

"No!" Cheryl answered, lightning fast.

Jimmy punched Porco. "You're a jackass."

It barely dimpled his huge arm.

"I don't know. Does it matter? We'd all be going as friends and hanging out together. We could put names in a hat. Normally, I'm sure we'd all find dates, but in this nutty school year, it'll take the pressure off if nobody finds anyone."

"Sounds good to me," Garret said.

"I'm in," Jimmy concurred.

Judging by their faces and the way they agreed so quickly, Porco already discussed it with them and had their buy-in. Largely, he was selling the idea to the girls. They exchanged glances back and forth and nodded.

"Sure," Nicole said.

Leaning backward, Porco thrust his arms in the air. "All right, it's settled." He straightened up and pointed at the group. "Everyone has a couple weeks to find a date. Otherwise, it'll be friends to the end."

Luckily, I had Piper to go with, and didn't have to worry about scurrying for a prom date. It'd be fun watching everyone else try their best over the next two weeks, then seeing who got paired together.

Chapter 25

Friday Night Match: November 23

They scheduled a rare Friday night wrestling match. Lately, it's been two meets on Saturdays, and one or two during the week. The grueling schedule had taken its toll. At the end of practice yesterday, my arms felt as heavy as telephone poles. After tonight's competition, we had a party to go to and the rest of the weekend off. I desperately needed the break.

We were up against Lipschitz High School and had home field advantage. After two periods I led 9 to 4. I never wrestled this kid before, but I knew I was better than him, and by now, he did too. So far, I couldn't pin him. He was a tall, thin, Black guy, and tougher than he looked—beating him on points would have to do.

The referee motioned for me to take the down position. I got on all fours and glanced at Myckal. She wore light blue, floral print jeans, and a black satiny tank top. Her legs were crossed and the top one started to bounce. Ever since I admitted to her that she had great legs and begged her to never wear a skirt at the scorer's table again, it's become a running joke between us.

She gave me a sly smile and I grinned back. We did this when I possessed a huge lead. If I had a tough opponent, I wouldn't risk splintering my concentration by messing around. In those cases, my eyes focused straight ahead. Didn't have much to worry about tonight, however.

The Lipschitz wrestler took his place on top of me. Breaking eye contact with Myckal, I arched my head back, and looked into the crowd. I blinked twice and couldn't believe who was in the bleachers. Was this a joke?

Glaring at me with the ugliest expression ever was that white-eyed prick, Hector Wolfe. What was he doing here? He went to school somewhere near Binghamton, about three and a half hours away. There's no way he should be in Big Dune, but there he was, mocking and pointing at me.

The ref blew his whistle. Just like that time with Myckal, I didn't react. The Lipschitz guy smashed his forearm into the front of my elbow. I collapsed onto the mat. He landed hard on me, and his shoulder crashed on top of my head. The wind blasted from my lungs and a flash of white blinded me.

All I could do was lay flat on my stomach, hoping my senses cleared before he pinned me.

The crowd and his teammates sensed he might be able to do it. The noise level ramped up a lot louder. He became super active, jumping from one side of me to the other. After a minute, he slipped his hand past my arm and had me in a half nelson. Grunting and driving into me with all his might, my shoulder approached the forty-five-degree angle mark.

"Es-POH-Sito!" Coach Slaz screamed.

That woke me up. I was stronger than my opponent and powered my way back to my stomach. He scored two points for that move and came within an eyelash of four. I peeked at the scoreboard, 9 to 6.

We still had a minute to go. I couldn't afford to stay flat like this and give him a chance to catch up. I decided to set a dangerous trap. If it backfired, he might get those four points or even the pin.

He went for the half nelson again and I let him have it. His team roared, believing I was washed up. He put all his weight and strength into forcing me onto my back. Instead of resisting him, I went with the momentum. Rolling with the move, we kept going and I flipped *him* onto his back.

"Oh crap," he cried.

My arms wrapped around his shoulders, and my chin drove into his pecs.

The referee awarded me two points for the reversal and two more for almost pinning him. He slipped out of my grip at the last instant and maneuvered to his stomach. It was over. The score now stood 13 to 6 in my favor. A loud buzzer sounded twenty seconds later. The ref held my hand up in triumph—a major win on my part, and I ran to my teammates for congratulations.

Still, way too close to call.

After a bunch of high fives and pats on the back, Coach Slaz grabbed me by the arm. "What happened to you out there, Luca? You had him completely under control, then he almost beat you."

Inhaling and exhaling deeply, I tried to regain my breath. I placed my hands on my hips and bent over at the waist for a second. When I stood up, I pointed at Hector. "You recognize that jerk?"

Slaz followed my gaze, tilting his head. "That's Hector Wolfe. He beat you in States last year. What's he doing here?"

"Wish I knew."

****

We defeated Lipschitz High 28 to 20. I showered and sat on the bleachers, leaning back and waiting for Pablo. My green and white letterman jacket was unbuttoned with my hands in my pockets. As captain, he and Slaz often debriefed afterward. Pablo pinned his guy in the second period.

My hair was combed and soaking wet. Pablo was my ride, I wasn't going anywhere until he came out.

Ten minutes later, he walked over. "Good job tonight."

"Yeah, you too."

We didn't have a chance to talk about my near miss. He was warming up at the time but saw the final score. I stood and we headed for the exit.

"I have something to tell you—" Pablo started.

"You'll never believe who was in the stands tonight. That douche bag, Hector. Of course, he was wearing his Shultsville Wrestling Camp Champion t-shirt."

"I know. I invited him."

I did a double take not believing what I heard, then took a step back and stared at him. "If you told me you were abducted by aliens and they forced you to perform in some kind of E.T. Vegas improv, that'd make more sense than what just came out of your mouth."

"Would there be like, space dancers in the show?" he asked.

"Yes, and they're all totally hot. But they all think you're a jackass. None of them will be sleeping with you. Hopefully, they suck out your eyeballs. What the hell are you talking about? You invited Hector?"

After forcing out a deep breath, he looked me in the eye. "I wanted to tell you earlier but with this crazy schedule I skipped lunch to make up some math. We didn't see each other the rest of the day. Anyway, the Iowa coach called me last night."

"And?" I raised my arms in a *so what* gesture. He knew I couldn't stand Hector.

Dropping his chin to his chest, he continued. "You know how I'm flying out at six in the morning for a campus tour. I guess Hector is, too. He lives in some hick farm town upstate. They don't have any direct flights there. Their coach asked if Hector could crash at my house tonight and we'd fly out together." He raised his voice and eyes. "But he's flying back on his own Sunday night. We're not going home with each other."

As if that made it better. "That's good. Will you be *blowing* Hector while you're down there?" My eyebrows drew in and I crossed my arms. "Why would the coach ask you to do it?"

He rubbed the back of his neck and paced in a circle. "Sounds like Hector wants to commit to Iowa while we're there. We're probably going to be teammates next year."

My body froze, my mouth fell open, and my gut hollowed out. I knew Pablo was touring Iowa this weekend, but that's all I thought it was, a tour. But he just referred to Hector as his new teammate.

"There's more," he said.

"More? What else could there be?"

"Coach Flanholtz called Slaz. Northwestern heard about the asbestos crud and canceled our campus tour."

"Until when?" My heartbeat thumped so hard in my chest it hurt my throat. Every worst fear I had flew through my mind. Was this fate? Did it mean I'd have to face Hector after all? I still had no way to beat him. Plus, he was the biggest ass and trash talker ever. More importantly, was my scholarship gone, too?

"He doesn't know. Said we could call him after the new year, once school's out."

"But if you *fall in love* with the college this weekend, would you commit to them anyway?"

He shrugged.

Feeling nothing but hurt and pain, I closed my eyes. If Pablo gave his verbal to Iowa, would Northwestern still care about me? Probably not.

"One last thing."

Flatly, I uttered, "Go ahead."

"I invited Hector to the party tonight."

What the heck? Stepping away from him and scowling, I pointed, then ran in the opposite direction.

"Come on man. Don't be like that.... Luca... Where are you going?!"

Chapter 26

The Couch

I sprinted halfway across the parking lot. As a wrestler, I had great stamina and could go five miles before getting tired. I stopped when someone called my name.

"Luca, is that you?"

Pausing under a humming streetlight, I tented a hand over my eyes to shield the blinding glare. "Myckal? What are you doing out here?"

The driver's door to a red Honda Civic stood open. I never saw her car before.

"Finishing up some manager stuff with Slaz. You just missed him, he walked me out. What are you doing around this late?"

"What time is it?" I strolled over the aging, cracked asphalt. Weeds and grass spiked their way through, while cigarette butts and candy wrappers outlined spaces where kids had parked and hung with friends. You could tell the car owners by the trash they left behind.

She checked her watch. "Wow. It's so much later than last year. Ten-thirty, already. That's what happens when you have a crazy asbestos schedule and can't start wrestling until seven-thirty. Where are you heading without a car?"

"I was waiting for Pablo. He had a meeting with the

coach, too. Do you have any plans, tonight?"

"Well, this was it." She chuckled and waved her arms at the school.

The distant sound of light traffic moved along the highway. It had to be in the thirties, I could see her breath.

I raised my chin. "Let's go to a party."

"Now?" She tilted her head and looked at me like I was crazy.

"Why? Do you have to be home anytime soon?"

"Well, no. But didn't you say you were waiting for Pablo?"

A low airplane flew overhead, but no sign of Pablo anywhere. Even if there were, I wasn't going with that jerk.

"Screw him. Let's go." I stepped to the passenger side.

She owned one of those fancy cars with a button to unlock the doors. After we both buckled in, she asked, "Where to?"

"Do you know how to get to The Couch?"

A chuckle escaped over her lips, and it grew into a great smile. "You mean that place really exists? I thought it was an urban legend. You know, the myth of where the bad seeds at John Marshall tap a keg with Bigfoot."

Grinning and shaking my head, I replied, "No, it's very real. How about the Big Dune Bowling Alley, ever been there?"

She bit her bottom lip, looked to heaven to try to place it, then nodded. "It's on Route eighty-two, right?"

"Exactly. Park in the back and we'll walk from there."

"All right. The Couch it is." She started the car, and

we zipped out of the parking lot.

Every town in America had a place where teenagers could safely drink without the police ruining everything. Ours was The Couch.

Behind the bowling alley, there's nothing but weeds, trees, and paths for miles around. If you knew which trail to follow, it was better than going to *Narnia*. About a mile back there were four old sofas assembled in a square. No one knew who put them there, no one knew how long they were there, and no one knew who named the place The Couch.

If we kept the group under a hundred people, the cops left us alone. We could safely park at the bowling alley and even build a small fire.

One of the great things about The Couch was that it had a ton of motorcycle trails corkscrewing away in all directions. The police never sent more than two officers, and they were easy to spot, approaching with their big bouncing flashlights. Plus, a giant thorn bush guarded the trailhead. The cops always seemed to stick themselves and yelp in pain. As long as you weren't passed out drunk on one of the couches, you had plenty of chances to escape.

On the way over I told her about Northwestern and being offered a scholarship if I won the state championship.

"Between you and me," I said, "they really want Pablo. They're only talking to me because we're best friends, hoping that'll lure him there."

She snuck a glance at me while driving. "You're better than you give yourself credit for. You always put yourself down when you compare your career to his. I'm sure they want you just for you."

"Thanks," I whispered. My eyes almost teared up. I leaned my head back on the seat and looked out the side window so she couldn't tell. *Legs* by ZZ Top came on the radio.

About ten minutes later Myckal parked under a streetlight in the crowded bowling alley and shut off her car. "So, what happened in your match tonight? You were doing so well. But in the third period you seemed distracted. Again."

Exhaling a big sigh, I turned diagonally to face her. "That's when I saw that idiot, Hector Wolfe, in the stands. He stared at me with this stupid grin, waving and laughing at me—trying to psych me out. He loves to play head games."

A sly expression curled her lips. "As long as you're not trying to blame this one on me." She batted her eyelashes and peered at her legs. "I'm not wearing a skirt, and I did that *just for you.*"

"Thanks, wiseass."

She giggled.

"And I love your flower jeans, too. I appreciate you putting them on, *just for me.*"

"Hey, whatever I can do for the team. But seriously, don't you think Pablo will visit Northwestern with you before he makes a decision?"

Massaging my temples to prevent a headache, I frowned and tried to keep my voice from sounding choked up. "I don't know anymore. I thought so. But when he said he invited Hector tonight, he called him his teammate. I'm not expecting him to attend a different school for me. If he really loves Iowa, he should go there. I just thought I'd get a chance to visit Northwestern and make my case before Pablo leaves us all behind."

Spacing out for a second, I gazed straight ahead. Myckal reached over and brushed a hair from my forehead. The orange streetlight cast a fuzzy glow and the neon purple bowling sign lit up her dark car. We smiled and stared at each other.

It felt good to unburden myself and share my pain. But I sensed a twinge of guilt. Was I sharing it with the right girl?

Despite the cold, somebody turned up the temperature in here and it snapped me to attention. I switched my tone to upbeat and slapped the tops of my legs. "So, are you excited for your first Couch party?"

"I am." She nodded.

"Good. Let's head out."

After she locked her car, I led the way to the back right corner of the sloping, uneven parking lot. A bunch of pebbles scraped under our feet.

"It's cool that we have a full moon tonight," I said. "Just walk where I do. There should be plenty of light to see where you're going."

"All right. I'm trusting you with my life."

"No problema. I won't let anything happen to you."

We entered the high weeds, but stayed on the wide, ruddy trail. After twenty feet, the tree line began. No one in the parking lot could see us anymore—that was the beauty of The Couch. We were safe from prying eyes. We followed the path quite easily until we traveled up a small hill. A bunch of tree roots stuck out and crisscrossed the trail. I stumbled on the way down then sped up to keep from falling on my face.

"Careful back there." I said, trying to preserve my honor. "I think a bear or maybe a mountain lion attacked me. I couldn't see which."

"Thanks. Very graceful and manly of you. I think you scared that dangerous predator away. Or he could be hiding under those roots you tripped over. But I see why you're a wrestler and not a figure skater."

"Uh oh. Look how quick they turn on you. One minute I'm going to Ivy League schools and maybe the Olympics, and now I'm Maxwell Smart."

"Hey, if the shoe phone fits." She shrugged and smiled. "Seriously, do I have to worry about wild animals this deep in the woods?"

"Just the drunk ones."

The path curved to the left and right a couple times, and it didn't take long for us to see the dancing light from the fire. Then, we heard the party.

"Watch yourself on this next part. It's Mother Nature's way of protecting us from the police. You have to duck under these branches on the left and leave the trail for a few steps."

"Okay. But how does it protect us?"

I kept peeking over my shoulder to make sure she maneuvered it correctly.

"The cops never seem to learn. If you continue on the path to the right, you get smacked in the face by these huge invisible prickers. If you hear an adult screaming in agony—start running."

She laughed, keeping her head down and cautiously placing every stride. "Does that happen often?"

"I've only had to do it once. Maybe twice. But those were gigantic parties in the summer that got out of hand. In the winter it's too cold for a blowout like that. Only twenty or thirty people will show tonight. We'll be fine."

During the summer, people lugged kegs or beer balls back here, but at this time of year, it was BYOB. We didn't bring anything, so I counted on the charity of others.

"Promise you won't leave me," Myckal said. "If there's a police raid, you have to come find me before you run."

Holding back the final branches for her, we passed under the tree without a scratch. I put my right hand on my heart and took her left hand. "I promise to protect you and keep you from spending a night in the town jail. Even if I have to sacrifice myself to the constable gods. I will safeguard your honor from ever having to say, 'I'm sorry, your honor. Luca made me do it.'"

As my right hand dropped, it found its way into her hand. She must have reached out and grabbed it. Or did I do it? We studied each other in the moonlight for a beat too long. I needed to lower my gaze from her magnetic eyes, and I tried dipping my chin to my chest. Nothing worked. She knew I had a serious girlfriend. But the way she looked at me right now, I swear she wanted me to lean in for a kiss.

My nose started to itch like crazy. Probably, the pollen from being in the middle of the woods. Except, it was winter. I scrunched my face trying to scratch it. It only made matters worse. There was a simple solution— just let go of her hands. Except they felt so warm and awesome.

A voice shouted to us. "Who is that over there?!"

She sighed but didn't break eye contact. "It's Luca and Myckal, *Porco!*"

"Get over here, you two!"

Myckal impressed me by yelling at him. Lucky he was there. Piper was a hundred miles away, but I'd never do anything to risk what we had. She was the best thing to ever happen to me. My thumping heart sent a warning to my brain that I had better listen to it and get myself out of this situation.

We both smiled and finally released each other. From this distance, no one could see us holding hands. It's a good thing, too. I didn't want anyone getting the wrong impression and starting some stupid rumors. We were just friends.

As we got closer, my legs were still wobbly from staring at Myckal. On the far side of the party, I saw some familiar faces. "Nicole and Cheryl are by one of the couches. You okay if I leave you with them for a while?"

"Of course. Why? What are you doing?"

"I'm getting friggin' wasted."

Porco, Jimmy and Garret huddled by the fire. "Luca!" they cheered as I approached.

My mouth had gone dry, and I was dying of thirst. I ripped a bottle of vodka out of Garret's hand and guzzled it like water.

Chapter 27

Hectoring

About an hour later, I accomplished my goal of being one hundred and ten percent trashed. A few brave souls sat on the gross couches. Most of us shied away, afraid of the critters hibernating inside. These weren't the original four. Every so often a different couch materialized and the sorriest one ended up on the fire. No one ever took responsibility.

Several different groups stood around, hands in pockets, joking. The back of my ears burned from the freezing night air.

I half sat, and half leaned on a giant boulder. As much as I tried to get comfortable, it hurt too much. Its craggily ends dug into my butt and felt ice-cold. Every time I slid to adjust my position, dirt embedded in my jeans.

Somebody brought a boom box. *Stairway to Heaven* by Led Zeppelin blasted out and Pablo joined us at the crackling fire.

"I'm surprised you showed up with your girlfriend," I said.

"Why, is Stacey Lampert here? I didn't see her." He looked over my shoulder for his hot prom date, eyes aglow.

I stumbled off the boulder, pointing at him with my

beer hand. "No, not that girlfriend, your other one."

"Oh, you mean that *Hector's* my girlfriend." He took a drink of his beer. "Look, dude, I'm just doing the Iowa coach a favor. But he might be my teammate one day. He did win States last year, and according to him, they really want him."

Porco asked, "Is this the guy that beat Luca in the semifinals?" He angled his eyebrows down and creased his forehead, sending Pablo a sideways glance.

"That's not my fault."

"What?!" we all said.

Pablo held up his hands. "I didn't mean it the way it came out. I'm not saying it's not my fault that he beat Luca. I didn't ask to have him sleep over and take him to the airport in the morning. I'm really serious about going to Iowa and I figured it wouldn't hurt if I helped out the coach. That's all. I didn't expect this to piss you off."

Garret piped in. "He's sleeping over at *your house*? Isn't that taking things a little far? Couldn't they have put him up at the Big Dune Motor Inn?"

"That place is so greasy. Half the rooms rent by the hour," Pablo said.

"What do you care?" Jimmy asked. "If he has to sleep in someone else's slime, he'll feel right at home."

Porco spit dip into an empty beer bottle, then interjected. "Let's not give Pablo a hard time, gents. He's probably got a lot to do before his flight."

"Thanks, Porcs," he said.

"Tickle fights with his new girlfriend and makeovers 'til dawn."

I grinned. It felt nice for my friends to back me up. Pablo was the de facto leader of our group, and usually, everyone took his side. But not tonight.

"You guys know what I'm talking about," Pablo said. "I'm not trying to diss Luca. I'm just trying to figure out the future. Like we all need to be doing."

Even in my drunken state, the prospects of Northwestern kept popping into my vodka-addled brain. Rather, that my chances kept diminishing. Alcohol usually takes my troubles away and cheers me up. But it was backfiring so far.

Missing out on a full school year really sucked. Weird things invaded my thoughts—spirit days, dress-up days, changing the decorations in my locker, and award nights. Thanks to asbestos, they were all gone. Even though my parents never came to a single award's dinner, a hollow pain filled my chest. I'd never have one again.

Pretty soon this would all be over, too. It felt like we were missing out on so much, as if someone was punishing us, but we didn't do anything wrong.

"You know what, Pablo?" I slurred.

He grimaced and took a deep breath, afraid of what might be coming. "No. What?"

"First thing Monday morning, I'm changing the decorations in my locker." I staggered away, searching for another group to join.

Taking two laps around the party, I occasionally stopped and laughed with other friends but kept my momentum going. If I stayed too long in one place, the world might start spinning off its axis.

Finally, I saw Hector. On the other side of the fire a girl leaned her back against a tree. His hands rested above her head, like a greaser in a fifty's movie. I wandered in that direction. No idea what I wanted to say to him, but something had to be said.

About twenty feet away, I realized he was talking with Myckal. They were next to a big evergreen bush. I tiptoed over and got down on one knee, confident neither of them saw me.

I was in full view of the rest of the party. If anyone looked over, they'd wonder why I was kneeling on the frozen ground. I gagged and made believe I was puking, but no one noticed. It didn't matter, I felt like a spy, outsmarting the Russians, or at least my dopey friends.

Inching closer, I tried listening in.

"Why would you defend that guy? I beat him so easily last year. He's lucky he won't have to wrestle *me* again. And what'd you say is the problem with your school?" Hector asked.

"Asbestos," Myckal answered sharply.

"Yeah, asbestos. That's it. Maybe he'll win since I'm not in your tournament." Hector put on an evil smile. "You're the team's manager, right? So, you know a lot about wrestling. Wouldn't you rather be with the State Champion, instead of the guy who lost to the State Champion?" He chuckled at his own remark.

"Ugh, no. And *why* did Pablo introduce us?" Myckal snarked.

"I told him I wanted to meet some hot downstate chicks. When I saw you, I said, *bingo*, I want to get to know her. Aren't you glad he did?" Hector grinned and leaned closer.

"Actually, the next time I see Pablo, I'm thinking about kicking his ass."

"Oh, ho, ho. You're feisty, aren't you?

"Do these kinds of cheesy lines work on the girls in your school?"

I edged farther into the bush. Myckal was handling

herself extremely well and defending me better than my so-called best friend.

"Yeah, they do. They *appreciate* winners where I come from." He brought his hand up, like he was about to brush the hair out of her face.

I pictured the worst happening. If he tucked it behind her ear, they might get married one day— probably have a minivan, too. I tumbled out like a drunken sailor, startling them both.

"Hey, look who it is. I was wondering if I was going to see you tonight," Hector said.

While he was momentarily distracted, Myckal ducked under his arm and slipped away.

"Hey, where do you think you're going?" He spun around, realizing too late that she had snuck off a few steps. With a creepy grin, he reached out and grabbed her butt.

Myckal whipped her arms backward trying to cover herself from him. But he was too quick and pulled his hand back. She whirled in an arc and smacked his face. A red handprint instantly formed.

Laughing, he rubbed his cheek. "What did you do that for?"

"You're a pig." She stormed off and disappeared somewhere behind me.

I spread out my arms. "Well, here I am, wedding boy. You better say sorry to Myckal."

"Wedding boy? What does that mean?" He smirked and moved his chin back and forth, stroking it. "Doesn't matter. What happened to you against that Lipschitz wrestler? I would have pinned him in the first period. You're lucky you won on points. When you finally saw me in the stands, I thought he had you." He ignored my comment about apologizing.

"Yeah, but did you ever think about this?" I took a big looping punch at him.

Hector stepped to the side and allowed me to fall flat on my face. I wished that's all that happened. On the way down, my cheek barked the side of Myckal's tree.

I got up from the cold dirt, picking little bloody pieces of wood from my face. I wasn't cut bad, but the way my head throbbed, I'd probably have a black eye tomorrow.

Putting up my fists, I was ready to fight. Hector laughed, realizing that in my present condition, I posed zero threat. But when I swung again, he shoved me hard against the tree.

There's nothing like a fight to attract every teenager's attention. Within a second, a circle formed around us. Pablo sprang between Hector and me, a hand on each of our chests.

"Keep your boy back, Pablo. Otherwise, he might get hurt." Hector tried some lame taunting, pointing with both hands.

"What's wrong with you, Luca?" Pablo grabbed my shoulders and led me away. "What happened?"

Myckal ran over, her eyes wide with concern. "Look at your face. Are you okay?" She took a tissue from her purse and wiped dirt and wood shavings from the scratches in my cheek.

All my friends gathered behind me, except the one who used to always have my back. Pablo stood in front of me, glaring like I had done something horribly wrong to him.

All he had right now, was stupid Hector, looming over his shoulder.

I stared at them, so disappointed in my best friend. A few seconds later, I shook my head. "No matter what happens, Pablo, there's one thing you should never forget."

He sneered. "Yeah, what's that?"

"Iowa's colors are black and gold. Keep it in mind when you paint each other's toenails." I headed for the trail. Myckal and the rest left with me.

Chapter 28

Phone Call

I called Piper on Monday night. Lately, it was impossible to reach her over the weekend. It's weird. At the beginning of the semester, we'd talk for hours on Saturday and Sunday.

When I got home from practice earlier, I showered, and my hair was still drying. I had on a t-shirt and sweats, wishing I could go to bed after we hung up. But with only four weeks left in the school year, teachers were killing us with homework. Although, Northwestern seemed like a long shot, I still had to study as if it were in play. That amped up the stress level big time and my stomach churned with acid. Looking at the stack of books on my desk, I might be up until midnight.

Sure enough, I ended up with a black eye from my scrape with Hector, and the whole school heard about it. Checking in the mirror, I grimaced, it still hadn't faded. It was so embarrassing walking through the halls all day. Everyone stared.

As a wrestler, part of my self-esteem was tied up in my ability to win on the mat or in a fight. I used to tell myself Hector might be able to beat me in a match, but I could take him on the streets. Now, all I had were doubts. Actually, they were worse than doubts. He outwrestled me twice and humiliated me at the party.

I decided not to reveal my weekend festivities to Piper. Usually, we shared everything. But she's made her opinion of me fighting abundantly clear. When it accompanied alcohol, that ticked her off even more.

Ten days from now, she'll drive home for the prom. She was worried about the weather and wanted to be safe, so she's coming down on Thursday. I couldn't wait to see her. Fooling around in Toma's Dress Shop still sent tingles down my spine.

Hopefully, my eye would heal by then. Worst case scenario, the County Championships were this Saturday. I could claim somebody smacked me in the head during a match.

"So, what else is going on?" I asked her. We'd been talking for about fifteen minutes. I had no desire to discuss my argument with Pablo until the end of our conversation. Right now, I enjoyed hearing about her week.

Don't Fear the Reaper by Blue Oyster Cult played quietly in the background. Ever since junior high I put a cassette in the stereo when I called a girl. Music made me sound cooler. At least I didn't feel like I had to crank it anymore. In seventh and eighth grade, it blasted so loud I couldn't hear my girlfriend.

A heavy sigh came through the phone. "What day is the prom again?"

I scrunched my eyebrows together. What a weird question this late in the game. "It's not this Friday. It's next Friday, the fourteenth. You told me you circled it with a huge heart on your calendar."

Loud quick breaths made their way through the receiver.

"Are you still there?" I asked.

"I have a question for you."

"Okaaay."

She cleared her throat. "Jonesy asked me to his winter formal."

Since she decided to let that hang in the air a few seconds, so did I.

"That didn't sound like a question," I eventually said. My pulse thrummed so hard, I felt it up my arms.

"I suppose you're right," she agreed, a little tongue-tied—likely biting her nails. "It's just as friends. But it's on the fifteenth. Would you be okay if I went with him?"

My mind blanked.

"Are you still there, Luca?" Her turn to ask the question.

I sat on my bed, hunching forward. The phone in one hand, my head in the other, while shock and disbelief stabbed me in the chest.

"What about our plans? Jimmy's having the after party. That goes until three or four in the morning. Then we were going to the city on Saturday with everyone else. See the tree and then… get in some kind of trouble." I let out a nervous chuckle, hoping she would take her question back. She didn't really want to go with Clive, did she?

She exhaled. "You could still go with your friends. We went to Jimmy's last year so I wouldn't be missing out if I skipped that. Plus, I don't want to be the only college kid there. And maybe, I'm not so crazy about looking for trouble. So, I would just drive back up to school Saturday morning."

That stung.

"You didn't used to mind. You used to think it was kind of fun." My mouth went dry as kindling and an

214

intense thirst burned my throat. "Why would you leave so early on Saturday?"

"Well, I'll be tired from driving home on Friday, going to your prom and then driving three hours back on Saturday. I'll need a nap before his formal. Then a nice, slow shower. It'll take me almost as long to get ready for that as the prom. Plus, I have a hair appointment at five."

Even though my blood was boiling, I did my best to maintain a calm, even tone. "I thought you were coming home on Thursday. You have a hair and make-up appointment with Donna on Friday afternoon. You loved the way she did them last year. I know I did."

"Ohh, you're sweet."

"Now, I'm sweet?" I felt hollow inside.

"You sound mad." Her initial nervousness had disappeared, and she seemed way too casual. "Look, I have a test on Friday in my one-fifty Sociology class. But don't worry, that should give me plenty of time. I'll just do my own hair and make-up. Hopefully, I'll make it to Pablo's by seven for pictures."

My lips curled back in disgust and my gut tightened. "Of course, I'm mad. I don't give a damn about Clive's formal. I don't know how you could possibly want to go with him, even *as friends.* But I really don't understand how you could ask to do it the same weekend as *our* prom."

"I thought you liked Jonesy and wouldn't have a problem with it. You sound a little jealous, Luca. I didn't think you were so insecure about our relationship."

"Ha. That's a joke. I may have thought he was a cool dude the first time I met him. Lately, he's just been a douche."

"And when did you decide this?" Her voice turned

sharper.

"Around the time you started calling him *Jonesy*."

She stayed quiet. I could picture her face twisting in anger, but I was on a roll.

"How can you accuse me of being jealous? I barely said two words to Andrea, and you flipped out on me. Clive knows damn well when the prom is, and he still has the balls to ask *my girlfriend* to his formal? Are you telling me there are no other chicks in Albany, like Andrea or Jenny? I'm really thinking about kicking his ass the next time I see him."

"That's your answer to everything!"

I regretted threatening Clive the moment the words were out of my mouth. I knew she'd defend him.

"Plus, he would never go with one of those tramps," she stated.

"Why do you keep sticking up for him? When I was at your dorm, I said that he probably slept with Jenny, and you got so pissed off. Now you're mad about it again."

"What are you suggesting, Luca?" Anger dripped out of the phone like rusty-pipe water.

"I'm not suggesting anything. I just want to know why *my girlfriend* wants to go to some moron's formal and why she's so offended that he would sleep with *those tramps?*"

"Well, maybe I'd rather go to his formal than some stupid prom!"

"Good. Why don't you then?"

"MAYBE I WILL!" She slammed the phone harder than I'd ever heard anyone do it.

I took a baseball off my dresser and whipped it across the room, busting a hole in the paneling.

"What the hell was that?!" My father boomed from upstairs.

"Nothing!"

He hammered down the foot of the recliner, ready to come rushing down here and rip me a new one when my mother stopped him. "I was spying on Luca in the laundry room. He's fighting with Piper. Just leave him alone for now," she said.

They probably thought I couldn't hear them. It didn't matter. My muscles quivered and my whole body tensed. Collapsing onto the bed, I screamed into my pillow. Piper and I never fought like that before. I couldn't believe she wanted to go to Clive's lame formal.

I wasn't sure if I had a prom date anymore—or a girlfriend.

Chapter 29

Lunch Plans

So far, this week sucked. I thought everyone heard about my black eye—apparently not. It's Wednesday and I was still explaining it.

Pablo and I hadn't talked since he took Hector's side and basically left me high and dry with Northwestern.

Right now, I didn't care about any of that. Ninety-eight percent of my thoughts revolved around Piper, and our big blow-out. The other two were about sex. Since Piper was the only one I'd ever been with, it hurt even more.

Two minutes after she hung up, I phoned back to apologize. She must have taken it off the hook—nothing but busy signals all night. On Monday, I called about a million times, she never answered. On Tuesday, I called two million times, she didn't pick up then either.

I left a ton of messages. All of them basically the same. "I'm sorry. It was all my fault. I'm stupid. I'm begging you, please, still come to the prom with me. And oh yeah, call me back."

She hadn't. I've never been so miserable in my life. I couldn't eat, couldn't sleep, and the thought of studying was a joke. Every time I closed my eyes, I heard *Jonesy asked me to his winter formal.* Or when my heart really wanted to punish me, it replayed, *Well, maybe I'd rather go to his formal than some stupid prom!*

I felt bad for my teammates. I went overboard in practice and knocked the hell out of anyone I wrestled against. Even the guys in heavier weight classes complained that I took things too far. Pent up rage had a way of doing that.

"Guess who just got asked to the prom?" Nicole announced as she entered the cafeteria.

Everyone was at the table. Pablo sat at one end, I took the opposite end.

"Really, who?" Cheryl asked.

"Me. That's who." Nicole beamed.

"No duh," Cheryl said. "I mean who asked you?"

Nicole sat next to me, all smiles. "Greg Crossman came up to me a few minutes ago. Right after Math."

"He's cute," Cheryl said. "But doesn't he go out with Sarah Stewart?"

"Not anymooore." She twirled her finger in the air. Everyone clapped and congratulated her.

She stood and made a few curtsies. On her way back down, she said to me, "Hey, grumpy."

Staring at my soda can, I ripped the little metal tab off the top, slicing the tip of my finger. "Greg's a cool guy. You two'll have a lot of fun." I sucked out the wound.

"Yeah, *we will.* Okay, Cheryl, Myckal, when are we going dress shopping?"

Porco held up his arms. "Hold on. Before the chicks start making plans, let's go over things real quick. Thanks to Greg Crossman's desperation—"

"Screw you, Porco," Nicole yelled, grinning.

He sneered and pointed at Nicole and Myckal. "As I was saying, now that Greg has taken away my threesome, the only two people left without a date are Myckal and me."

"I wonder who planned that?" Jimmy called.

"Slag off, dude. So, it's all set. Myckal and I will be going as friends, and the rest of you losers will have to waste time entertaining your dorky dates."

He looked up and down the table. One by one they all nodded.

"You cool down there, Luca?" he asked.

"Sounds good." I sat there, crushing my can.

"I think we need to hear from poor Myckal," Garret claimed. "She's the one that'll have to spend the night with you. Are you sure you want to go through with his plan?"

She happened to be sitting next to Porco. "Ahh, there's no one I'd rather go with." She slid her arm around his huge bicep and planted a kiss on his cheek.

While turning as red as his Jello, he shrugged that shoulder, pointed at Garret, and sunk his teeth into a chiliburger. With a full mouth, he mumbled, "See moron, I told you she was cool with it."

"Poor girl," Garret said.

"Why? I like Porco." Myckal used a teasing and sultry voice. She wiped her pink lipstick off him.

For a split second, she made eye contact with me, then turned away. The girls resumed their shopping plans, the guys set a date to go to Anthony's Tuxedos. I ignored them all. My brain switched to next year. Most likely, we were all headed to different schools. Whenever older kids came back for the occasional Couch party, I'd watch how they reunited with their old cliques. They seemed more like distant relatives than the tight groups they used to be. Very few people seemed able to keep their close friendships together.

Would we?

A light punch grazed my shoulder.

"Can I talk to you for a second?" Pablo stood there, looking gloomy.

"Sure." I motioned for him to sit.

"Not here. Outside."

I shrugged and followed him through the doors, then blew into my hands. The weatherman said high thirties and overcast today. Neither of us had coats. We took a few steps away from the building, but I stopped, not wanting to venture far from the heat.

"Dude, how long are you going to stay pissed at me?" he asked.

With zero desire to look him in the eyes, I glanced at the sidewalk. "Why don't you tell me about Iowa?"

His tone of voice perked up. "I wish you had gone with us. You would not believe the weight room they have *just* for the wrestling team. And the main gymnasium, where they hold their matches, it's more like an arena. The coach was totally cool and maybe the most intense person I ever met. He said it's not like our matches where only family and friends come. They sell out almost every seat. He had us watch a movie about the history of the program and all the championships they've won."

"What about your sweety-pie, what did he think?"

Narrowing his eyes, Pablo glared, but didn't correct me. "Hector loved the place. He kept trying to give the coach his verbal commitment."

"Tried, what do you mean, tried?"

"The coach seemed to like him, but he told Hector he had to win the state championship this year to earn a scholarship."

"What'd Hector say to that?"

"You really want to know?" Pablo slipped his hands into his pockets then hopped up and down to get warm.

"I can guess." I frowned.

"He said no problem. He didn't have much competition in his weight class and has already beaten everyone that he might face."

"What a jackass," I moaned.

"I know man. He's a douche. Plus, I didn't hear the story about him and Myckal until after I got back. If I'd known he grabbed her ass, I would've kicked *his* ass. And I already apologized to her."

I let half a smile curl my lips. Hearing my best friend criticize Hector after the way he defended him at The Couch reduced a little stress. So, I decided to move on.

"What did the coach say to you? Did you give him your verbal?"

He paced in front of me. "He wants me to go to Iowa, a lot."

"Did he say you have to win States, too?"

"Actually, no, just the opposite. If I skipped the tournament this year or even lost my leg in a shark attack, they'd still offer me a full ride."

I leaned up against the wall, trying to act cool and immediately regretted it. The bricks were freezing. "Ahh, cold. So, you committed?"

Scrunching his lips together, he shook his head. "No, I didn't."

"What are you talking about? You just said you loved the place, and the coach wants to have sex with you. You'd be crazy not to.?"

He laughed. "When I hesitated with my verbal, he

asked if there were any other schools I still had to visit. I told him me and you were checking out Northwestern."

"You did?" I crinkled my eyebrows together, really surprised. "Look man, I don't want you jeopardizing your chances at Iowa for me."

Pablo held up his hand. "I'm not risking anything. I said we'd take a tour right after the new year, and I'd get back to him after that."

My face softened and a warmth spread across my chest, even into my freezing throat. "You'd really do that for me?"

"You know you're my boy. We've been best friends forever. There's nothing I wouldn't do for you."

Shaking my head, I peered at the ground. My foot found a tiny snowball to play with. I almost teared up. Between my fight with Piper, Pablo basically apologizing, and the stress of trying to get straight A's, my emotions were all over the place. But I couldn't let him see that. "What did the coach say?"

"That I'd look stupid in purple."

We shared a laugh. I hadn't smiled in a while.

"Seriously, he said it's no big deal. I have a spot on their roster, no matter when I tell them." Pablo patted me on the shoulder. "You know, our first night in Iowa a couple guys on the team took us out to a freshman bar. Sweety-pie got so wasted he admitted you're the only one who ever gave him trouble."

"He did?"

"Yeah, and remember this summer when you wrestled him at camp. He *was* puking his guts out. He rolfed at the end because he was so fatigued. That's the key to beating him."

"What is? Spicy food?" I scratched my cheek and

then rubbed my chin like a detective, trying to decipher his logic.

"Tiring him out. He's won every match by pin this year. Most of them have been in the first period. A couple times he's gone to the second, but he hasn't wrestled in the third period all season."

"How does that make me feel better? He's destroying everybody. Plus, now he's got a scholarship riding on States." I frowned at the prospect of ever facing him again.

"He didn't destroy you. You got him to go the distance and he won on points, but he threw up right after. You just have to keep the match close until the third period, then make your move."

Tilting my head to the side, I pursed my lips. "At camp you told me to dive at his legs immediately."

"Yeah, that was dumb. Don't do that if you face him in States. Although, it may not matter because thanks to asbestos, we still don't know what our tournament will be like."

"This whole year basically blows, all because of that stupid substance."

"So, we're cool, man? You and me?" Pablo held out his hand.

"We've always been cool." I shook it, then wrapped my other arm around him, the way guys do a hug, without doing a hug.

He hugged me back—dude style, too. "Good. Because I'm freezing my ass off. Let's get inside."

Chapter 30

Tourney Update

While rummaging through my wrestling locker, I discovered an old damp singlet hiding underneath a bunch of putrid sweatpants. It hadn't been washed in weeks, neither had my sweats. Putting it up to my nose, I gagged a little, but it reeked less than anything else in here. I shrugged, threw it on, felt clammy all over, and went to the mats.

Pablo and I warmed up together before practice. When it was my turn, I'd throw a hold on him, he wouldn't fight back, and it helped perfect my technique. When it switched to his turn, I wouldn't resist, and he worked on his approach.

Crumpling him into a move called the cradle, I forced Pablo's shoulders down and pinned him. This late in the season, the mat always smelled like a sweaty butt. We're supposed to mop it once a week with disinfectant. But no one ever changes out the water in the slop bucket. It sits there all year. The rookies simply roll it out, swab the mophead around a little, and ring the brown gunk back in. The mat acts like a sponge and re-absorbs a bunch of Herpes and Hepatitis germs. No wonder wrestlers have bad acne.

"Piper hasn't returned any of your calls this week?" Pablo asked, his head squeezed between my bicep and his thigh like a pretzel.

Letting go of him, we popped up to our knees, facing each other. Since these routines were at half-speed, it gave us time to talk and catch up. Other guys came out of the locker room, paired-up, and went through their own dry runs.

I shook my head. "Not once and I've left more messages than I can count." It felt good having my best friend back to talk over things. But as each day passed, I grew more and more emotionally numb. My limbs weighed a ton and my wrestling moves were sluggish.

"We're getting down to crunch time bro. I hate to ask this, but are you sure she's still coming? Prom's only eight days away."

I blew out a long breath, full of pent-up frustration. "If I'm being one hundred percent honest—no. I hope like crazy she is and I still have faith, but I'm getting scared."

Because of all the drinking I'd done at parties lately, I thought I might have to cut weight and practice in those disgusting sweatshirts and sweatpants. But when I'm stressed, I can't eat. Any extra pounds I may have put on were long gone thanks to my neurotic Piper Kraft starvation diet.

Coach Slaz sauntered out in his green and white uniform—our school colors. "Bring it in, gents."

Everyone hustled over on all fours. Once we were on the mat it seemed more natural than getting up and walking. We sat in a semi-circle. A few guys finished lacing their wrestling shoes and ended up in the back row. As captain, Pablo had a responsibility to always be in the front, so today, I was right there with him.

"The county championships are Saturday," Slaz

began. "We have one or two wrestle-offs at the end of practice, otherwise, you all know who's representing each weight class."

My record stood at thirteen and zero and I'd be the favorite at one-hundred-and thirty-four-pounds. I won this tournament last year, and was very proud of it. However, winning it again only punched my ticket to States. My entrance to Northwestern required a victory at both championships.

He cleared his throat. "I just got off a phone call with the details of our state tourney. Enough schools are participating to have a competition, but New York isn't recognizing it as the official state championship. That'll be held next April. Since we'll be out of school, we obviously can't be in it.

"However, our event will be called the Greater New York Regional Wrestling Championship. Those of you who win on Saturday will represent John Marshall as the Weed County Champion."

Pablo raised his hand. "How's that going to work for the guys trying to earn a scholarship?"

That's why we loved him as our captain. As a two-time state champion, he could go anywhere he wanted. He asked that question for the rest of us.

"I'll be happy to call any of your future coaches and explain the craziness going on," Slaz said. "Hopefully, they'll accept a win there as good as a win at States but there's no guarantee. It's up to each individual college coach to make that decision, but I'll do what I can for you."

Only the starters would be wrestling in the county championship, and only the winners went on to this weird regional thing. It affected maybe three or four of us. The rest of the guys looked bored.

As I ran through the names of the wrestlers I'd face, my heart raced. I had a great shot at winning it all. Coach Slaz and Coach Flanholtz at Northwestern knew each other for years. Hopefully, Slaz could work his magic for me.

I didn't want to get ahead of myself and count my chickens before they hatched, but I couldn't help imagining life next year in Evanston, Illinois. Wind and snow from Lake Michigan would pelt me in the face and I'd suffer horrible bouts of the flu. It was going to be awesome. Tensing my arms and clenching my fists, I tried to calm down before getting too excited.

"This Greater New York contest will be held next Friday, December fourteenth, right here at John Marshall. We're lucky they chose us to host the tournament."

All the seniors grumbled and complained.

Slaz held out his hands to calm us down. "What's all the noise about?"

Royce Kedell, a thick-haired, Black kid—our chunky one-hundred-and-seventy-six pounder raised his arm. He'd most likely win the county championship for his weight. "That's the day of the senior prom."

"What are you worried about, Kedell?" Slaz frowned and snapped his pen on the clipboard. "The tournament begins at ten-thirty in the morning and should be over by five or six. From what I understand the prom goes from eight until midnight. You'll have plenty of time to change into your dress."

"Oooh, burn," emanated from the team as well as laughter.

Kedell's neck muscles tightened, and his chin thrust

up. "But, Coach, the prom's not just about the dance. There's pictures beforehand, picking up your date, limos—"

"Don't forget your hair and make-up, Kedell."

That kind of comment couldn't be ignored by a bunch of wrestlers. The muffled noises of guys near him giving him the needle, drifted over. But not too bad. He was one of the bigger kids on the team—and on the wrestling mat, might makes right.

Slaz said, "Normally, I'd ask any of the County Champions wrestling in the State tourney to stay and support your teammates. But since this is the wackiest year ever and it is prom day, you can leave as soon as your last match is over. That's the best I can do for you."

Kedell nodded.

"All the asbestos schools are participating in our state tournament," Slaz continued. "But that wasn't enough to satisfy the wrestling committee. A few upstate counties and schools have agreed to take part so that New York would sanction it. Booger Hole County near Albany is sending a couple representatives, most notably from Butt Hill High School. That's good for you Esposito."

Every eye fell on me, and a prickle zipped down my spine. Trying to sound excited, I grinned. "Why's that, Coach?"

He studied his clipboard. "Don't you remember who's all the way up in Butt Hill? Hector Wolfe."

My eyes bulged and I sat upright. "What?!" The momentary exhilaration I just experienced, disappeared in an instant. My mind flashed to last year and the pain of losing to Hector thundered through every nerve cell.

Slaz scratched his nose. "Yeah, the guy that beat you

in States. I hear things inside Booger Hole are very strong and entrenched. Assuming he can dig around up there, and when things get tough and the competition really starts running, if he can find a way to pull out a big one, he'll be their champ."

My mouth fell open and my breath caught in my throat. "Sorry, I meant to say… What?!"

He narrowed his gaze and crossed his huge guns across his chest, with his clipboard clutched in front. "This is good news for you, Luca. You get to have your revenge against him while you're winning States. Nothing will ever feel better than picking him off."

Pablo nudged me, giving a thumbs up and trying to appear confident. Yesterday, he presented a plan to beat Hector. For a wrestler as talented as Pablo it made sense, and he could do it. But I wasn't as good as Pablo.

My shoulders dropped and my head fell between my knees. I didn't want to believe what came out of Slaz's mouth. My chances at Northwestern were disappearing and I still had no idea if Piper was coming to the prom.

December fourteenth might be the worst day of my life.

Chapter 31

Monday, December 10—Five Days to Prom

The weekend went about the way I expected. Since I returned as last year's county champ and was undefeated going into the tournament, they gave me the number one ranking. That meant a first-round bye. Later, I won my first two matches by pinning my opponents. In the finals, I faced a guy I had pinned earlier in the year.

As the match wore on, he was wrestling way harder than in our first meeting. That happened a lot in tournaments. Some people rise above their skill level and put on the show of their lives. Others choke under pressure. It all depends.

At the beginning of the third period, the score stood at 4 to 3, way too close for comfort.

I began in the down position and escaped after a minute, earning one point—5 to 3. We circled and danced around each other, neither gaining an advantage. If he landed a takedown, that would be worth two points and he'd tie up the match. With about thirty seconds left, his coach screamed that he was out of time. He'd have to shoot at my legs.

Making believe I was tired and about to stand up straight, I timed his move better than he did. He lunged forward. I pancaked my body on his head and shoulders and scooted behind him before he could react. Two more points for me. The clock ran out and I captured my second Weed County Championship, 7 to 3.

Normally, that'd be the highlight of a wrestler's high school career. With bigger goals on my horizon, it still only qualified me for our state tournament.

They announced all the winners during first period. Five of us had won—a very impressive showing for John Marshall and Coach Slaz.

For the rest of the day people patted me on the back and said congratulations. It was pretty cool. Except, I still hadn't heard from Piper, so my stomach burned and tumbled in knots.

At home that night, I left the dinner table without touching a thing.

"Aren't you hungry, honey?" my mother asked.

Placing my plate in the dishwasher, I said, "Not really. I have to keep the weight off." My mom bought it and I went to my room. Our cocker spaniel, Lil, scrambled down the stairs with me and I snuck her my slice of meatloaf. She almost took off my finger.

Faithfully by Journey played on the stereo—Piper's prom theme. When I'm down in the dumps I enjoyed listening to love songs, sad songs, and even watching sad movies. Somehow, they hurt and helped at the same time.

Fifteen minutes later the phone rang. I'd been running to pick it up all week—only to experience crushing disappointment when I heard a voice other than Piper's. I stopped doing that yesterday, figuring she'd call when she wants to.

"Luca, telephone," my thirteen-year-old brother, Vic, yelled. We had two phones. One in the kitchen, and a cordless. As much as we begged our parents, they couldn't bring themselves to go completely wireless.

My pulse quickened, hoping it was her. I took a deep breath to settle my nerves, in case it wasn't. "Who is it?"

"I'm not your answering machine," the little twerp called.

I remained laying on my bed, tossing a baseball in the air and catching it. It was almost cold enough down here to see my breath. "Is it a girl or a guy?" I had ton of homework in front of me, probably be up all night, but I wasn't up to starting it yet.

"With your loser friends, who can tell?"

"Do me a favor and bring me the phone," I said.

"No way, I'm not going in your sucky room."

Getting to my feet, I lobbed the ball into my mitt and placed it on the dresser. I didn't shower after practice. A dumb move—if I did that a couple times a week, my acne broke out. I didn't want that ever happening, but especially not with the prom and all the pictures we'd be taking. Presuming, of course, I still had a date.

With States coming up, Slaz worked us extra hard, sweating our tails off. I peered at myself in the mirror, some pimples starting to show on the left side of my chin—I cringed. I took a whiff of my shirt, the same one I practiced in. "Ugh, nasty." I backed away from myself. My eyes watered and I grabbed a towel, planning on heading to the bathroom after the call.

I opened my door and stepped into the laundry room. "Who's on the phone?"

My brainless brother imitated a girl's voice. "*It's Piper.*"

I did a double take. He tried holding the phone away from me. I snatched it and shoved him against the dryer. He tripped over a clothes basket and his head banged into the hollow part of the washing machine, reverberating into a loud *gong.*

"Hey!" He held the back of his skull and sat up.

Covering the mouth end of the receiver, I pointed down at him. "You're lucky I don't beat the crap out of you. You know I've been dying to talk to her all week."

While lying in a pile of my parent's dirty underwear, he cupped a hand over his mouth to yell. "I hope you break up with him, Piper! He's been crying over you for days!"

"Hello, Piper." I sneered at him, but tried sounding affectionate to her.

"Hi, Luca."

"Do you mind holding on a quick second? Promise me you won't go anywhere. I need to take care of one small thing."

"I promise," she said.

"Okay, thanks." I was so happy and encouraged that she called. But a force awoke deep inside me. I had an obligation to older brothers everywhere. Vic's taunts couldn't go unanswered.

As he started standing up, I kicked his legs out from under him. He stumbled backward, landed in the basket and his head crashed into the same spot on the washing machine—booming much harder and louder this time, possibly denting it.

"What's going on down there?" My father bellowed from his recliner. We didn't have anything to worry about. Once he put his feet up and slid the seat back, he wouldn't move for years. A tsunami could be on its way, as long as he stayed above the water line, he wasn't un-reclining. A little dent wouldn't change things.

Not wanting Piper to overhear us, I covered the

handset again. "You're going to have one less idiot son before the night's over, that's what!"

The little turd got up and tried punching me. I placed the phone down and threw the cradle move on him. Bunching him into a ball, I forced him to the floor and pressed my armpit directly over his nose. "You like that smell? Do you like that smell?"

Wrangling to get his head free, he shouted, "Don't go to the prom with him, Piper! He's a jerk-off!"

"That's it." I picked Vic up, kept him squeezed tight in a circle, and tossed him into the dryer, slamming the door closed.

"I'm telling Dad," his muffled voice called out.

"Go ahead. I'll high-five him for buying the extra-large dryer. You know what, I'm turning this thing on."

"No!" He smashed out of there and scampered upstairs. A pair of my father's ripped boxers clung to his shirt.

Shutting the bedroom door, I took my hand off the receiver, and sat on the bed. "Hey, Piper." I used the friendliest voice I could muster.

"Hi, Luca. What was that all about?" She sounded somber.

"Nothing. My dumb brother was being a brat, so I threw him in the dryer."

"You didn't." She raised her volume, like she was worried about the creep.

"Just kidding. You know me, I'd never do that. He says hi by the way."

"But Vic answered the phone and already said hi."

I shrugged. "What can I tell ya? He's not very bright."

Neither of us said anything for five excruciating

seconds.

"I'm so sorry, Piper. About everything. I shouldn't have yelled. I've been miserable all week not talking to you." My heart raced and I rushed through those words. I wanted the apology out immediately, so she knew how much I regretted my part in our last conversation.

"I'm sorry, too."

What a relief. My shoulders slumped as I let that feeling sink in, like a deadweight slid off my back. As much as I hoped she'd apologize too, part of me feared a breakup during this chat. I closed my eyes and let out a huge sigh. "I called you right after we hung up. I wanted to say sorry that instant. When you didn't pick up, I left a few messages. Did you get them?"

"You mean a few thousand. You didn't have to keep calling and leaving more and more of them. When I didn't phone back, I thought it'd be obvious I was mad and needed time to calm down and think."

"I'm a guy. Nothing's obvious to me."

She snorted back a laugh. Felt great to hear it.

I wedged the phone between my shoulder and ear and crossed all my fingers. "Does that mean you're not mad at me anymore and you're coming to the prom on Friday?" *Please, please, please,* I muttered under my breath. It'd kill me if she said, no.

"No and yes."

"Huh?"

"No, I'm not still mad at you. And yes, I'm coming to the prom."

"Whew, *thank youuuu,*" I said.

She chuckled but not as freely as usual. Still, I took it as a good sign. Things looked positive in the world again. Probably shouldn't venture down this path so soon, but sometimes I can't help putting my foot in my mouth.

"What about Saturday? Are you coming to the city with us?"

"I don't know." Her breathing came off loud and labored.

"What do you mean?" I dropped my head between my shoulders.

"When we got off the phone, I was so mad at you. The next time I saw Jonesy I told him that you were okay with me going to his formal. He knows it's just as friends."

Clenching both fists, I used a sharp tone. "I never said I was good with it."

She used an even sharper tone. "*Luca.*"

I was about to say something I'd regret when I literally bit my tongue. Jumping off the bed in pain, I hopped in front of the mirror and stuck it out. Teeth marks appeared, redness framed them, and it bled a little. Exhaling in short bursts like a machine gun, I tried to calm myself down.

"Okay, look. I'm not thrilled that you said yes to him. But I'm not going to tell you that you can't go—"

"Oh, you're granting me your permission?" Sarcasm trickled through every syllable of that sentence.

I paced around the room like an Olympic sprinter doing laps. "That's not what I mean, and you know it. All I'm saying is that if I told you I was going to a different prom with a girl from Ackerman, you might not be that keen about it, either."

"Is that what you want, to go with another girl?"

"*Of course not.*" It took every ounce of strength not to scream my head off.

She didn't respond.

A frozen smile plastered my face. "Look, right now I'm just thrilled to be talking to you and that you're coming on Friday. Can we leave things at that?"

A few more painful seconds dripped by.

She huffed and her voice came out cold. "Robyn's waving to me. She needs to make an emergency call and I have to get off. Finals are in two weeks. I'm going to be studying late every night until they're over and won't be able to speak on the phone. I'll call you if I have a chance."

Unable to process what was happening, and pressed for time, my eyes darted back and forth. "Oh, okay. Umm. I love you."

"Lo—" The phone went dead. She sounded so rushed, I wasn't sure I heard the words *you too*, or even *love* for that matter.

Paranoid or not, and replaying the last part of our exchange in my mind, I wondered—did I still have a prom date?

Chapter 32

A Huge Favor—Two Days Before States and the Prom

I walked into first period, U.S. History. Ms. Maroney had been out for over a month, supposedly with horrible headaches from the asbestos. I didn't want anyone to get sick, not even her. Couldn't say I missed her, though.

Hi. I'm Mr. Krieger. Your Substitute Teacher was written on our blackboard. Ms. Maroney had kept it washed and clean with almost military precision. No one's done it in her absence. The ghosts of yellow chalk marks were etched up and down with yesterday's notes peeking through. The ledge running along the bottom held erasers in need of a good pounding and miles of allergy-filled dust.

Mr. Krieger had a beard and John Lennon glasses. With his feet up, he leaned back in Maroney's chair, reading a guitar magazine. Slush dribbled off his boots, right onto her desk calendar. I grinned on the way by.

We had four minutes before the bell.

"Hey, Myckal."

She was already in her seat.

"Luca, my favorite wrestler." She beamed at me. "Hurry up and sit down before anyone else comes over. I want to run something by you."

"Okaaay," I said.

She checked around to make sure no one could eavesdrop. Porco's desk was behind hers, but he hadn't arrived yet. As long as other kids continued to drone on, three-ring binders snapped, and the pencil sharpener grinded away, we should be fine.

"So, are you ready for States?" Myckal asked. "Or at least what we're calling it this year?" She wore a really cute black and white plaid dress—more black than white. It had overalls on top with a black turtleneck underneath. It was thigh length, and with black knee socks, she exposed an adorable amount of skin between the two. I wondered if she was cold. It flurried today.

Thinking about Hector forced me to blow out a deep, nervous breath. For luck, I crossed my fingers on both hands and held them up. "Two more days. So, what do you want to talk about?"

Her eyebrows creased together, and she crossed her legs. "Tell me how you think your bracket will play out."

I shrugged. "Slaz went over our records and who we'd most likely go against. In my weight class, only two wrestlers are coming in undefeated. Me and your buddy, Hector."

Recoiling at the name, she picked up her purse like a shield. "I hope you kick his ass on Friday. That guy was so nasty at The Couch."

I angled forward and slid my chair closer. "Why, what happened?" A slight yellow bruise remained under my left eye. At least it's not still black.

"Argh. I wish Pablo never brought him."

"That makes two of us," I said.

She shook her head and pursed her lips. Her thick spiral curls were down but she had a white scrunchy on top. It set off a pair of great blue eyes. "Before you came over, he was telling me how all the girls at Butt Hill are into him because he's the State Champion. There's no way I believe that. But he claimed he has all these groupies that practically worship him and if I wanted, I could be John Marshall's local representative. He was such an ass."

"Well, he obviously likes you."

"Gross—no thanks." She slapped my shoulder.

We were close enough to the cafeteria to inhale greasy breakfast smells and an empty hole formed in the pit of my stomach. I had overslept and missed breakfast.

Her eyes narrowed and she turned to the side. "Are you worried about going against him?"

"To be honest? Yeah, I am. He's the returning champion, and he'll definitely be ranked number one. If I'm lucky, I'll be ranked number two. That means I won't have to face him until finals."

"You can take him." She smiled and lightly squeezed my forearm, holding her fingers there a couple seconds before pulling away. Her nails were painted, alternating between green and white, our school colors.

"Hasn't happened yet. He won in our semifinal match last year and then at camp he beat me again."

Her touch felt nice. I wouldn't call her the biggest flirt in the world, but she was ranked near the top. Better than me, for sure. Since she knew about my girlfriend, and we were just friends, it was all harmless. But I needed to be quick to keep up with her. She seemed wound up about something.

"Just be confident. You're a really good wrestler and you've gotten better throughout the season. If you have a good plan, I know you'll do it."

"Thanks. But you're acting a little weird right now. What's going on?"

She cleared her throat and made stronger eye contact. "I think I have a way to help you out. If you want my help, that is."

"Why? What did you have in mind?"

Sliding up in her chair, she glanced around. "Since we established that he wants me as a groupie, my idea is super crazy. So, don't be afraid to say, no."

"Don't be afraid to say no, huh? Well, I doubt very much I would *ever* say no to you. So, you have me seriously intrigued."

She let out a deep sigh and used a softer voice. "Suppose you wanted to distract Hector during your match. Can you think of anything that *I* could do, that might give you an edge?"

My eyebrows furrowed in deep thought, then released. "Maybe. But I'm afraid to say it out loud."

"Why?"

"I don't want you taking a swing at me."

A devious smile crossed her lips. I'd seen it at the lunch table many times. Usually right before something sarcastic flies. She put the end of her pen in her mouth, bit it for a second then waved it at me. "We both know Hector's a perv and a big ass-face. Right?"

"Ass-face? That's putting it mildly."

"Well, it got me thinking about that day at the scorer's table. After you imposed a dress code on—"

"Hey, that wasn't my fault." I put up my hands, hiding behind them. "You have amazing legs. I couldn't concentrate with those things around. Most guys would've melted if they were in my position."

She cocked her head to the side. "What position was

that?"

"Umm, kneeling on the mat, right in front of you."

"Actually, you were on all fours."

When she pointed downward, it pulled my eyes to the top of her knee socks. I gulped and quickly looked up.

"And I think you said I had an incredibly sweet pair of legs."

I did a double take. "You remembered my exact quote?"

"Certain things stick with a girl." She shrugged.

"Fine. Incredibly sweet. I may have even said gorgeous. But you can't blame me for what happened. You're like a giant eye-magnet that guys can't resist."

"Aww." She fake swooned and wore a shy smile. "Now look who's being sweet."

"Whatever." I stretched out the word and made a "W" with my fingers. It was one of her favorite tricks. "You know, last year, my Psych teacher gave us advice about what to do if a pretty girl walks down the hall. When I noticed you in my wrestling match, I tried using the same technique."

"You think I'm pretty, Luca?"

"Didn't you agree not to take everything I say and fire it back to me in the form of a question?"

"Sorry, it kind of happens naturally," she teased. "So, what about your Psych teacher?"

"Anyway," I lengthened that word, too. "The class was discussing teenage hormones and how boys should conduct ourselves, so, we don't come off whacky in front of girls. He claimed there was a difference between appreciating a pretty girl and becoming a weird stalker dude." The scent of her perfume drifted over me—

orange blossoms and some other cool spices.

She lifted her chin. "What was his advice?"

"He said when a pretty girl passes you, if you turn your head and look at her two times, then you've gone too far." I held up two fingers to play up the point.

"Hmm." While wrinkling her nose, she squinted and slowly said, "I guess I agree with that."

"Right. So, when the girl goes by, you better make that first look count."

She giggled. The sound of it made me smile.

"Are you ever going to tell me what your crazy idea is, or do you just enjoy torturing me?" I asked.

"Didn't you learn anything in Psych? Girls love to torture boys."

"Somehow, I think you may have gotten an A in it."

She flicked her hair back. "Okay, here goes. What if I wore something a little *distracting* during your match and it just happened to catch Hector's eye? Would that help you out?"

After letting out a small, pleasant laugh, I scratched my chin. "Considering he is the biggest loser in the world, and he'd come in totally overconfident, I'm sure he'd love to check you out instead of focusing on me. So, yeah, that would help. But I'd never ask you to—"

"Because I'll do it."

My jaw hit the floor. "Really? You will?"

"Of course. I'll do anything to get back at that jerk."

"Huh?"

Biting her bottom lip and nodding, she said, "He crossed the line when he grabbed me at The Couch. I'd love to get my revenge. And I have *just* the outfit."

"Well, it is a crazy idea. But I don't want to put you in a position where you'd feel uncomfortable."

She shot a darting glance at me. "Duh. This was my plan, remember? I want to get even with the idiot."

Feeling a mixture of shock and gratitude that she offered to help me out, I tried to temper things a little. "You could just wear what you had on that day." Then my confidence grew, and I decided to needle her. "You know, when *I* couldn't take my eyes off you."

If she could throw off Hector's attention, even for a few seconds, it might give me a fighting chance. Because up until now, I had no way to beat him.

She tapped her pen against the desk and a slow smile grew on her lips. "Let me get this straight. Not only am I willing to do you this huge favor. Now you want to dress me up, too?"

Myckal knew as much about wrestling as anyone. As manager, she had to pay attention to every match. Slaz, Pablo, and Myckal met each week to review everyone's performance. She wasn't there just to give statistics. Pablo said he and Slaz always asked her opinion.

Unless she truly thought I could beat Hector, she wouldn't suggest this strategy. Otherwise, she'd have him leering over her for no reason. What would that accomplish?

No one's ever done anything like this for me. She made me believe in myself and the inside of my chest warmed up.

I raised my hands in surrender and leaned backward. "Okay, I'll leave the wardrobe choices up to you."

A sly grin lit up her face. "Good idea. And we'll see who the groupie is."

Chapter 33

Florist—The Night Before the Prom

Anthony's Fine Tuxedos was the only tux shop within thirty miles. Last year, Piper and I ended up there on prom day, hoping they still had a tux for me to rent. I prayed it was any color except, yellow.

Luckily, Anthony had a black one in my size. I tried to pay for it and rush out of there, but he insisted on sizing it for me. While in the back of his store, Bryce, the jack-off quarterback snuck out of a dressing room and clocked me in the face with a perfect punch.

Before I knew what happened, I crumpled to the floor. He promised me it was only a warning shot, and Pablo and I would suffer a lot worse at the prom. He and his dopey backup, Brayden, laughed as they walked out, leaving me laying amongst the dust bunnies.

When Piper checked on the ruckus, she found me on my butt. Unfortunately, she did a lot worse. She chose that moment to interrogate me about why I broke up with her ten months earlier. She wouldn't let me up until I gave her a straight answer.

My journey to the store this year was far less exciting. We got measured and paid for the rentals. Because of States, Pablo and I wouldn't have time to pick them up on prom day. Jimmy would handle it.

For flowers, we went to the Duke and Duchess mall.

Most everyone chose a corsage of carnations, roses, and baby's breath, with a boutonniere to match. As for the colors, they all had specific instructions from the girls. But not me.

I ordered the identical corsage as last year—a Radiant Orchid. Hopefully, Piper'd think it was romantic to get the same one.

Kedell, from the wrestling team, was right. Going to the prom was a lot more than attending the actual dance. The leadup had a lot of meaning. By waiting until the last minute, I blew that with Piper's prom. This time, I wanted to enjoy as much of it as possible. Jimmy volunteered to pick up the flowers after the tuxes. But I preferred to do my part. Plus, my nervous anxiety churned inside me. I didn't want to be alone with my thoughts. I couldn't just sit around and stress about Hector.

Pablo and I would relax later tonight by watching *Ferris Bueller* and *Die Hard*. I volunteered to go to the video store before heading to his house.

The florist was probably in his thirties, with black hair, thick muscles, and looked like a TV star. "Can I help you lad?" Same Irish accent as last year—a real wiseass as I remembered.

I figured I'd start the banter before he did. "Where's the cute girl that took our prom order? Can't I be waited on by her?"

"That cute girl, laddy buck, is my wife." He tilted his head and grinned. "And believe me, a little pip squeak like you couldn't handle a woman like her. She'd tear you to pieces. Now, you said she took your instructions for the prom. Is it too much to think you came here with your receipt?"

Reaching into my pocket, I took it out and snapped it back and forth, pulling on each end. "Here you go."

Stepping under the light, and reading it with squinting eyes, his brows raised. "Five corsages and boutonnieres. It doesn't look like you paid for them yet. That'll be one hundred and twenty-three dollars, and I only accept cash."

It didn't make sense. We paid for the tuxes and flowers when we ordered them. That way whoever picked them up didn't have to try to collect the money. Because someone wouldn't have the dough when the time came. I felt like I couldn't breathe.

"No, no, we already paid the day we came in. Can I see the receipt? I'm sure it's stamped somewhere on it."

I reached for it, but he held it high in the air. He was taller than me and with the counter in the way, I couldn't get at it.

"Relax laddy. You should see your face. You've gone totally white. I know we charged you already. That's what you get for saying you wanted to deal with the cute girl instead of me. Did I mention she's *my wife*?"

My hands flew to my chest, and I regained my composure. "Don't ever do that to me again. There's no way I could ever come up that kind of money."

He winked and walked to the back of the store to get our order, and returned with three shopping bags. "Let's confirm everything real quick, shall we?" He took them all out and compared each one to the receipt. Every corsage was in a clear plastic case with its accompanying boutonniere. They all looked beautiful, tightly constructed, and expertly put together. The boutonnieres had long pins to attach to the tuxes. Each corsage had a wrist strap with fancy ribbons.

"What's this, who's the big spender with the orchid? Magenta with streaks of white and darker pinks. Just lovely," he added.

"That's mine." I beamed with pride. "Don't you remember me from last year? I got that same one for my date." My heart warmed up, picturing Piper wearing it. For tonight, at least, I'd only consider positive things, like her looking gorgeous in that maroon dress. Tomorrow, I could stress about her possibly not coming to the prom, or if she did, not going with us to the city.

"Of course. Aren't you the lad who ordered the corsage for the prom?" He wagged his finger in my direction.

With a wide grin and a loud voice, I said, "That's right, that was me."

He cocked his head and smirked.

I sneered. "You don't remember me, do you?"

"Sorry, kid. Do you know how many high schools there are around Big Dune, and they all have proms with wee ones that look just like you. Unless you shopped here every month, it'd be difficult for me to place ya."

My shoulders sagged, a little disappointed. I tried one last time to jog his memory. "I came in on prom day. We started talking. You gave me a hard time for waiting until the last minute and didn't think I'd know the color of my date's dress, but I did. Actually, I didn't, but I thought I did.

"Then you overcharged me for the Radiant Orchid because you claimed it was the only thing you had left that would match her dress. The shop was a lot messier than now. You told me it got that way on prom day, which was worse than the trading desk on Wall Street, where you used to work."

He slowly nodded, and his eyes lit up. "Yes. Waiting until the last second. Typical of ya, isn't it? Told ya to tell her that ya picked it out because it matched her eyes. Did ya follow my advice? And did it work?"

Practically hopping up and down, I answered. "You got it. That was me. I did and you were right, she loved the compliment. We actually became boyfriend and girlfriend after that."

"They always do. But I don't think I can take all the credit for getting you two together. So, last year you shopped on prom day for the corsage and this year you're picking it up a day early, what gives?"

"You must have heard about the asbestos mess we're dealing with. Tomorrow's not only the prom but they scheduled the state wrestling championship too. I didn't know if I'd have enough time to pick up the flowers after the tournament."

"A champion wrestler are ya?" He scanned me up and down. "Never would have guessed it, not with your scrawny build."

My mouth opened to throw an insult back his way, then I realized he was joking. "Why, did you wrestle?"

He nodded. "National collegiate champion."

"Really, what school?"

"University of Dungarvan."

"Never heard of it."

"Irish champion, lad. There are schools outside of America, ya know? Do ya want to learn one of my secrets? It's legal, but they hardly teach it over here."

"Of course. What is it?"

"With your state championship tomorrow, there's not much I can show ya. Ye need to rely on what your coach has taught. But people who watch these tournaments often complain that they're boring. Both lads are so good it's difficult to score any points. But a time will come when you'll end up on your feet, grappling back and forth to get position to shoot at the other's legs. That's when ya do this."

With lightning speed his hand flew at my ear, then stopped an inch away. I didn't have time to duck or block it. Chills shot through my shoulders and arms. He could've dropped me, no problem.

"As long as ya hit him in the ear pad, it's legal," he claimed. "Being slapped there is way louder than you can imagine. When ya want to confuse your opponent and throw him off balance, slap him." He nodded and handed me all three shopping bags.

"Thanks man, I appreciate it."

"Good luck, laddy. Just remember, catch him hard in the ear. But be careful. If ya miss and tag his face, your referee will deduct a point. It may cost ya everything. That's the way life is. If ya wait too long, ya might miss out. But if ya jump early, you'll never know how things would have come out after."

Chapter 34

Winter Weather

Prom day and States finally arrived. I'd never been so nervous in my life. Piper and I still hadn't talked since our make-up-slash-argument the other night. Barely sleeping a wink, I woke up without an alarm clock to a nauseating, jumpy feeling. I kept shaking out my hands and clearing my throat. My feet felt too large for my body—I must have tripped three times before breakfast.

I arrived early to History. No sign of Mr. Krieger yet. Would we have a sub for our sub?

With her books held in front of her chest, Myckal zipped into the classroom. "How are you feeling, Luca?" She had her hair down. Often, a white scrunchy or a clip held part of it in place, but not today. It looked great and professionally done.

"Wow, check out your hair. Aren't you gorgeous this morning? Who's the lucky guy?"

She pushed up on one side of her thick black curls. "Funny and thanks. This glamour shot is just for Porco." She curtsied and sat down. "I got it done yesterday. I would have rather gone today, but with the tournament, that wasn't happening. I've been up for hours teasing it back out."

As manager of the team, Slaz gave her an oversized, John Marshall Wrestling sweatshirt. Unlike us, she didn't have to buy it. She wore that, plus black jeans and black ankle boots. Her ensemble looked very cute, but not exactly what we discussed.

"You've been up for hours? Girls are crazy, do you know that? But good for Porco," I said and smiled. "Remember, Pablo's house at seven for pictures. You gonna have enough time to get ready after States?"

Chairs scraped along the floor as kids took their seats. A lot of other girls came in with ponytails— probably waiting for their own hair appointments.

Shaking her head and smirking at me, she said, "It's such a piece of cake for you boys, and you don't even realize. Anyway, Coach Slaz says no problem. Kedell is our last wrestler at one hundred and seventy-six pounds. Even if he makes it to the finals, I should be able to leave by five at the latest. Hopefully, four-thirty. And I can't believe I'm going to finally meet the famous Piper. I've heard so much about her. I'm dying to see the girl that made an honest man out of you."

"Yeah right." With all my crazy energy, it was hard to give anything but short answers.

"Good thing she drove down last night." Myckal arranged her books and pens on her desk.

"Why's that?"

"Didn't you hear? A small storm's hitting us from Canada. Not a blizzard or anything, but Albany's going to get about six inches of snow. We'll get two or three. Do you think the tree at Rockefeller Center will be all white?" She reached forward and gave my right tricep a slight pinch.

I barely felt it through my sweatshirt. My eyes widened with concern. She was excited about our trip to the city tomorrow but my stress level amped up, worrying over the weather.

"No, I didn't hear about any storm. Piper was supposed to drive down last night. But she has a test today. She's borrowing a car and coming home right after. I was hoping she'd be at my match against Hector."

If it were any other weekend I'd tell her not to drive in the snow, but it was the prom, she couldn't miss that.

"Oh, I'm sure she'll be there to cheer you on." Myckal tried to sound convincing. I wasn't sure if either of us bought it. She waved her hand in dismissal. "Besides, the weather guys are always wrong. She'll be on the road long before it starts, if it snows at all."

"Argh. Not going to get strung out about it. I can't control the weather, and today I'm only concentrating on things I can control." A deep sigh escaped my lungs as I stared out the window. No snow yet, but there were a lot of gray clouds.

"See, that's the right attitude. Stay positive and Hector won't have a chance."

We had about two minutes before the bell. I perked up in my seat and raised my tone of voice. "Speaking of Hector…" I spun a circle with my right hand. I let the rest of that sentence go unfinished, hoping Myckal would complete my thought.

"What about him?" She shrugged and raised her hands to shoulder level.

So much for that idea. Nodding at her, I squinted and checked her out, head to toe.

"What?" She sounded self-conscious.

I really didn't want Porco walking in and learning what we were up to. This was our little secret. I glimpsed around to make sure we wouldn't be overheard. "I don't want to comment on what you chose to wear, especially after the way you kicked my butt for it the other day, but I was hoping for—"

"You were hoping for what?" She creased her eyebrows together and looked at me sideways. Then she spun her fingers back at me.

"I was hoping for something a little more—"

"A little *more*?" She asked and snapped her gum.

"You're not going to make this easy on me, are you?"

Her face went blank with the biggest *what are you talking about* expression.

"Fine. I don't know exactly how I thought you'd dress to distract Hector, but it begins with the *letter S.*"

Her chin rested on her hand. "Hmm, what starts with S. Sweet and wholesome?" She blew a bubble.

I shook my head.

She pointed at me. "Sultry?"

"That's closer."

"Skanky. You were hoping for skanky."

"No!"

With a big grin, she sat straight up and sounded offended. "Slutty? You wanted me to dress slutty?"

"Definitely not!"

"Don't worry, it's plenty slutty." She leaned back and crossed her arms.

"Really?"

A few people glanced our way. Even though I tried to keep quiet, she didn't, and she may have caused me to raise my voice.

Angling forward, she smiled and bit her bottom lip. "Yeah, Hector's not going to know what hit him. I stopped at the girl's locker room and put my outfit in there. It's a little white skirt, with a—"

"No, no, no. Don't tell me." I thrust my hands in front of me like a bunch of armor. "All this talk about you dolling yourself up in *hot sexy* clothing is going to have the opposite effect. You'll have me fixating on you all day and I need to think about wrestling and wrestling alone. The plan will backfire before you get a chance to work your magic on Hector."

"Don't worry. I'm saving it until later." She narrowed her gaze. "It may not be appropriate to walk around school in it, anyway." She uttered that last sentence in a breathy whisper.

"Using that throaty voice isn't helping me, either."

We chuckled.

"Honestly, Myckal. If this is going to make you feel uncomfortable, you don't have to do it. Plus, I would never ask you to wear something *slutty*."

"Please. You didn't. Besides, it's not exactly that, but it should do the trick. And when they hang that state championship medal around your neck, you're going to owe me big time." She jabbed me in the chest.

"Sounds good. I'll save a dance for you, tonight."

Slapping my shoulder with the back of her hand, she pulled away like she was offended. "You're going to owe me a lot more than that, buddy."

We smiled.

"Okay, two dances. By the way, when I was thinking of you, my S word was sexy. And seriously, thanks."

Her eyes lit up.

Chapter 35

Maroney's Class

Porco walked into History with quick, deliberate steps. Trying to be stealthy, he pointed at his shoulder with his thumb, meaning we should look behind him.

"You've got to be kidding me," I said, not wanting to believe my eyes.

Ms. Maroney clomped through the door with her hair in a bun and a thick leather folder across her chest. She'd been absent for over a month and, quite frankly, I hoped she'd be out the rest of the year. She's my least favorite teacher ever and had always hated me.

"Nice to see you too, Mr. *Espuzito*. I'm going to imagine that comment was directed my way. I'll send a blue slip to administration letting them know you were disrespectful. With your record, I wonder how many detentions that will earn you. And thanks to your outburst, the class will have a pop quiz today."

The grumbling began right away, and everyone shot me dirty looks. Ms. Maroney plopped her items on the desk, took out a stack of papers and held them in the air, signifying the quiz. It didn't take her long to mispronounce my name.

Teachers used blue slips for infractions that didn't require an immediate trip to the office. A day or two after they sent it, an aide would pull you out of a different class to visit the vice-principal.

"Thanks a lot, Luca," someone on the other side of the room called out.

We still had a minute before the bell. Ms. Maroney sneered as she took her seat. Some people actually said hi to her as they came in and asked how she'd been.

I didn't look to see who thanked me. My eyes glared at the teacher. A couple seconds later Porco kicked the back of my legs. Slowly, I turned toward him.

"Yesss?"

"Cut it out," he whispered. "She already nailed you for one detention. If you keep it up, she'll find a way to have you kicked out of States."

"How did you know what I was doing?"

He snorted a small laugh. "Because I know you and I know her. Now watch your ass."

"He's right, Luca." Concern flowed from Myckal's voice. She tapped her foot and twisted her hair. "Don't do anything to get in trouble."

"Fine." I turned back around but instead of looking at Maroney, I focused on people coming through the doorway.

Once the bell rang, she stood and walked to the other side of the room, passing out the papers. "I was going to give you this as homework. But thanks to Mr. *Espuzito*, let's see how everyone does on the quiz."

The complaint level cranked back up. But she was full of it. There's no way she was ever going to give the assignment as homework. Her style would be to test us the second she got back. I grabbed my quiz and got to work.

With fifteen minutes left, I completed all the questions and waited for the rest of room to wrap up.

Despite Maroney's best intentions, I found it easy—my straight A record would continue unblemished. The quiz distracted me for a while, but the anxiety of the tournament wouldn't be denied. My body temperature ran from hot to cold and I kept spinning my pen on my desk.

An announcement came through the loudspeaker. "This is Mrs. Wild. Please excuse the interruption. Would the following members of the wrestling team come down to the gymnasium? They're all county champions and are competing in the state championship being held at John Marshall today. We wish them good luck on their way."

Five of us made States. She announced us by weight class. I bit the inside of my cheek until my name was called. "At one hundred and thirty-four pounds, Luca Es-Poh-sito." Unlike Maroney, Mrs. Wild said my last name perfectly.

The class broke into applause.

"Go get 'em Luca."

"You can do it man."

"You got this, bro."

Those and other encouragements came my way.

Chills flew down my spine as I stood and gathered my things. Trying to remain humble, I fought the smile curving my lips, but it forced its way out and I waved to everyone.

"And will team manager Myckal Chase come to the gym as well."

Joking around, people clapped for Myckal and encouraged her too. She collected her books and curtsied to the class. They laughed and hooted for her louder than me.

Grinning, I waited for Myckal to proceed past me up the aisle. I patted her on the shoulder and followed behind.

When she turned in her quiz, Ms. Maroney said, "Thank you. Pass my best wishes to all the wrestlers for me."

"I will." Myckal beamed and placed a lock of hair behind her ear.

When it was my turn, I tried handing my paper to Maroney. She didn't take it.

"Where do you think you're going?"

"To the gym. Didn't you hear the announcement?" I scratched my chin and frowned in confusion.

Wearing a crabby expression, she crossed her arms and refused to take my quiz. "I most certainly did. I heard them call for Ms. Chase and, as manager, she's excused to represent the school. I did not, however, hear your name. Now, take your seat, Mr. *Espuzito*."

My jaw dropped.

Porco piped up from the back row. "Ms. Maroney, they announced Luca and Myckal. Maybe you didn't hear it because we were all cheering for him."

Several others nodded or said things like, "Yeah, that's right."

"Did I ask for your assistance, Mr. Porco?" she barked.

Not wanting to earn his own detention, he placed his hands in the air and leaned back in his chair. The rest of the students instantly fell silent. I heard two noises, the red secondhand humming around the clock and my heart beating inside my chest.

Maroney remained perched on the ledge of her desk, one leg in front of the other.

The muscles in my neck twitched and my mouth went dry as a bone. I started to point at her, but Myckal elbowed her way between us. She placed her hand on my chest and pushed me hard, back toward my seat.

Initially, I didn't want to move, but she whispered through clenched teeth and forced me to step backward. "Don't you *dare* give her the satisfaction. She knows damn well they just called your name. There's only ten minutes left in class. The tournament doesn't start for an hour and a half. Now sit your butt in that chair, keep your mouth shut, and go down when the bell rings." She shoved me in the seat, and I slammed into it. "You can thank me later."

Myckal smiled at the rest of the class, then leaned past me to whisper to Porco. "Keep him under control. It's your job."

His big paws slapped the top of my shoulders and remained there, in case I tried anything stupid—like getting up.

Holding her head low, Myckal rushed out of the room.

"That's the first smart thing I've ever seen you do, Mr. *Espuzito*. I didn't realize Ms. Chase had such power over you." She roamed to the other side of the class. "Hand your quizzes to the front, please."

It took all the effort I possessed, not to answer her back.

Porco leaned forward and whispered, "Stay pissed, man. Save that rage for the wrestling mat."

Chapter 36

Warmups

My hands shook as I undid my lock, and a lonely clang echoed in the tiled, empty locker-room—blue for some reason. Every movement seemed difficult. My muscles felt like clumsy blocks of granite. I changed into my uniform, probably the one kid wrestling today in sneakers as opposed to proper shoes. I put on my sweatshirt and went into the gym to find Pablo, Kedell, and the rest of the guys from our team—I couldn't take being alone.

Things looked pretty bizarre out here. Three wrestling mats with scorer's tables in front of them took up most of the floor space.

Two side mats were rolled out for warmups. They were kept far apart so opposing wrestlers didn't have words before a match and get into a fight. One mat was in the back gym where we practiced every day. As host, John Marshall would use that one and the visitors would stretch on the mat by the front of the gymnasium.

That wasn't the bizarre part. Since the prom was tonight, and in this very room, the prom committee spent all last night decorating. A ton of green and white fabric netting hung far above our heads. It reached from one side of the basketball court to the other and cinched in the center of the ceiling. Hundreds of green and white helium balloons floated up there. They were also tied to every possible door handle. Two huge banners, in script lettering hung on opposite walls. *John Marshall Class of 1991* and *A Night to Remember...*

It had to be the fanciest wrestling championship ever.

As expected, Hector was ranked number one at one hundred and thirty-four pounds, and I was number two. Pablo had the number one ranking at one hundred and fifty-six.

Because of the wacky structure, two counties didn't send wrestlers at my weight class, so Hector and I each had a first-round bye. When the second-round started, I won my match 10 to 4. An impressive win at States. Since everyone was a county champion, the scoring tended to be on the low side. But Porco's advice worked. Using my anger and rage against Maroney helped rack up a lot of early points, and I hung on for the victory.

I won my next match 5 to 3, earning a trip to the finals. The two guys I beat were both excellent high-school wrestlers, but not quite college material. Maybe I was good enough to earn that scholarship.

My collision course with Hector looked unavoidable. I didn't check the standings to see how he did. I'd be pleasantly surprised if I didn't have to stare at his ugly mug later, but that seemed unlikely.

At three-thirty in the afternoon Pablo and I relaxed on the bleachers—lounging backward with our feet up. He pinned all of his opponents. The preliminary bouts were over, and the final matches had begun. Since we were under a crazy time crunch with the prom, all three mats kept going. Normally, we'd only use the center one for finals.

"It started snowing," Pablo said.

"What?"

"I can see through the gym doors. It's coming down pretty hard."

"Crap." I let out a long breath and came forward, leaning on my elbows.

"Why? What does it matter?" He furrowed his eyebrows.

"Did you notice Piper's not here? She was supposed to drive down last night but she had a test at one-fifty. I'm worried about her making it, for a lot of reasons."

"What gives?"

I finally told him about our fight and my fear that she might not even come. It felt good to get it off my chest. At the same time, the anxiety of the situation overwhelmed me—and I didn't think I could get any more nervous.

"Let's not worry about her," he said. "I know Piper pretty well, I'm sure she's on her way. Right now, you have more pressing things to focus on. I checked the board. Hector pinned both of his opponents in the first period."

"Excellent, just what I needed to hear. That he annihilated everybody. You didn't even pin everybody in the first period. Got any other good news?"

"It is, dummy. He probably hasn't broken a sweat yet. I'm sure he's cocky and thinks he's going to blow you away. Make him work harder than he ever has before. If you keep up a strenuous pace, and the score low, by the third period he'll be out of juice. Just make sure you have some left. That's when you make your move. Build up some points and take the lead. Remember, you're in better shape than him."

"What if you guys end up as teammates next year? Won't you feel guilty about helping him lose?" I joked.

"Cut it out. You know my loyalty's always been to you. I want you to win your championship more than I want to win mine."

We high-fived.

Coach Slaz approached. "Start warming up, Luca. You too, Pablo. Things are moving faster than we're used to."

High stepping to the bottom of the bleachers, I rubbed the back of my neck and grabbed my walkman. Ozzy was ready to go. He always helped get rid of my nerves. By the time the matches ahead of me were over, I'd hopefully be loose and fired up, with *Crazy Train* leading me onto the mat.

After pulling off my sweatshirt, there's always a second when I felt like a gladiator. I'd drift into la-la land and stand there in my singlet, believing I could do anything. Every twitching muscle was under my control. Then reality would hit, and the anxiety of life would torpedo its way into me—usually with some nausea. Why couldn't that zone of confidence last forever?

Watching Myckal squeeze and navigate her way through the crowd snapped me back to the real world. She had changed out of her jeans and into a white miniskirt. I made a show of looking her up and down. "There you are. And *very nice*," I teased.

The skirt had a black zipper in the back, a thin belt with rhinestones, and the hem split into a cute little leg slit. Her winter boots had been replaced with white ankle socks and sneakers. The wrestling sweatshirt gave way to a pale blue, zip up hoodie. Her legs looked really tan.

"What? Oh, this is nothing." She casually waved me

off. "Just wait until your match. We'll see if I can't get Hector's eyes to pop out of his head."

A tense chuckle escaped my chest, and I blew out a trembling, stress-filled breath. I couldn't believe this was Pablo's third championship. The pressure was paralyzing. Who would want to endure this more than once? The thrill of victory better be worth it. Glancing around the stands, I searched for Piper, hopeful, but doubting I'd see her.

"Thanks again for doing this for me." I held up my palm and high-fived Myckal. "All right. I'm going to head over to the home gy—" A sour taste invaded my mouth. "Where the hell does he think he's going?"

Across the way, Hector threw on his head gear and with his straps down to show off his giant muscles, he jogged toward the John Marshall back gym, where *I* was supposed to stretch. Naturally, he would violate that small etiquette and start his manipulations early. Before running through the doors, he peered in my direction and stuck out his tongue, doing his best Gene Simmons.

"I'm going to kick the crud out of him right now." I sneered and took a step.

Myckal grabbed my bicep. "Hold on. Let him go."

"Why?"

"When you told me he likes to play head games, I got an idea. I figured he might try to warmup in our space. Don't worry. I have this covered." A sneaky smile curled her lips and she waved to the other side of the gymnasium.

Basketball players and cheerleaders sat on the far bleachers. They had a five o'clock game at Ackerman and kicked back, waiting for their bus.

"It's a good thing you're still friends with your ex-girlfriend, Jodi," Myckal said. "She agreed to do you a big favor."

Jodi Griffin was the head cheerleader and she waved back at Myckal. Faith and Hope, the two girls who caught me buying condoms waved, too.

"I wouldn't exactly call her my ex. We dated for like a month in tenth grade. But what are you talking about?"

"I told Jodi what a big jerk Hector's been. You were probably too drunk to remember, but she was at The Couch that night—Faith and Hope, too."

"Fantastic. They all saw me make a fool of myself."

"Actually, it is fantastic. Before Hector hit on me, he was hitting on Jodi. She thought he was the crudest and most stuck-up idiot in the world. He made some vulgar comments about the twins, too."

"Sorry, not seeing the fantastic part," I said.

"Cheerleaders have to warmup before a game, too." Myckal pointed at them. "Earlier, I ran over and asked Jodi if they could do their stretching in the home gym. Right in front of Hector."

"You didn't?" I raised my eyebrows.

Biting her bottom lip, she nodded. "Ah-hah. Usually, they limber up at the school where they perform. But just for you—*and him*, they agreed to play some mind games of their own."

I couldn't believe that Myckal had arranged this. All the cheerleaders took off their varsity jackets. With Faith, Hope, and Jodi out front, they marched in a straight line toward the home team gym, their arms swinging in unison. They looked gorgeous in those tiny uniforms.

Pablo must have seen us talking and came over. "What are you two smiling about?"

"Check it out." I nodded in their direction. "Myckal convinced the cheerleaders to stretch in the back with Hector."

To see that far away, he tented his hand above his eyes. "Well, you don't want one of them pulling a hammy, now, do you?"

"Right. Safety first." I cocked my head to the side, agreeing with him.

"If there's enough time," she said. "They might practice a few routines back there, too."

Thanks to Myckal, our plan was falling into place, better than I'd ever hoped. Too bad I didn't have one of those curly mustaches, or I'd be twirling it. With the cheerleaders straining and bending in front of Hector, there's no way he'd stay focused on our match. "I'd hug you Myckal, but I'm sweaty and gross in this uniform at the moment."

She pushed me away, joking. "Eww, no thanks. Save it until you beat him."

"You got it." I smiled.

"And remember, I'm not done with him yet. Just wait until later."

Chapter 37

Championship

I stood on the center mat, Hector on one side and me on the other. My heart palpitated faster and harder than ever before. The referee, Father Roy, was busy at the scorer's table. He was my parish priest and officiated all the major tournaments in the area. Apparently, he won the national championship in India for his college. Definitely not someone to mess with.

Taking long deep breaths, I tried filling my blood with oxygen. If we didn't begin soon, I might pass out from the panic coursing through my veins. My whole future rested on the outcome of this match. So did Hector's. It meant a scholarship to Iowa for him and one to Northwestern for me. No matter what, I'd wrestle like my life depended on it. Slaz towered behind me, massaging my shoulders and arms.

"Coach, I can't wait any longer." I strapped on my head gear. "I'm going to go prowl inside the starting circle."

He looked at me cross-eyed. "Why would you do that?"

"When I wrestled Hector at camp, Pablo told me to immediately shoot at his legs. He was waiting for it and took me down, no problem."

"That was dumb advice."

"I know. I hate Pablo. You should bench him. Anyway, I want Hector to think I'm so psyched up I'm going to try it again. But I'll fake him out this time."

"Fine. Esposito. There's nothing left to say. You can beat this guy. Mind what you have learned. Save you it can."

My body tingled with adrenaline. "Thanks, *Coach*." I ran to the circle and jumped up and down several times, like I couldn't wait to attack. When I peeked over, Hector grinned at me.

What was the holdup at the scorer's table? I glimpsed that way and Myckal winked. She took off her sneakers and socks, reached into her gym bag, and removed the sexiest pair of stilettos I'd ever seen. After strapping them on, she got to her feet, adjusted her mini-skirt, and sauntered over to the Butt Hill manager.

Following a few seconds of debate, Myckal exclaimed, "I have a different wrestler at one hundred and thirty-four pounds."

"I'm telling you, that's Hector Wolfe. He's up now." The Butt Hill manager pointed at their side.

"Nope." Myckal shook her head, her raven hair flowing. "I have someone else at this weight class. We'd better check with your coach."

Father Roy and their manager tried to say something, but Myckal ignored them. With a clipboard in hand, she strolled like a runway model across the mat.

"What can I help you with?" Hector's coach asked her.

"Sorry to bother you, sir." She tapped on the scoresheet. "But is this Timmy Bohn? It says he's wrestling for you at one hundred and thirty-four pounds."

270

"Go get 'em Luca! You can do it man!" The basketball players and cheerleaders encouraged me on their way to the bus. I watched Hector's gaze. Despite the intensity of the moment, he couldn't look away from those short playful skirts.

A smile curled my lips, Myckal's too.

With a gruff voice the coach said, "No, you've got it backward. This is Hector Wolfe and Timmy Bohn is my heavyweight. I'm sure my team manager told you that. Now can we please get on with things?"

"Sorry, my mistake," she replied, her voice as sweet as syrup. She turned to leave, but not before waving each of her fingers. "Good luck, Hector."

"Wait a minute, young lady. You knew this was Hector Wolfe all along?"

"Oops." She shrugged.

That put a scowl on the coach's face, and he raised his voice. "One other thing. Your shoes are not appropriate for a wrestling mat. Those sharp heels could slice a hole right through it."

"No problem." She glanced at Hector then to her stilettos. Her blue eyes sparkled like stars. Reaching down like an actress in a steamy movie, she bent at the waist and leisurely undid her straps. After stepping out of each one, she dangled them over the back of her shoulder. With a seductive sway, Myckal strutted her way to the scorer's table. Hector zeroed in on her legs, tilting his head for a better view.

"Concentrate, Wolfe." The coach smacked the back of his skull. "You've got a championship to win."

"Lay off, Coach. This guy's no problem." Hector glared at me, then bounced in place.

To keep from cracking up, I turned away from them

271

and gave her a thumb's up.

"There's more," she mouthed.

Father Roy waved for Hector to join me in the middle of the mat. He wore his priest's collar at the top of his referee's uniform.

"Shake, gentleman."

As if sensing a dramatic moment had arrived, the crowd noise kicked into a higher gear. This was bigger than a state championship. Hector squeezed my hand, leaned in, and whispered in my ear. "You're about to be a four-time loser."

Earlier, I decided to laugh at his trash-talking and snorted a chuckle.

The whistle blew. Throwing my arms forward and ducking my head, I bluffed shooting at his knees. He pancaked down, thinking he trapped me. I moved forward, but he was back on his feet quicker than a mongoose.

Instead of going for his legs, I smacked him in his ear pad. His hand flew to it, and I could tell by his expression, it was as loud and nerve-wracking as my florist claimed. But he recovered so fast, I couldn't do anything with it.

For the rest of the first period, we grappled standing up. It was excruciating and neither of us gave an inch. With thirty seconds left, Hector tore through my defenses and took me down, earning two points. I immediately stood and broke out of his grip for an escape, receiving one point. The buzzer sounded.

The score was 2 to 1 in his favor. I began the second period in the down position. I refused to look at Myckal. The whistle tweeted. I faked going for a reversal, Hector reacted, and I stood up, pulling away from him. Another escape—2 to 2 now. He was the strongest guy I ever wrestled. A couple times he almost ripped my shoulder out of its socket.

Up close, his angry white eyes contained little black dots like BB's—red streaks too. No one else scored before time ran out. The scoreboard buzzed. Period two was over.

I tried to catch my breath, panting super hard. Every inch of my body throbbed with pain and fatigue, as if my muscles were about to tear away from my bones. This was the toughest match of my life. I ran dangerously low on stamina. If Pablo was right and I was in better shape, Hector had to be totally spent. His face was flushed, and he dropped to his knees, looking ready to puke.

I'd start the third period in the up position, and doubted I had the strength to keep him from escaping and taking the lead. Father Roy motioned at Hector to get into place. Instead, he ignored the instruction, and stood up. Then he bent over, his hands on his knees, laboring to breathe.

Father Roy had to toot his whistle to get him moving. "Let's go. You're down."

Circling behind me, Hector stalled and scrounged for energy. "It's not going to work, wuss bag," he whispered into my ear pad, gulping for air. "There's no way you can stop me. One more point and I win. Again." He bumped into me, then got on all fours, with his head down. It sounded like he was gagging.

"You, okay?" Father Roy asked him.

Hector struggled through a few coughs and finally nodded, raising his head.

I stood off to the side, my hands on my hips. Out of the corner of my eye, Myckal slowly unzipped her hoodie, directly in Hector's line of sight. She arched her back, bit her bottom lip, and accentuated each movement of her shoulders, twisting and turning to remove her jacket. When it came off, she held it by two fingers, then let it drop to the floor. She had a low cut, white tank top underneath. It showed off her tan and toned arms.

I checked on Hector. He was spellbound, almost hypnotized by her. She angled her body to the side. In slow motion she leaned forward and let her deep red fingernails dance on her calf. She tickled it, then sat straight up. One leg, suggestively, crossed the other, exposing more of her amazing thighs. When the top leg started to bounce, his jaw had dropped and his eyes bulged.

This was my chance. My breathing grew rapid and shallow. Blazing with anger and frustration, I hustled into place. The whistle blew. I counted on Hector staring dreamily at her, and not reacting.

Half a second at most, that's all I'd have. My hand zoomed behind my back, winding and coiling up. With all my might, I whipped it around and caught him flush on the jaw with the bottom fleshy part of my thumb and kept driving forward until my bicep crushed the side of his head.

He collapsed onto his stomach. Not wasting an instant, I threw a half nelson on him and flipped him on his back. The whistle blew again. I expected Father Roy to smack the mat, indicating a pin. Instead, he awarded me two points for a near fall, meaning an almost pin. He signaled to the Butt Hill coach and called an injury time out. Hector was barely conscious.

"Get over here, Esposito," Slaz yelled.

Hector sat up looking dazed and confused. Their

assistant coach put smelling salts under his nose. He grimaced, but hardly stirred.

Their head coach screamed at Father Roy. "That was a dangerous cross face. Didn't you see the way he hit him? He wound up to kingdom come."

Two thwacking sounds advanced the scoreboard—4 to 2. I had captured the lead.

"What's he yelling about, Coach?" I asked, catching my breath. I had never been part of an injury timeout before and didn't know the rules.

"That was one heck of a blow you dished out." Slaz had a sly grin on his face. "Anything you want to tell me?"

I shrugged.

"That's what I thought. Keep an eye on the scoreboard timer. Hector gets one and half minutes for an injury time out. If you *had* thrown an illegal move, he'd have another two minutes to recover. But the ref didn't see an illegal move, so Hector doesn't get it."

"Here you go, Luca." Myckal handed me a jug of water.

"Thanks." With extreme caution, I looked into her eyes *only*. I didn't dare check out what she was wearing. I wanted to quench my thirst and chug it, but drinking too much would risk a cramp, so I took a small sip.

At a painfully slow pace, the clock ticked away. "What happens when it gets to zero?" I choked out. It was difficult forming complete sentences.

Their head coach kept arguing.

"Don't worry about the referee. If he hasn't changed the score by now, or tossed you out for throwing a punch, he isn't going to. As for Hector, if he can't continue, then you win automatically."

My face must have lit up, because Slaz admonished me. "Let's not get excited. Hector's starting to wake up… Hold on now, the doctor's checking on him."

"Why does that matter?"

"If he thinks Hector has a head injury, he can grant him five more minutes to rest. Since that's where they're concentrating, I'd say it's a safe bet. You're up by two points. When you get back out there, do whatever you can to keep him from scoring. Even if he escapes, the score will be four to three in your favor. If he doesn't take you down, you'll be state champion. Think you can do it?"

"Yes, sir." Chills flowed through me, and goosebumps broke out everywhere. I was never so excited to get back on the mat.

He patted the side of my face.

This could still backfire. If Hector took the five minutes, he'd regain his full strength. I would have squandered all that effort tiring him out. So much for Pablo's theory.

The scoreboard buzzed—Hector's minute and a half was up. The doctor shook his head.

A short whistle tweeted, and Father Roy waved his arms in the air. "He looks concussed. It's over. I'm not letting him continue."

Jumping up and down, Hector screeched and protested. "No frigging way! I can beat this guy! He's nothing! There's no way I'm losing to him!"

To his coach's credit, he wrapped Hector in his arms and told him it wasn't worth a brain injury.

"You won, Esposito!" Slaz yelled.

I couldn't believe it. All the hard work and worry had come to a wonderful end. I hugged Slaz harder than anyone, with moisture flooding my eyes. When we stopped, Myckal was right next to me. Gross and sweaty or not, I threw an arm around her, and the three of us embraced on the side of the mat.

Actual tears and gasps poured out of our group. Father Roy blew the whistle. A match wasn't officially over until both wrestlers met in the center. The ref holds each of our wrists, and after a second, he raises the arm of the winner.

It sucked for the loser but was supposed to foster a sense of fair play and sportsmanship. I was beaming and so happy, grinning ear to ear. I hopped and skipped out there. An ugly expression darkened Hector's face.

Father Roy hoisted my arm. Nothing had ever felt so good. As soon as it came down, I looked at Hector and went hurtling through the air. He had been clenching his other fist and slugged me with a perfect right hook. My feet flailed toward the sky, and I flopped backward, landing hard on my back. Myckal ran onto the mat to check on me. My face instantly swelled, already in a lot of pain.

Father Roy's whistle blew in long angry bursts. "You're disqualified! You're disqualified!"

Hector's coaches charged to the center and pulled him away.

"You suck, *Espuzito*! I'LL KILL YOU FOR THIS!"

I got up laughing, then cupped my hands over my mouth. "Losing by injury is one thing. Good luck explaining to Iowa that you were disqualified for fighting!" Sprinting off the mat, I grinned. I'd never been punched so hard in my life. I knew I had a blackeye. But I *loved it.*

Chapter 38

Getting Ready

Pablo's parents had a huge, white, colonial style house. His bedroom was downstairs, next to the playroom. A few new posters were tacked to his brown paneling—Michael Jordan, Rambo, a Ferrari, and some hot blonde in a bikini. I didn't recognize the girl, but *very nice*, I'd have to find out where he got her.

I arrived late because of the tournament, so everyone else was already here. Last year I spent some time alone in this room, getting dressed for the prom and contemplating the day's events. This year too. Which day was crazier? I couldn't answer that question until after midnight. We still had a long way to go.

For Piper's prom, I spent the first half of the morning chasing her around school, trying to convince her to go with me. She kept saying no. It became so bad I pulled the ultimate promposal, getting down on one knee, and begging her in the middle of a crowded hallway.

That was only the beginning. We had to drain my bank account, buy a dress, rent a tux, get her hair done, find flowers at the last minute, and end up here for pictures. We still had the most insane prom and battle with the football team ahead of us, not to mention Bryce's stunt with the eggs. It was exhausting just thinking about it.

What about today? Could I have won without Myckal's help? I wasn't sure. She played her part beautifully—and literally. Her trick with the cheerleaders was pure genius and she definitely distracted Hector on the mat. She gave me the edge I needed at the perfect moment.

When he punched me in the face, that was the cherry on top. Despite keeping my cheek iced, it stung and everything around my eye had turned purple. It's the same blackeye he gave me at The Couch, so it swelled and reverted to its former size awfully quick.

I adjusted my bowtie in the mirror and relaxed my smile. Draping the championship medal around my neck, I lifted my chin, puffed out my chest, and exhaled a gratifying sigh. It looked sharp over my tux. Even flashed myself a thumbs up.

Still tingling with excitement, the chills of winning hadn't washed away yet. Pablo's last two state championship medals hung on his dresser. They were the same style as this one—a red, white, and blue ribbon with a gold medallion at the bottom and the carved outline of New York State. Only the date differed. Mine said 1991, even though today was December 14, 1990.

This would have been the best day of my life, except for one big thing. I still had no idea where Piper was. *She's going to show. She's going to show.* I kept muttering it to myself, trying to believe in positive thinking.

Pablo had a phone in his room. I sat on the bed and dialed her number. To my utter surprise someone picked up.

"Hello."

"Robyn, is that you?" My heart thumped in my chest. All my other calls went unanswered. I really didn't expect to reach anyone.

"Hi, Luca." She sounded reserved.

"I can't believe I got ahold of you. Do you know how many times I've left messages? Of course, you do. You probably listened to half of them." I spoke way too fast but was so excited. Then something hit me. "Wait a minute. I don't think I ever heard you call me Luca before. What's going on? Do you know where Piper is?" Fear lifted the hairs on my arms and neck.

"Sorry, I don't. She's been so depressed and torn up over your fight. I haven't seen her since this morning."

"You have no idea where she could be?" All the self-doubt I ever possessed stampeded over my body. My rib cage felt like an elephant stepped on top of it, and the heaviness spread to all my limbs.

"She was supposed to borrow her friend Jill's car for the weekend and drive down. I don't even know if she picked it up. If I knew Jill's phone number, I'd call her for you."

Piper couldn't be punishing me over our last fight, could she? Not with the prom on the line. She told me she'd be here. But what if she chose Clive over me? That'd be the worst thing ever.

Closing my eyes, I asked the big question. "Is she still coming to the prom?"

"I honestly don't know. When she woke up today, I'm not sure *she* knew. She wants to, she loves you so much, but she's been so confused lately. When the phone rang, I was hoping it was Piper telling me she arrived there safely."

"I can't believe this is happening." My neck bent

forward, and my forehead rested in my hand. My throat and eyes both hurt, like when I was a kid and used to cry. But there was no way I was doing that.

"It started snowing this morning," Robyn said. "I'm worried. Did you try her parent's house, or page her? Her original plan was to go there, get dressed, and meet you at Pablo's by seven."

"I did both. There's no answer and she hasn't called. It's snowing here, too."

She tried sounding upbeat. "Do me a favor. Have her call me if she—I mean when she gets there. Let her know I'm pissed. She's got us all worried because she didn't write a note or tell anyone when she was leaving."

My breath sputtered out. "Okay, I will. And thanks, Robyn."

"I almost forgot. How did you do in States?"

"I won." I felt a little embarrassed, didn't know why.

"Congratulations. Now that you can go anywhere you want, does that mean you're not coming to Albany next year?" she teased.

"I don't know about being able to go anywhere, but Albany looks like a long shot."

"I guess so. And, Luca."

"Yeah?"

"I really hope you enjoy your prom. You're a great guy. You deserve a special night."

"I appreciate you saying that."

"No problem, Jailbait."

As I hung up, the door opened, and Pablo entered with a huge smile. "Who was that?"

"Robyn."

"What did hot Robyn have to say?"

"Super-hot Robyn has no idea where Piper is."

He shrugged. "Okay, so nothing's changed. We're still operating under the assumption that she's on her way. Worst case, she shows up after the limo, and my parents tell her to meet us at the school."

"You're right. She's probably just caught in traffic. If I remember correctly, she knows how to get to John Marshall."

He slapped me on the back. "Excellent. You ready to get started? Everyone's waiting, including their parents. How about we go take some pictures?"

The sounds of whooping, laughing, and yelling came from the living room. A rush of adrenaline woke me out of my stupor, and I drew a mental line in the sand. I wasn't going to sit around and act depressed until I knew for certain there was something to be bummed about.

When we walked upstairs, every guy had a black tuxedo. Last year there was a mix of black, white, and gray. The girls looked amazing, way better than us.

I grabbed my boutonniere from the fridge, but left Piper's corsage inside. No need taking it out.

"Do you want some help with that?" Myckal had approached without a sound. She wore a dark-green velvet dress, strapless, with ruffles, and knee length. I ran a finger along the line of my shirt collar and pulled it out a touch. It suddenly got warmer in here.

"Yeah, thanks. I like your corsage. The red roses are pretty, but you should have made Porco spring for the expensive orchid."

"Right? I think that was the least he could do, considering I saved him from being dateless." With a few quick strokes, she fastened the orchid to my lapel.

The other girls had their hair up, but Myckal's curls

cascaded on her bare shoulders.

"You look really beautiful. But what's that green thing around your neck?"

"Boys are so clueless. I don't know why we put up with you. It's called a choker and that's my grandmother's broach in the middle."

I shifted from one foot to the other, trying my best to remain still. I scanned the room, no one was watching us, but it felt like they were. My stomach fluttered a little. I chalked it up to winning at States and being nervous about Piper.

"Well, between that choker and your dress, all I can say is—wow!"

It seemed like she skipped a breath after my compliment. "Thanks. You look great too. Piper's a lucky girl, even if she doesn't realize it."

My mouth opened, but nothing came out. A hot prickling feeling traveled down my spine and made my back itch.

"How about we take a few pictures of our two state champions?" Pablo's father said. An expensive camera hung around Mr. Salinas' neck. Pablo's parents were rich, and his father's hobby was photography. The other parents stood behind him. Mine didn't show, but they never came to things like this, they did even come to the championship. By now, I didn't expect them to—it didn't bother me.

A large bookcase adorned a whole wall of their living room. That's where he wanted us to pose. Last year, we set up in front of Mrs. Salinas' flower garden, but that was during May, and the sun hadn't set yet.

"Then they can take off those stupid medals and we can finally par-tay," Porco emphasized. Everyone else cheered.

Pablo and I stood side by side smiling for a couple shots, then we draped our arms over each other's shoulders.

With an elegant accent, Mrs. Salinas asked, "Luca, didn't you have a blackeye at last year's prom, too?"

"Yeah. Figured I might as well get one again. That way nobody can tell the difference between prom photos."

She shook her head and gave me a wry grin.

Mr. Salinas lowered his camera and kept his focus on us. He had a glorious mustache. "Very good, now let's have their dates join them. Stacey, you go in front of Pablo, and Piper, you stand in front of Luca, but each girl should be a little off centered."

My eyes flashed around the room—desperately hoping to find her. Had she snuck in without me knowing? The answer came quick—no. He must not have realized she wasn't here. As fast as my heart rate shot up, it painfully thumped back to normal.

Like a stunning ballerina, Stacey glided over, all smiles. She wore a dark blue dress. The top resembled a cami with inch wide shoulder straps, and it cinched at her waist. The bottom half was kind of like mesh, and it went just below her knees. She had lacey gloves on, too. If the voters could see her now, she'd win prom queen in a landslide. Glad I already voted for her.

After she got into place, a few awkward seconds passed. Everyone stared and then averted their gazes, embarrassed for me. My face started to flush. Finally, Myckal came to my rescue.

"Why don't I take Piper's spot? Until she gets here." She used a lighthearted tone of voice and stepped into position.

"Perfect," Mr. Salinas said. "Everyone face my way, and guys, place one hand on the small of your date's back."

Touching a girl in one of these fancy dresses was absolutely incredible. Myckal's velvet dress curved to her body, and she gave off a buzz that was impossible to resist. Her breathing deepened when my hand fell on her hip then curled halfway around her ribs. I was tempted to walk my fingers higher and tickle her. If it was Piper, I would have.

My muscles froze as she took half a step back, pressing into me. Our bodies touched. My knees brushed her dress and maybe her legs—rocketing my pulse rate. My non-existent poker face may have brightened, because Cheryl and Nicole's eyes both widened, possibly realizing this was an intimate moment in danger of going too far.

Nicole piped up first. "Cheryl, let's jump in there with our two favorite champs. Stacey and Myckal can't hog them all to themselves."

Cheryl bit her bottom lip. "My thoughts exactly. Our handsome big shots are off to Iowa and Northwestern. Who knows when they'll grace us with their presence again?"

"Yeah, right," I said.

After we looped our arms around the girls, Mr. Salinas snapped a couple pictures, then we took some with the other guys. We removed our medals and for the next forty-five minutes, everyone else posed with their dates for typical prom photos.

I snuck away and plopped down at the kitchen table, sitting limply and feeling lonely. No one seemed to notice my absence.

"How about one out in the snow?" Mr. Salinas suggested.

Mrs. Salinas countered. "No, the girls will ruin their hair."

"Yeah, one quick one," Pablo demanded. "We'll run in front of the Christmas trees and then we'll dart back in before anyone gets wet."

"Let's go for it," Nicole agreed.

Worried, panicky expressions spread over the other girl's faces. But when people followed Mr. Salinas downstairs, they gripped their arms through each other's elbows and trailed behind.

The outdoor light was on in the side yard. Snowflakes lazily dropped on us, and laughter soon broke out. Tons of Christmas lights decorated their trees and shrubs. A beautiful Manger Scene lit up an area in front of an evergreen bush. Santa's sleigh and nine reindeer were perched on the roof, about to take flight. We got into place and that was the final shot of the evening.

The girls hustled back inside taking tiny steps—a couple of them slipped in their sexy shoes. Luckily, no one went down. We threw snowballs at each other.

"Limo's here," Jimmy yelled. "Time to go."

I dashed upstairs to the front window and my heart sank further. No Piper in sight.

Chapter 39

Prom

The limo ride to the prom rocked, but there wasn't enough room for everyone inside. Maybe we didn't plan this correctly. Two girls took the backseat and three went on the left side. The right side had a long, illuminated bar with crystal glasses. Sadly, nobody stocked it.

The guys had to sit on the floor. They obviously vacuumed it beforehand, and I didn't mind huddling down here one bit. Being surrounded by so many gorgeous pairs of legs felt like a dream come true.

"Who wants champagne?" Stacey held out a bottle. Somehow, she snuck it in, although where she hid it, I could only imagine.

The privacy window kept us safe from the driver. *I Still Haven't Found What I'm Looking For* by U2, played on the radio.

"Oh, absolutely, let me have that." Pablo elbowed me out of the way and reached over my back.

Good thing I was flexible. The way he crushed me, I could've lost a liver. He had a difficult time tearing off the foil and undoing the wire.

"Do you know what you're doing?" Jimmy asked.

A second later the cork ricocheted off the back window and caught Garret on the forehead. A little champagne spilled down my back.

"Awesome."

"Excellent."

"Woo hoo."

"That's cold," I called.

Garret's hand went to his head. "That friggin' hurt."
Everybody laughed.

"Let me see that thing." Porco took ahold of Garret's
forehead. "Oh, ho. It's welting up already. Lucky it
didn't catch your eye."

Garret punched Pablo in the arm. "You're lucky,
jackass. I would've killed you if it did. Here, give me the
bottle."

Pablo pulled it away. "Sorry, about your melon,
man. But since Stacey brought the champagne, she gets
the honor. Here's to the Class of 1991 and the most
excellent prom ever!"

Cheering and applause broke out. Stacey took the
first drink. It must have bubbled up on her because a tiny
bit flowed out of her puffed out cheeks. Smiling and
wiping it off her chin, she handed it to Nicole. The girls
passed it around themselves then gave it to Garret.

When it got to Porco he made another toast. "Here's
to Pablo and Luca. Our two state champions!"

More clapping and hurrays.

By the time the champagne made its way to me,
there was maybe an eighth of a bottle left. "Yeah baby!"
I chugged the rest of it.

"You okay way down there on the floor, Porco?"
Myckal asked.

He tickled her ankle and his fingers slid to the
bottom of her calf. "Are you kidding? All these smoking
hot girls in amazing dresses, right in front of me. Do you
know how many dreams I've had like this?"

Guess I wasn't the only one. She leaned forward and smacked him on his back, first with her right hand, then with her left. He cowered and we all chuckled.

About ten minutes later we pulled into the school parking lot. A row of limousines idled in front of the gym entrance, letting kids out. John Marshall had the typical high school spoke and wheel architecture. The main office inhabited the center and several hallways shot off like spokes. The gym and cafeteria were at the same end.

When it was our turn, the driver opened the door and held up an umbrella. The guys crawled out first and waited for their dates to emerge. Since I was alone, I should have just run in. For some reason I lingered as snow covered my hair and shoulders. The girls had their hands through the guys' arms, probably to keep their balance as much as the affectionate embrace. Everyone walked at a slight angle, like hunchbacks trying to keep the snow off their bare shoulders, and tuxes. Nobody wanted to cover up their formal attire with a bulky winter coat.

Scanning the parking lot, there was still no sign of Piper. My heart sunk some more.

"Luca, you coming?" Pablo yelled from the school door.

Stacey ducked into the building. They were the last two to go in. I felt zero urgency to get out of the snow. The back of my ears burned a little from the chill and my legs weighed as heavy as telephone poles. Hands in my pockets, I shrugged and trudged with slow, sluggish steps. My ankles burned from the cold.

When I got there, Pablo threw his arm around my shoulder. "You good man? You ready to party?"

He wiped the snowflakes off my tux, and I knocked

some out of my hair. For the first time it really hit me, next year he'd be at one school, and I'd be at another. He was most likely Iowa bound, no matter what happened with me. In that split second, a hint of sadness dabbed his eyes, like it occurred to him, too.

Once inside, the heat raised my spirits and I refused to mope around until Piper showed up. I wouldn't focus on waning friendships, either. There'd be plenty of time for that after the prom. "Let's do it dude! Let's make it a night to remember!"

"You got it baby," he agreed. We high-fived and paraded under a green and white balloon archway.

"I think you were supposed to do that with Stacey. It's more tender that way."

In one quick breath, he pinched my butt and planted a big kiss on my cheek. "But you know I love you the most."

"Get the hell away from me." I pushed him off, laughing.

Stacey came over. "Hey, that's my date. What are you trying to do, Luca, make me jealous?"

"You know what, Stacey. You can have him and don't feel the need to ever return him."

After he winked at me, Pablo bowed to Stacey, she curtsied, and he held out his hand for her. When she offered it to him, he kissed it, they interlocked fingers, and he led her to the back side of the archway. She placed her hand through his arm, and they entered together—a king and queen arriving at their kingdom. Who knew? By the night's end, they probably would be. They glowed like a coronation was on its way.

You'd never know they held a wrestling tournament here a few hours ago. Everything looked so different and beautiful. On the ceiling, glittering strings of lights branched off in all directions, some going into the cafeteria and others into the gym. Green and white balloons floated everywhere with tons of streamers hanging down, too. A white gazebo with ivy vines stood in the right corner of the lobby. The prom committee hired a professional photographer. Our group lined up to take pictures in it. Kids ran over and snapped a few with their disposable cameras.

Since I had no one to pose with, I checked out the cafeteria. They set up a bunch of high, round tables covered in white tablecloths. I headed for the serving stations, fixed a small plate of stuffed mushrooms and meatballs, and snagged a can of soda.

Right away, a million people asked where Piper was. *I wish I knew*, I wanted to say. Instead, I claimed, "She's on her way. Just running late because of the storm. She'll be here any minute."

Fifteen minutes later, I walked back out. My group had just finished at the gazebo.

"Where'd you get those?" Myckal snatched half a mushroom off my dish. She placed it in her mouth with exaggerated movements. Her fingers lightly graced the area around her lips, then she dotted the tip of her tongue.

In the past, a move like that would have sent my spine tingling. But at my uncle's wedding, Piper had explained the finer points to me. "As provocative as it may appear, Luca, we're not being flirtatious or trying to turn you on. We just don't want to ruin our lipstick. Not everything is about you boys."

"That's what she said," I had replied at the time, earning a playful punch in the stomach.

With a dripping meatball in my soda hand, I pointed

toward the cafeteria. "The appetizers are in there. It's set up pretty cool. But let's head into the gym and grab a table before all the good ones are gone."

"Agreed," Porco said. He and Myckal led the way.

The big bright lights were off—never been in here without them. There were strings of white lights, the disco ball, and flickering candles used as centerpieces. If Piper were here, I'd be thinking about magic and romance.

Round tables were arranged to form three sides of a square, creating a large dance floor in the middle. The DJ set up her booth at the end of it, and a decorated Christmas tree stood behind her. If I remembered right, she was the same pretty Black girl that DJed last year.

Waiters and waitresses scurried about, bringing dinners to students already at their seats. The tablecloths alternated by color—green then white.

"How about here?" Porco pointed at a table one row back from the dance floor.

"Looks good," Pablo said.

We all grabbed a chair. The girls set their purses in front of them. One lonely seat remained empty, right next to me.

A waiter swung by and took our orders. We had a choice of chicken, prime rib, or vegetarian.

"I'll take two prime ribs," I said.

The waiter glanced at the open chair. "Two, sir?"

"Yeah, my date's on her way."

"We're not supposed to bring entrees out until the person's arrived. We're using the cafeteria to keep everything warm. Would you like me to hold it in the back for her?"

Friggin' A. Even the waiter wanted to know where

Piper was. If I had to come clean with someone, might as well be him. *Against All Odds* by Phil Collins played from the speakers.

I asked the waiter, "Tell me buddy, have you ever focused on these lyrics before?" Then I mouthed the words, *You comin' back to me is against the odds*.

"What's that?" he asked.

I slapped the empty chair. "Take a seat for a minute. Listen to this next part with me."

His face scrunched. "You know we're really busy, right?"

"Two minutes won't kill you. I can't talk to these numb nuts about my problems. They're having too good of a time. I don't want to bring them down."

"Sir, have you been drinking?"

"Come on. What have you got to lose?"

Scanning the surrounding area, probably for his supervisor, he shrugged and sat next to me. "Just my job."

"Good man. That's the spirit." I patted him on the back.

Pointing in the air, I made believe we could see the words and started singing the painful lyrics.

The DJ had the music cranked so loud, I had to raise my voice for him to hear me talk. "Between you and me. I'm not sure Piper's coming. I'm hoping she is, but we got into a big fight the other day and never officially made up. I still love her, and it'll kill me if she doesn't show. How long do you think I should wait for her?"

The rest of the table glared at us, but they couldn't hear what we were saying.

"Hold on man, here it comes." This time the waiter pointed in the air. He bit the nail on his index finger and wore a pained stare. "This is my favorite part."

He sung with a deep, beautiful voice, like an opera singer—a hundred times better than mine. He placed his arm over my shoulder, and we swayed to the music, both of us joining in. For a moment in time, it was just me and the waiter—alone in the universe.

With tears in his eyes, he stood and poked me in the chest. "You know what, man? I'm going to get you those two prime ribs. A couple cheesecakes, too. And no matter what happens, brother, don't ever give up on love!"

I shook my fist in encouragement. My friends looked at me with disbelieving expressions—raised eyebrows, slack mouths, and wide eyes.

"What the heck was that?" Pablo asked.

I cocked my head to the side. "What do you mean?"

Chapter 40

Last Dance

Shout by The Isley Brothers came on. Our whole table flew to the dance floor and boogied to it—jumping, sweating, and high fiving our tails off. It was the most fun I had all night.

When it ended, red, green, and yellow strobe lights transformed the atmosphere from fun to romantic and the DJ put on a gooey love song. Everyone paired up with their dates. I was the only idiot without someone to slow dance with, so I moped back to the table.

"Hey, Luca. Want a sip?" Steve Platis bumped into me and forked over a metal flask.

Glancing in all directions, I didn't see a chaperone. I took a seat, figuring I'd blend in better, and brought it to my lips. The hot taste of tequila burned down my throat.

"Thanks, man." I snuck it back to him.

"Plenty more where that came from." He raised his eyebrows, took a swig, and slipped the flask into his breast pocket.

"Hey, Sandy looks hot. You two coming to Jimmy's party?" I asked.

He flashed me a thumbs up. "You know it." He left in the direction of the punchbowl.

A group of girls passed behind me, their heels

clicking toward the restroom. I checked my watch, 11:15. Forty-five minutes left.

Being the only single person with a bunch of couples officially sucked. Even with such little time remaining, I didn't dare ask the obvious question. Had I been stood up at my prom? That was one for the books. Not many people held the honor. Plus, I'd get destroyed for it on Monday—probably never live it down.

Staring at the dance floor was far too depressing. I had to get out of there and took off for the exit. Mrs. Wild stood beneath one of the baskets. She had a fancy gold dress on. Never saw her in anything like it.

"Luca, congratulations on winning today." She surprised me by leaning forward and hugging me. "I'm so proud of you. Come see me on Monday. We'll make an appointment with Coach Slazne to talk about Northwestern."

"Thanks, I will."

Chills about my victory flowed down my spine and momentarily made me forget about Piper. Then I wandered into the lobby and all the pain, anger, and self-doubt slammed back. I decided to venture outside on the steps and hang my head in defeat.

Two smokers swung the door open, coming in from the icy cold. A nasty, stinging draft rushed by. I couldn't imagine what it did to bare shoulders. Every girl in the vicinity rubbed their arms and shot them dirty looks.

Tons of balloons hovered near the exit. Each time the door opened it must have created a vacuum, sucking them out of the gym. With the photographer long gone, the gazebo looked lonely in the corner. Since I couldn't deal with the freezing snowy steps, I decided to sulk in there.

We Are Family by Sister Sledge sounded muffled this far from the speakers. After a while, I lost track of time.

"Want some company?" Myckal asked. Where had she come from?

Scooting to the side, I patted the bench. "Sure. But won't Porco be missing you?"

With her arms crossed, she sat next to me, barely leaving a centimeter between us. "I can't take another fast song right now. He is by far the most embarrassing and horrible dancer in John Marshall's history. Why do you guys even let him go to school here?"

"He's really big and can kick everyone's ass?" I took my jacket off and draped it over her shoulders.

Sliding her hands through the sleeves, she nodded. "Thanks. And I guess that's a good reason. So, is there anything exciting going on in the prom gazebo?"

"Actually, about five minutes ago Jennifer Muraven started screaming her head off. She found her date in the nurse's office, making out with his ex-girlfriend."

"Really? Maybe we should get Porco to kick his ass for her."

I chuckled. "Maybe we should."

About thirty seconds of awkward silence passed between us.

"I still can't believe we had States earlier today," she said.

"*I* still can't believe what *you* did for me earlier today," I said.

Scrunching her nose, she spoke with a soft tone. "Me? I didn't do that much."

"Are you kidding? The stunt with the cheerleaders was totally brilliant. And the way you grooved at the scorer's table—you made Hector lose his mind. If I wasn't in on the planning, you would have turned me into a puddle. Right before the third period, I was so exhausted, I thought he had me. I don't know if I could've done it without you. I'm going to owe you forever."

A "Hmm," escaped her throat, and she squirmed a little in her seat. A grin briefly appeared, but she tried to conceal it. "I'm glad you won today, but it wouldn't have mattered if you lost. Even though you've been focusing on the championship for months, I hope you know, you're so much more than just a wrestler."

Blinking really fast, I tried to process what she just said. No one ever expressed that to me before. Piper's been encouraging and positive about my chances, but she never told me my world be okay if I lost. Everything's been about getting that scholarship.

When my blinking stopped, we made eye contact and locked onto each other for a few seconds too long. Geez, she had great eyes. Then she looked away and changed the subject. "Well, I don't know how they did it, but this place doesn't stink like a musty wrestling mat anymore."

Since she seemed a little uncomfortable, I moved on, too. "I think it smells like a normal hallway, only magnified. But you have to compensate for the prom and do a little math. Multiply all the cologne and perfume by ten, then subtract out the acne cream."

"Everything smells better when you win." She giggled and ran a hand through her thick hair, then gave my knee a quick squeeze. "Why are you out here all alone, and not inside with us?"

Exhaling a deep long breath, I shrugged. "Just

coming to grips with being dumped." My voice cracked and my eyes moistened. They stung like I had been swimming at the shore.

She took my hand. It felt great, like at The Couch. I wanted to interlace my fingers in hers, but I held back. "I'm so sorry, Luca. I don't know anything about Piper, but you deserve better than this. I heard the story about last year. How you made sure she had such a great prom. This is a horrible way to repay you."

Struggling to respond, I opened my mouth, but nothing came out. On my second attempt, I at least found the strength to clear my throat. "Thanks." All night I labored to keep Piper's prom out of my mind, afraid the memories would crush me. Now, they hit like a speeding comet. Piper was so irresistible in that little black dress. Dancing to *Faithfully* and telling each other how we were falling in love was the best.

These past couple weeks without her have been so confusing. My confidence level in the female department plummeted to non-existent. Hearing one of them stand up for me lightened my heart. Maybe I wasn't doing everything wrong, even though it felt like it.

I sparked up my tone of voice. "Speaking of prom dates, I still don't understand how you ended up with Porco. I thought a bunch of dudes would have asked you."

She let go of my hand. Raising her feet in front of her, she tilted her head, peeked at those sexy stilettos, and lowered them back down. "Well, a couple *dudes* did ask, but I said no."

"Why would you do that?"

Her baby blues stared right through me. "I kept waiting for the *right guy* to ask."

Whoa. My stomach fluttered like crazy, and my pulse raced like NASCAR. What did she just imply? The current song ended. Neither of us glanced away.

The DJ took to the mic. "Your votes are in and right at the stroke of midnight, we'll announce the winners of your Prom King and Queen for 1991." She put on *Heat of the Moment* by Asia.

Myckal licked her pink, sparkly lipstick and swallowed. "Isn't it weird that we're the class of '91? I mean it's still 1990 for two more weeks." Her voice came out breathy.

She was flirting with me, right? When you have a girlfriend it's easy to miss signals from other girls, at least for me it was. Being wrapped up with Piper for so long, I only saw Myckal as a friend. Now, I wanted to check out every inch of her in this dress. But if I broke eye contact, she might vanish into thin air.

"I danced at their prom last year. Believe me, you don't want to be the class of '90. They're a bunch of tools," I said.

My breathing shallowed, and I *accidentally* slid closer. It might have been the lamest pick-up move of all time. Our thighs brushed against each other, but she didn't pull away. Wow, that tiny bit of her leg felt amazing. Did she want me to try anything further?

Gazing deep into her eyes, I got my answer. First kiss time had definitely arrived. I shivered, but not from the cold. I wanted to lean in so bad, but wussed out and shook my head at the last instant. "I'm sorry. I can't. Even though part of me wishes things were different. I still don't know what's going on with Piper."

Nodding, Myckal got to her feet. Her lips pressed into a straight line. "Yeah. I'm sorry, too. She doesn't know how lucky she is." She gave my jacket back and let her hand trail over my shoulder.

I reached for her, trying to grab-hold, but it was too late. Those fingertips had disappeared. Her sweet and flowery perfume lingered behind—paralyzing me. Leaning against the wall of the gazebo, I pounded the back of my skull against it. How could I be such a moron?

Pablo swooped in and crashed into my side. "What just happened between you two?"

I made the sound of an explosion, hunched forward, and dropped my head into my palms. Coming back up, I said, "Nothing, man. We almost kissed. Then I backed away because I'm still holding out hope that Piper's walking through that door. Am I stupid?"

He checked his watch and smacked the back of my head. "Yes, you're stupid. I hate to say it, buddy, but you're insane. How far in the prom do you have to wait before reality sinks in? It's eleven-thirty, now. How's eleven-forty-five, or one minute to midnight? When will you realize she ain't coming?"

I'd love to be with a great girl like Myckal, but how do I turn my back on what I have with Piper? My thoughts were scrambled, and I scratched the top of my scalp. "It's just hard to believe Piper did this to me. I thought for sure we'd be the one in a million to survive a long-distance relationship."

"Sorry, man. You didn't. She's been drifting away all semester. She should've been at the tournament today, and she should be here right now. You recognized it the first time you played quarters. You've been living in denial and didn't want to admit it. And having a jackass like *Jonesy* sniffing around her hasn't helped.

You two never fight, but it's all you've been doing lately. The question is, what are you going to do about Myckal? She obviously likes you."

All I could do was stare at the floor, hoping I'd find the answer there. But the splintered wood offered up no solutions. Slowly, I turned toward him. "Wait, you knew about Myckal?"

"Yeah, bonehead. Everybody does."

I tapped my fist against my jaw. "Always the last to know."

"Like I said, you're an idiot. So, what now?"

"I don't know, man. Myckal's way too cool of a chick to be a rebound girl."

He smacked me again. "So, don't use her as a rebound. Where does it say you can't go from one serious girlfriend to the next?"

"First off, ouch, and, stop hitting me. What if I wait until the prom ends? If Piper still doesn't show, then I can talk to Myckal at Jimmy's party."

"Do what you want, dude. At best, you have thirty minutes left. Probably less because the DJ's going to have to start the king and queen ceremony before midnight. Supposedly, they're announcing us for winning States, too. And you're about to waste one of the most romantic moments of your life." He punched me in the arm and trekked off.

With or Without You by U2 echoed through the lobby. Bono's voice hit like a hammer. I've been waiting all night for Piper. Actually, I've been waiting months.

She really wasn't coming. It played in my mind and broke my heart. I loved her deeply. It'd take a long time to get over this. But Pablo was right, time was up. So, what about the final half hour of the prom? I might be crazy, but I had to give Piper one last try.

A pay phone hung on the wall, right inside the cafeteria. Rifling through my tuxedo pockets, I found a bunch of change. Dialing the number to her dorm room was more gut-wrenching than facing Hector. My fingers trembled. I pulled on my shirt collar and checked around. I didn't want anyone eavesdropping. But I had to find out if Robyn heard from Piper and that she was okay. Maybe there was an innocent explanation after all.

One ring, I squeezed my eyes shut.

Two rings, heart palpitations. It felt like I was choking.

Three rings, it sounded like a sonic boom.

"Hello."

It wasn't just a hello, laughing and shrieking cackled out of the phone, followed by Clive's voice. "I can't believe it, Piper just pointed and got burnt with her favorite rule. That's never happened before. Classic."

They were playing quarters.

A chorus of, "Drink," arose, and I swallowed back the pain.

Next, I heard Piper use her *joking around* voice. "Come here, you."

"Oh. *Absolutely*," Clive said. Their loud puckering thundered in my ears.

I was almost too embarrassed to respond, but the words slipped out. "Hello, Robyn." Part of me wished I had slammed the phone down and run away. Nothing ever hurt like this.

"Oh. Hi, Luca." She practically yelled her greeting. It wasn't for my benefit. The noise in their room dried up—total silence. I imagined a panicked expression on Piper's face. Robyn's voice shrilled higher. "How's the prom going?"

I didn't know how to feel, but I didn't want to be jealous. Lowering my head, I shook it back and forth, not believing the whole situation. If she wished to be with Clive, why not just break up with me? It was obvious she no longer wanted to be boyfriend and girlfriend, but why humiliate me like this? That's what stung, not that she chose his formal over my prom.

That last part might not be exactly true. It was a killer. I had a lot of soul searching to do. But what about right now? I had almost wasted the whole night for someone who hadn't put me first all year. This was *my* senior year. She didn't show for the state championship, and she left me stranded at my prom.

The clock was ticking. Meanwhile, one of the most awesome girls ever was on the other side of those gym doors.

"Enjoy your quarter's game," I said, and hung up the phone. Hearing their kiss sealed it for me. As the receiver clicked down on our relationship, a surprising avalanche of relief washed over me and knocked me out of my funk—like I received a cheery shot of adrenaline. I didn't realize I was holding that emotion in.

Smacking both of my cheeks, I rushed back into the dimly lit gymnasium. I weaved around people, scooted past half-empty tables, and ended up at the DJ booth. She cupped her ear to hear me over the music, then smiled and nodded.

It was my turn to sneak up on Myckal. She sat at the table laughing with Cheryl and Nicole. Her eyes popped when she saw me.

I held out my hand. "Let's dance."

Reaching for it, a ghost of a smile curled both of our

lips, and I led her to the dance floor. Since she didn't immediately reject me and run away, I decided to try a little dance move and held up our hands. Luckily, she twirled underneath. A tiny thunderbolt of optimism hit from above. Maybe I hadn't blown it with her, too.

My right arm went around her waist. Touching her made my breath catch and my knees as weak as jelly. Her left hand rested on my shoulder. Her other hand stayed in mine and felt spectacular. My fingers folded around it, like they belonged there all along. My thumb caressed the back of her hand.

The DJ lifted the microphone. "Myckal, someone named Luca must think you're pretty special. He requested your prom's theme song. *Take My Breath Away* by Berlin. Tell us, does he take yours away?"

Her mouth fell open. "What did you just do?"

Chills shot everywhere. "Did I ever tell you how incredible your eyes are?"

Biting her bottom lip and shaking her head, her breathing deepened and her chest rose and fell inside that awesome velvet dress. Holy cow!

I chuckled and lightly tapped the bridge of her nose. "What about this adorable line of freckles? How come I never noticed them before?"

She stopped and her voice cracked. "What about Piper?"

"That's over, Myckal. I'm sorry I didn't see it earlier."

"You don't have to apologize."

I placed a lock of her hair behind her ear. "Yes, I do. I messed up big time. I should have made tonight all about you. I want to change that and make every last second about you. You're absolutely the coolest person

I ever met, and definitely the most beautiful. I just wish I realized my feelings about you sooner. If you let me, someday I'll find a way to make up for it. We only have a little while left tonight, and I've never wanted anything more—but will you please dance with me at *our prom*?"

Her gorgeous face beamed.

This time, I leaned all the way in, and we kissed. It was like heaven. A little slow at first, then her tongue started to play and frolic. I couldn't help but smile through it. She pressed herself against me. There's nothing like the feel of a hot prom date in a gorgeous dress. Wow, did my hands ever want to explore.

Our lips peeled apart. My heart thundered and electricity gushed through every ounce of my body. Her cheek rested against my shoulder. She fit so perfect. I kissed the top of her curls. Her cherry fragrance swept over me, inflaming the dream and attraction. We danced and swayed to the music. Strobe and disco lights shimmered like stars in a faraway galaxy. I closed my eyes, trying to transport us there—aching to be alone with her.

I had almost wasted the whole night—I should have offered my heart to Myckal sooner. Now, I refused to squander any more time.

When I opened my eyes, Myckal stared up at me. We made out like the greatest couple ever.

Skyrockets burst inside the prom.

A word about the author...

R.H. Bird is the author of Promposal. He grew up in New York, worked on Wall Street and retired early as a stockbroker. He lives in Las Vegas with his wife and three daughters. They all love alpine skiing, scuba diving, and improv.

Thank you for purchasing
this publication of The Wild Rose Press, Inc.

For questions or more information
contact us at
info@thewildrosepress.com.

The Wild Rose Press, Inc.
www.thewildrosepress.com